Also by Melissa Albert

The Hazel Wood

The Night Country

Tales from the Hinterland

OUR
CROOKED
HEARTS

MELISSA
ALBERT

PENGUIN BOOKS

PENGUIN BOOKS

UK | USA | Canada | Ireland | Australia
India | New Zealand | South Africa

Penguin Books is part of the Penguin Random House group of companies
whose addresses can be found at global.penguinrandomhouse.com.

www.penguin.co.uk   www.puffin.co.uk   www.ladybird.co.uk

Penguin
Random House
UK

First published in the United States of America by Flatiron Books 2022
Published in Great Britain by Penguin Books 2022

001

Printed and bound in Great Britain by Clays Ltd, Elcograf S.p.A.

The authorized representative in the EEA is Penguin Random House Ireland,
Morrison Chambers, 32 Nassau Street, Dublin D02 YH68

A CIP catalogue record for this book is available from the British Library

ISBN: 978–0–241–59254–0

All correspondence to:
Penguin Books, Penguin Random House Children's
One Embassy Gardens, 8 Viaduct Gardens, London SW11 7BW

To my wonderful, fiercely loving mother,
who is not the mother in these pages.
If I ever wrote you into a book,
you'd be a heroine.

A nightmare is witchwork.

—ELIZABETH WILLIS, "THE WITCH"

PART I

CHAPTER ONE

)

The suburbs

Right now

We were going too fast. Too close to the trees, weeds feathering over our headlights, whisking away.

"Nate." I gripped the passenger seat. "*Nate.*"

Fifteen minutes ago we were at an end-of-year party, jumping up and down with our hands on each other's shoulders, and all the time I was thinking, *I should break up with him. I should do it now. I have to break up with him now.* Then he cupped my face in his hands and told me he loved me, and I was too startled to tell even half a lie.

I followed him out of the house, over the lawn, into his car, still saying all the useless things you say when you've bruised someone's ego and they think it's their heart. He slammed too hard into reverse, then sloshed over the curb peeling away, and still it took me a block to realize he was drunk.

At a stoplight he fumbled with his phone. For a few taut seconds I considered jumping out. Then he was off again, an old Bright Eyes song blasting and the wind tearing it into pieces. The music stuttered as he swerved onto the single-lane road that wound through the forest preserve. Trees closed in and my hair whipped to fluff. I closed my eyes.

Then Nate shouted, not a word but a sharp, surprised syllable, cutting the wheel hard to the right.

The moment between swerving and stopping was weightless as a roller coaster drop. I rocked forward and my mouth clashed hard with the dash.

When I licked my teeth I could taste blood. "What the *hell*!"

Nate turned off the car, breathing hard, craning to look past me. "Did you see that?"

"See what?"

He opened his door. "I'm getting out."

The car was sprawled across the narrow strip between the road and the trees. "Here? Are you serious?"

"Stay if you want to," he said, and slammed the door.

There was a Taco Bell cup in the center console with an inch of meltwater in it. I swished it over my teeth and swung my legs out of the car, spitting blood onto the grass. My lip felt tender in the loamy air.

"Hey!" I called. "Where are you going?"

Nate was slipping into the trees. "I think she went this way."

"She? Who?"

"How did you not see her? She was standing in the middle of the road." He paused. "Completely naked."

My breath caught as I considered the paths you could take to end up in the woods at three in the morning, female, naked, and alone. Toothy grasses trailed over my shins as I waded in behind him. "Did you recognize her? Was she hurt?"

"Shh," he said. "Look."

We stood on a rise above the creek that ran through the trees, which could be shallow as a pan or deep enough to kayak in, depending on the rains. Just now it was somewhere in the middle, waist high and churning along beneath a gibbous moon. I knew it was about that high because the girl we were following was kneeling in it, submerged to her shoulder blades.

She was, in fact, nude. Hair center-parted and long enough that the moving water tugged her head back. I couldn't see her face, but the rest of her was an almost electric shade of pale. There was nothing nearby to signify she hadn't dropped to Earth from a star, or risen from a crack in a hill. No shoes on the shore, no cell phone on a balled-up shirt. The sight of her was out of a dream, almost.

Her hands were moving over her skin in this profoundly unsexual way, squeezing it, slapping it, like she was beating the feeling back in. She was making these guttural sounds I had no words for. Crying, I guessed.

I'd almost forgotten about Nate when he dug an elbow into my ribs and grinned, mean and quick. He thumbed his phone's flashlight on and held it out like a torch.

Her head twisted and I saw that she was around our age, maybe a little older, eyes dilated and mouth still curling around the end of a smile. She hadn't been crying. She'd been laughing.

Nate meant to make her feel exposed, but I knew he was really doing it to me, because it was shitty and he wanted to be shitty to someone right now. I could've left him, but if I were her I'd be more scared of a dude by himself. And she might need help. I was ready to offer it when she spoke first.

"Come out." Her voice was low, smudged and hardened by some unplaceable accent. It rose into a singsong. "Come out, come out, whoever you are."

She rose like a backwoods Venus, dirty creek water running out of her hair, down her body, beading through her serious seventies bush. She whistled, piercing and clear. "I said show yourselves, motherfuckers."

She was naked, she was alone, she couldn't even really *see* us, but just like that we were the ones who were afraid. I felt the tremor in Nate as he saw how this was gonna go. "Fuck this," he muttered.

The girl stepped onto the bank. She was large-framed and underfed, her hair a sticking mermaid curtain, but the thing I couldn't look away from was how she held herself, without the barest awareness of her body. Like she was a baby, or a bird.

With a blunt suddenness she raised her arms, conductor style with their palms held flat. We flinched, both of us, because it seemed like something was supposed to happen. When nothing did Nate tried to laugh. It came out dry.

She dropped into a crouch. Eyes turned in our direction, feeling along the ground until her fingers found a fallen branch, thick and a few feet long. Hefting it, she stood. Nate cursed, shoving his phone into his pocket, and the girl stopped mid-stride. With its light gone she could see us, too.

"Ivy, let's *go*," Nate growled.

"Ivy."

The girl repeated my name. The word in her mouth was heatless, heavy. I squinted at her, confirming she was a stranger.

"What's wrong with you? Come on!" Nate yanked my arm hard enough that my shoulder burned. Then he was stumbling away, swearing at every tree branch that swiped him, every divot in the ground.

Over my tank top I wore a washed-thin button-up from Community Thrift. I slipped free of it and tossed it in her direction before following him.

"Thank you, Ivy," she said, when I was almost too far to hear.

When I reached the road Nate was back in the driver's seat. He drummed his hands on the wheel. "Get in!"

I was cranked up and weirded out and scared enough to listen. The music restarted when he turned the key and we both reached to slap it off, then snatched our hands back as if any contact might burn.

I didn't speak till we were out of the trees. "That girl. Did you hear the way she said my name?"

He shrugged, barely.

"Did she know me?" I persisted. I didn't think I'd forget meeting a girl who looked like that, the colors of a lemon sucked dry.

"How am I supposed to know?" Nate asked sullenly.

I pulled the mirror down to inspect my lip and cursed softly. Already it stuck out like the peeled half of a stone fruit.

We drove the rest of the way in sticky silence. When Nate stopped at the end of my drive, I reached for the passenger door. He locked it.

I reared to face him. "*What?*"

He flicked the dome light on and sucked in through his teeth. "Oh, man, that looks bad. Look, I'm really sorry. Are you okay?"

"I'm awesome. Let me out."

"Okay, but—" He swallowed. "What are you gonna tell your mom?"

I gaped at him. Cigarette behind his ear, peeping at me through those eyelashes that made older women smile and say, *What a waste, on a boy.* I started, helplessly, to laugh.

His posture went rigid. "What's so funny?"

"You. You're scared of my mom, aren't you?"

"So what?" he spat. "You're scared of her, too."

I turned away, face burning. When I flipped the lock again, he relocked it. "Nate! Let me. The fuck. *Out.*"

Someone banged their fist on the driver's side window.

Nate jumped, eyes going wide. I think he expected to see my mother out there. But it was my neighbor, Billy Paxton.

I peered up at him. Billy lived across the street from me, but we'd never really talked. Especially following a painful incident back in junior high, memories of which still had the power to make me stop what I was doing and wince. He'd been at the party Nate and I came from, and I'd pretended not to see him.

Nate rolled the window down, touching behind his ear to make sure he hadn't dropped his cigarette. "What do you want, man?"

Billy ignored him. "Ivy, you okay?"

I leaned around Nate to see him better. "Uh, yeah? I'm fine."

He put a hand to his mouth. There was a stripe of white paint over his forearm. "Did he do that to you?"

"Are you for real?" Nate squawked.

I felt, suddenly, like I might cry. It was the pain, I told myself. The adrenaline, fizzing away. "No, no. It was a . . . car thing. I'm good."

Billy watched me a little longer. He was too tall for it, bent practically in half to see into the car. "Okay. I'll be right there." He pointed at his porch. "Just so you know."

"Thank you for your service," Nate said sarcastically, but not until Billy was up the drive.

I wrenched the door open, slammed it behind me, and turned. "We're broken up."

"No shit," Nate said, and gunned it down the street.

I lingered on the curb. My lip was throbbing, my body pounding with exhaustion, but it was laced with the feather-light euphoria of being *free*.

Billy cleared his throat. He was perched tensely on his porch, still watching me. Embarrassed, I lifted a hand.

"Sorry about that," I told him.

"Sorry for what?"

He said it quietly enough that I wasn't sure I was meant to hear. I almost let it pass. Maybe it was the pain in my mouth—needling, insistent—that made me turn.

"I'm sorry you thought you had to step in," I said, more sharply than I intended.

Billy stared at me. Then he stood, shaking his head. "Won't happen again," he said, and disappeared into his house.

My eye went to the darkened second-story windows. One of

them lit up a minute later and I looked away, regret and bottom-shelf vodka muddling queasily in my stomach. Time to get in bed, I figured. Before my night found one more way to go to shit.

Slow and steady I unlocked the front door, holding my breath as I opened it just wide enough to slide through. Then I let it all go in a strangled yelp, because my mom was sitting on the stairs waiting for me.

"Mom!" I dipped my head, bringing a hand to my lip. "Why are you awake?"

She leaned into the patch of moonlight falling through the window over the door. Her bright hair was tied up, her eyes safety-pin sharp. "Bad dream." Then she snapped to her feet, because she'd seen my mouth.

"What happened? Were you in an accident?"

My lip beat like a second heart. "No! I'm fine. I mean—it wasn't really an *accident* . . ."

The beam of her focus felt physical. "Tell me. Tell me *exactly*."

"Nate—swerved," I said. "His car went off the road."

"Then what?"

I thought of the stranger in the woods, slapping at her chalk-colored skin. "Then nothing. Then we drove home."

"That's it? That's all that happened?"

I gave a shallow nod.

"Okay." Her unnerving intensity was draining. The corners of her mouth twitched up, conspiratorial. "But Nate was drinking tonight, wasn't he?"

I swayed a little, trying to think. She'd seemed less dangerous a moment ago, when she was outright pissed. "Um."

She gave a curt *I knew it* nod. "Go to your room. Now."

I edged past her, up the stairs and into my room. Skipping the lights, I fell onto my pillows and closed my eyes. When I opened them she was above me, pressing an icepack to my mouth with her scarred left hand.

"Did you hit your head?" Her usual reserve was back; she could've been asking for the time. "Do we have to worry about a concussion? Tell me the truth."

I leaned into the icepack's chill. When was the last time she'd tended to me like this? When I tried to remember, blankness pressed in like an ocean.

"My head's fine," I mumbled. I'd entered that terrible purgatory place where you're still drunk yet somehow already hungover. "I told you, it wasn't a big deal. Nate's not even hurt."

"He's not hurt." Her voice was soft, and veined with rage. "While *my* kid looks like a prizefighter."

"Dana." Suddenly my dad was there, hand on her arm, his steady shape blocking the light from the hallway. I fought to keep my eyes open as he stepped forward and she retreated, out of sight.

"We taught you better than this," he was saying. "What made you get into a car with a drunk driver?"

"I don't know."

A heavy Dad sigh. "I'm getting a little tired of hearing that. Do you have any idea how much worse this could've gone?"

My eye kept catching on the ceiling fan spinning over his shoulder, trying drowsily to count the blades. "I don't know," I repeated. "Lots?"

I wasn't being a smart-ass, not that he believed me. His voice went on and on, patient and pissed. By the time he'd finished impressing my stupidity upon me, I was half asleep. I dropped into blackout land and stayed there till morning, kicking off the first day of summer break with a hangover and a busted lip.

And a mystery, waiting on ice in the back of my brain. But days would pass before I'd see the girl in the water again.

CHAPTER TWO

)

The suburbs
Right now

My phone rang and the sound of it drilled into my dreams, disguised as the screech of Nate's brakes, as the scream I didn't have time to let go of, as the cry of some night bird flying above me, keeping pace as I followed a girl pale as a fallen star through the black woods. Finally it tugged me toward consciousness, sleep receding like salt water.

I lay there a second, blinking the images away. I *never* remembered my dreams. Ever. No one believed me when I told them that, but it was true. I peeked at my phone screen through one eye before answering.

"Look who's not dead." Amina's voice was acid bright. "Were my fifteen texts not enough? Did you need twenty?"

"Don't yell at me," I said pathetically. My mouth ached. The dream still coated my skin like Vaseline. "I had a long night."

I drained the water glass left by the bed, then told my best friend the story. The party, the breakup, the girl in the road. My failed attempt to sneak in. I could feel her getting worked up as I talked.

"I'm gonna kill him!" she said when I was through. "Did you see what he was drinking last night? *Absinthe*." Her voice dripped with good-kid horror. Amina had big tattletale energy. "To be fair it was probably vodka with green food coloring, but still. Are you sure you're okay?"

"I'm fine. Seriously."

"Yeah. You sound fine."

There was a note in her voice I couldn't quite read. "So? What's wrong with that?"

"Just . . . you can be pissed, you know? You *should* be. He could've killed you."

"I *am* pissed," I said. Wasn't I? I poked at the feeling like it was a toothache.

She sighed. "Anyway. Nate sucks. I can't believe your mom caught you coming in. Was it awful?"

I scrubbed at my eyes. "It was fine. Why is everyone so scared of her all of a sudden?"

Amina paused for what I assumed was comic effect, but when she spoke again her voice was darker. More direct. "You know you can always come to my house, right? If you ever need to."

I already stayed at her place all the time. We used to switch off houses on Saturday nights, but a couple of years ago she'd started making excuses not to sleep at mine. She was one of those routine-addicted people—the multistep skin care, the specific tea made specifically by her father, the two pillows she had to bring with her just to fall asleep—so I hadn't pressed. But now I frowned. "Yeah, I know. But why would I need to?"

Another pause, then: "This girl you saw. She was *naked*? Like, completely?"

I narrowed my eyes at the subject change, but again I didn't press. "Yep."

"Standing in the middle of the road."

"I guess. I didn't see that part, I was too busy worrying I was gonna die."

Her voice dropped forty degrees. "I *will* kill him."

"Not if my dad gets there first."

"Or your mom. You know she'd help you hide a body."

"She would've killed the body she's forcing you to hide."

"What I do find interesting, though," she said craftily, "is the part where the hot guy from across the street came to your rescue."

"Amina," I said warningly.

"Yes?"

"Just . . . don't get too excited."

"I never get excited."

I laughed. "I'm going back to bed now. Love you."

"Love you, too," she said.

Before I could put my phone down it lit up with a text from Nate.

In my life

why do I give valuable time

to people who don't care if I

live or die?

Instagram poetry or sad lyrics? I refused to give him the satisfaction of googling it, but now I was too annoyed to sleep. I changed his name to NO in my contacts and headed to the bathroom to poke at my lip. My brother, Hank, walked in scratching his bare chest, then halted mid-scratch.

"What happened?" He shoved in next to me, peering at my lip in the glass. "Wait, is *this* why Dad was yelling at you in the middle of the night?"

I squinted at him in the mirror. "Way to ask if I'm okay."

"I was coming to congratulate you for finally getting in trouble for once. I just thought it'd be for a *fun* reason." He stared at my reflection. "You know what you look like? You look like that ridiculous dog from across the street, the time he ate a bee and his mouth blew up. Are you okay? What'd you do?"

I elbowed him away. "Ate a bee. Stop blowing your gross breath at me, it'll stick in my hair."

Hank *hah*ed a big mouthful onto the crown of my head and walked away laughing. He'd been home from his first year of college for less than a week and already I was over it. No food was safe from him, and if anyone asked him to do anything— pick up his shoes, clean a dish—he whined about how he was on vacation. I wouldn't get away with that shit for one hour.

"Ivy, you awake?" My dad's voice drifted up from below. "Come down here a sec."

I found him leaning against the kitchen counter in his appalling cyclist's Spandex, shoveling granola into his mouth. He smiled at me when I walked in, then winced. "Oh, sweetheart, your lip. That little turd."

I shrugged. Nate *was* a turd. He pounced on mispronunciations like a cat on a cockroach. He'd hold up his finger in the middle of a conversation, pull out a notebook, and start scribbling in it while you stood there like an asshole. *Sorry,* he'd say with this fake-apologetic smile. *I just had to get this story idea down.* Once I got a glimpse at one of these "ideas." It said, *Mag-*

ical island where all men die but one. Object of sexual obsession/ ascends to god?

But he was the junior everyone had a crush on. Saying yes when he asked me out seemed obvious. He'd had all these ideas about who I was—that's one of the perils of being quiet, people invent personalities for you—and I couldn't admit even to Amina that I *liked* it. I liked the person he thought I was. Cool instead of faking it, aloof rather than worried about saying something stupid.

My dad must've mistaken my grimace for hangover agony, because he pressed his own cup of coffee into my hand. "Let's talk about last night."

"I messed up," I said instantly. Dad was easy, he just wanted you to take responsibility. Hank would make excuses until he suffocated under the weight of his own bullshit, but I could play the game. "I had no idea Nate was drunk. He was supposed to be the designated driver."

Dad nodded. "That's a good start, but you still need to be aware. *You* have to stay vigilant, no one's gonna do it for you. What happened last night . . ." He shook his head. "Sweetheart, that wasn't like you."

I could've agreed right then and walked away. But the words hit me funny. Maybe because I'd just been thinking about Nate telling me who I was. And getting it all wrong.

"It wasn't like me," I repeated. "What would you say *is* like me, then?"

"Hey, I'm just saying we're lucky. We got a smart one. We never have to worry about you. Your brother, on the other hand." He tipped his head and made a comical face, I guess to imply it's funny when sons get into trouble. Daughters, not so much.

"Don't get soft, Rob. I'm sure she can think of a dozen ways to give you a heart attack."

My mom stood in the basement doorway. We both startled; neither of us had heard her coming up. Her hair was down and the white of her left eye was stitched with fine red threads.

"Dana." My dad took a step toward her. "What were you doing in the basement?"

She ignored him. "How's the lip, Ivy?"

The ibuprofen hadn't kicked in yet. It was killing me. "Fine."

My mom stepped closer to inspect my injury. Too close. There was an odd scent coming off her skin. Sharp, almost herbal. But it was early for her to have been in the garden.

Her eyes refocused on mine. "You're staying home today."

"What? Why?"

"Because," she said testily, "you're grounded."

Her gaze flicked to my dad when she said it. She always deferred to him on parenting stuff, in this flat, ironical way. Like we were play kids in a play house that he insisted on taking seriously.

"I am?" I turned to my dad. "Am I?"

He looked uncertain. "If your mother says you are."

"But . . . it's summer break. I didn't *do* anything."

"Well. You got in a car with a drunk driver."

"I didn't know he was drunk!"

"Next time you'll pay more attention," my mom said, then pursed her lips. "Please tell me you dumped his ass."

I felt flushed, irritated. And just the littlest bit triumphant. "Yeah. I dumped him."

"Good girl," she murmured, and started to leave the room.

"Hey." Gently my dad clasped her shoulder, turned her back to face him. "Are you getting a migraine?"

His voice was oddly accusing. And he was right, now I could see it. It had been so long since she'd had one. I'd forgotten the way the headaches made her mouth slacken, made the muscles around her eyes twitch. "I'm fine," she said. "It's fine. I already called Fee."

Fee was her best friend, basically her sister. Whenever my mom got one of her rare migraines, Aunt Fee brought over the gnarly vinegar brew they took instead of actual medicine.

"That's not what I'm . . ." He cut himself off, stepping away from her. "You know what, never mind. You'll do what you're gonna do."

He kissed the side of my head. "We'll talk more later. I'm heading out for a ride."

When the front door had shut behind him, I looked at her. "Is Dad mad at you?"

"Don't worry about it," she said shortly. "I'm heading upstairs."

"Mom. Wait."

I was getting greedy, I think. Having her wait up for me, punish me, give more than half a shit about my choice of boyfriend. It made me want more from her. I just wasn't sure what.

"Last night, when I got in. You said you had a bad dream."

She tipped her head. Not quite a nod.

I took a quick breath. "Was it about me?"

"Ivy." Her voice was soft. Uncharacteristically so. "I shouldn't have—it was just a dream."

But I remembered how *awake* she'd looked last night, how

nervy and alert, even before she'd seen my injury. "What was it about?"

She pinched the bridge of her nose, eyes fluttering shut. "Dark water, running water. And a . . ."

"A what?" My voice sounded faraway.

Her eyes snapped open. "Nothing." She tried a smile. "Fee would tell me it means change. But for her that's every dream."

I didn't smile back. I was seeing the girl in the woods again, crouching in the creek's black water. "Hey, Mom," I began, tentatively. "I—"

She shoved a finger into her eye socket. "Not now. Truly. I have to lie down."

I let her go. Wondering like I always did what I could've said differently, to make her stay.

CHAPTER THREE

❯

The suburbs
Right now

It was barely eleven and already the day was blistering bright, all the cars and mailboxes glittering in the sun. I sat on the front step, alternating sips of coffee and soupy June air. Billy Paxton's car was still in his driveway. I'd seen it from the window. And if he *happened* to come out, I could thank him again. Do a better job this time.

My phone hummed in my back pocket. A text from Amina.

AHHHH check Nate's feed IMMEDIATELY

"Oh no," I whispered. Another text came through.

It's not about you btw sorry!! Tell me when you've seen it

Nate had posted less than ten minutes ago. There was his pretty, punchable face in closeup, lips parted and lids at half-mast. A piece of the Dairy Dream sign was visible over his shoulder. With its black-and-white filter the photo could've been a movie still.

His mouth was swollen, smeared with gunmetal blood. A bruise was rising over one eye. The caption read, *You should see the other guy*. The first comment was from his little brother, Luke. *I hear the other guy was a parked mail truck.*

I stared until my jaw started to ache. I unclenched.

Well? Did you see it?

Yeah, I texted back. I saw it.

INSTANT COMEUPPANCE, Amina replied. She'd never liked Nate. WHO RUNS INTO A PARKED MAIL TRUCK???

I didn't reply. My phone buzzed again.

Am I being a monster? Sorry! I swear I wouldn't be happy if he were dead. I can 90% promise you I didn't park the mail truck.

Hahaha, I typed, then put my phone facedown on the concrete.

I touched a finger to my lip, feeling this inchworm of dread burrowing through my belly. It was unsettling, that's all. When karma worked so clean.

I heard a sound like Yahtzee dice rattling in a cup and smiled. You could always hear my aunt's truck before you saw it. The thing was older than me, a beater only she could drive, because there were about five tricks to making it run and one of them was prayer.

"Hey, Ivy-girl," she called as she pulled into the drive. She climbed down with a stuffed Women & Children First tote bag over her shoulder. "Lemme see that lip."

It was ninety degrees in the shade and still she was rocking the full Aunt Fee thing, dark lipstick and metal jewelry and that split curtain of heavy black hair. She leaned in to cup my chin, eyes narrowing, skin breathing the scent of vinegar and black tea and the chalky amber she rubbed on her wrists. "Look at that. Somebody's got a death wish."

I ducked out of her grip. "I do not have a death wish."

"Not you, that boyfriend of yours." She paused. "Ex?"

I nodded.

"Good. Your mom and I are flipping a coin on who gets to help him find Jesus."

"Would it make you feel better if I told you he just drove his car into a mail truck?"

Her eyes flicked past me, toward the house. "Did he, now. No one's dead, I hope? Or maimed?"

"He's fine. He messed up his face, though. Just like me."

She smiled slightly, though her eyes stayed flinty. "Payback's a bitch."

I nodded at the tote. "You brought Mom the gross tea?"

She pulled a little unmarked tin out of her pocket. "And salve for your lip. To be used *sparingly*."

"Thanks, auntie," I said, giving her a hug. Whatever was in the salve, it would work. She was the brain and hands behind the herbal remedies sold at the Small Shop, her and my mom's fancy-people headshop in downtown Woodbine. Her stuff had a cult status that kept the lights on.

She headed inside and I followed after, to try out the salve. It smelled like the underside of a log and tasted like Satan's ballsack, so I wiped it off and put the little pot in the medicine cabinet. Hopefully Hank would think it was lip balm.

When I went upstairs I could hear them talking through

my parents' bedroom door. My mom let loose this free, throaty laugh that made my stomach clench. It was a sound only her best friend could get out of her.

Sometimes I thought, if I didn't love Aunt Fee so much, I might be jealous of her. Sometimes I wondered if my dad could say the same.

I was waiting for her when she left, pretending to read a magazine.

"Hey." I lay the magazine over my chest. "Did Mom tell you how long I'm grounded?"

Aunt Fee tipped her head. "Into *The Economist* now, are we?"

"Yes," I said defensively.

"However long they ground you, it'll be fair."

"But it's summer break!"

"I can't hear you when you're whining," she said automatically, one of her favorite lines when I was little. Then she relented. "How about this. If it's longer than a week, I'll talk them into letting you have a city day with me."

"A *week?*"

"Just wait till *you* have kids, and one of them comes home bleeding from the mouth at four in the morning."

I flipped a page of the magazine. "What else did you talk about?"

"You, mostly. Your brother."

"Then why did she sound so happy?" I muttered.

Aunt Fee's mouth tightened. She worried about us, I knew she did, but she was too faithful to my mom to ever acknowledge it.

"Why don't you go up there?" she said instead. "Just . . . go visit with her. What's that game you two used to play, the one you made up? That rhyming game? She's feeling better now, you could go play it."

"Game?" I frowned at her. "What game?"

She tapped her middle finger to her thumb, uncertain. "Oh, what am I thinking of? I'm thinking of someone else."

"Who?"

"Use the lip salve, Ivy-girl. Sparingly. Eat something with iron, too, you're running low. And stay away from boys who don't treat you right."

She kissed my hair and let herself out into the heat.

I remembered, then, when my mom last had a migraine. The scent of vinegar on my aunt's clothes must've knocked something free in my head. It was just over two years ago. I could pin it to the day because of what happened the night before: the high school talent show. Aunt Fee had brought over the gross tea, and we'd talked about what went down with Hattie Carter.

Hattie Carter. The name landed in my brain like a black bird touching down on a wire. I hadn't thought about Hattie in a long time.

My temples ached dully. There was something I wanted to consider, some train of thought whipping past me too quickly, disappearing into a silvery fog.

I rubbed the ache away and went to my room, where I couldn't smell the vinegar.

CHAPTER FOUR

>

The suburbs
Right now

I didn't see my mom again that day. She must have felt better, though, because when I woke up the next morning she was gone. It was the first Monday of summer. I was grounded, carless, and alone.

By ten a.m. I was standing in the bathroom in an old bikini, painting bleach onto my hair. I'd had the stuff for a while, but not the guts.

It seemed like the thing to do after my first breakup. Plus Nate had been kind of gross about the redhead thing. *She's a girl with hair,* Amina had snapped at him once, *not hair with a girl.*

Truthfully, though, I'd gotten the idea to bleach it a long time ago. Probably around the thousandth time someone gushed over how much I looked like my mother.

My scalp burned as I sat on the edge of the tub in a shower cap, eyeballs pickling with fumes. After rinsing out the toner I stared at myself for the longest time.

Even wet, the hair was an old-fashioned platinum. Set against it my brows were two dark slashes, my healing lips the mouth of a video game assassin. I had my mom's straight nose, her belligerent jaw, but with the new hair I looked like my own self, too.

The bathroom mirror was three panels. I could see myself from three angles as I leaned toward my altered reflection. Glass greening, features blurring, my nose grazing the mirror's cool surface.

Something rippled in its left-hand panel.

I jerked my head toward it and for a moment I was looking at a stranger. My heart lurched, then I was laughing at myself. Thinly, a little nervous.

I thought I'd stopped thinking about the girl Nate and I saw in the water, her nakedness and her uncanny gaze. But she must've been bobbing in the back of my brain. Because for an instant I could have sworn it was *her* face in the mirror, her pale hair, reflected back at me.

I felt uneasy after that, or maybe just restless. I'd told Amina I was grounded, and around noon she sent a photo of herself holding up a plastic ice-cream spoon with a face drawn on it. Meet your understudy, Spoon Ivy! For the rest of the day she and our friends Richard and Emily sent pictures of themselves posing with Spoon Ivy at the Dairy Dream, the skate park, in Richard's car. At Denny's they posed her next to a coffee carafe, because they found it hilarious that I'd been fired after just a month waiting tables there, for sneaking extra shift meals. The last photo showed Emily's Saint Bernard, Claudius, with a mouthful of mangled plastic. RIP Spoon Ivy.

That bitch got what was coming to her, I replied, then headed out to check the mailbox. Maybe I'd get lucky and there'd be a magazine.

I could feel my thirsty hair bristling under the sun, drinking in humidity and releasing the acrid scent of ammonia. I was reading an article on my phone as I trudged over the concrete, so I almost stepped on the rabbit.

It was stretched out in the middle of the drive on a grease patch of blood. There was its body, strong legs splayed. And there, a few inches away, was its head.

I jerked back, closing my eyes, but the sight of it stayed. The cartoon points of its ears, the slow violence of that sever.

It was too clean to have been left by somebody's dog. Could one of our block's terrible children have done this? I thought of Vera, a death-obsessed eight-year-old I'd babysat for once and never again. Or Peter, who had a face like a cherub and once tried to sell his mom's engagement ring door to door. He was definitely the kind of kid who lit ants on fire.

Or Nate, I thought reluctantly. Pressing a palm to my stomach, to the unease roiling there. I remembered the burn in my shoulder when he yanked me back in the woods, the way his expression curdled when I laughed at him. In those moments, at least, he seemed capable of retribution. But could he have done *this*?

No way, I decided. For one thing, he was a vegan. Basically. I mean, he ate burgers sometimes. But he did *call* himself a vegan.

Still, there were rumors about him, and the blazing trail of angst and exes he left in his wake. The kind of shit that used to make me feel smug about being the one he wanted, as much as I cringed about it now. One of his exes shaved her head after they broke up. Another wore the same black hoodie every day for weeks, sleeves drawn down to her fingertips. People claimed she'd pinpricked his name over her wrist with a safety pin, but people were assholes.

I took a photo of the rabbit. It looked less sinister on my screen, all the blood and dread squared off, flattened away. *What would Amina do?* I asked myself, and texted it to Nate.

Do you know anything about this?

I was back inside, considering whether to call my dad about the rabbit, when Nate sent a string of replies.

Wtf is this

Why are you sending me this effed up photo?

ARE YOU SERIOUS WITH THIS

Go to hell Ivy

My head pulsed like he was right there, yelling at me. I was still untangling my response when I saw my mom's car through the window, pulling into the drive. Her tires just missed the bunny.

She stepped out in a black sack dress, hair piled high and lit redder by the sun. Her eyes were hidden behind big white-framed sunglasses, so I couldn't make out her expression. But I knew when she saw the rabbit.

She hunched. Shoulders curling forward like she'd been socked in the stomach, hands catching her knees. Just as rapidly, she straightened. The way her head twisted toward the house made me think of a predator scenting along the breeze.

Then she was running. Up the drive, through the front door. When she saw me in front of the window, her hands went up. Not in surprise. Not to shield herself. She held her palms straight out, crooking her fingers in a gesture that plucked at my guts like a guitar pick. It was an attitude so unreadable yet so obviously malevolent it sent a bolt of cold thudding down my spine.

Then her face slackened and her hands dropped. "Ivy!" she said. "Your hair!"

I touched it, the ragged white ends that curled at my chin and smelled of chemical.

"I thought . . ." She was panting. "I didn't recognize you."

"Sorry," I said.

Her eyes wouldn't settle, on me or anything. She kept pressing two fingers to the hollow of her throat. "Are you alone?"

"Yeah."

"Have you been here all day?"

"Um. Yes? I'm still grounded, right?"

She came closer. Her eyes were a lucid blue, like lucky Hank's. She touched her own hair. "You covered the red."

I shrugged. What, was I supposed to apologize?

"I don't like it." Her voice sliced cold and clean. "The blonde looks cheap on you. Between the hair and the lip, you could play one of those dead girls on *SVU*."

I bit my cheek and saw her seeing the hurt I couldn't hide. For a second I thought she might actually acknowledge it.

"I'm going upstairs," she said instead. "My head's still not right."

That was the closest to an apology that I was gonna get.

She stayed in her room until dinner.

The late light coming into the kitchen made it seem darker. My mom moved forkfuls of takeout around her plate, her right hand smooth and her left scarred from knuckles to wrist. She'd always had those scars but tonight they seemed to stand out, to pulse like swollen veins. It was so strange to me, suddenly, that I'd never been told how she got them.

My dad worked through a pile of gnocchi, struggling to find something nice to say about my hair. Hank kept his eyes on his phone the entire meal. I could tell by his smirk he was texting a guy, and probably not the one he was dating. Hank should not have been granted massive blue eyes and Kaz Brekker cheekbones. It was like giving a toddler a ray gun.

My mom cried out.

We all snapped to, Hank included. She pressed a hand to her mouth, spit something into her palm. A brief glance and she folded her fingers neatly in to hide it.

"Dana?"

She took her time looking back at my dad. Her balled hand was in her lap, the other tight around her water glass. "Hmm?"

He put down his fork. "What was that? What did you just take out of your mouth?"

She watched him steadily. "Shrimp shell."

"Are you sure? It looked like . . . could you have cracked a tooth?"

She pulled her lips back in a frozen smile. My brother and I glanced at each other, then away. "How do I look, Rob? Did I lose a tooth and just not notice? It was a shrimp shell."

"Fine," he said. That was the last word anyone spoke for the rest of the meal.

She was lying, of course. I'd seen it, too. The thing she'd spit out was a hard yellowish sliver. Not her own tooth, but some-body else's.

I'd say a rabbit's.

It was barely eight when I escaped to my room. I lay in bed sucking on ice cubes, flipping the pages of a graphic novel Richard had loaned me, but I kept seeing my mother. The way she'd looked at me before she knew it was me. The gesture she made with her hands that twanged like a discordant note I'd heard before. And the dead rabbit, the iced shells of its eyes.

"Ivy?" My mom tapped on the door, then opened it.

I swallowed an ice cube, wincing as it ran like an ice-skate blade all the way down. "What's up?"

"I meant to ask how you're feeling. Fee told me she gave you some stuff for your lip."

I hadn't thought about my lip in a while, because it had stopped hurting. When I pressed a pinky to it, the swelling was almost gone. "Yeah. It helped."

"Good. So. Your hair." She rapped again on the doorframe, then walked all the way in. "I think it suits you, actually. It's very old Hollywood."

I had zero to say to this bullshit backtrack. I watched as she took a dirty T-shirt off the floor and folded it, placing it on the foot of my bed. That wasn't like her: my mom didn't take care of our messes for us. And she didn't have the kind of nervous hands that made busy work out of nothing.

"The other night," she said idly, still smoothing the shirt, "you told me Nate swerved."

"Yeah."

Now she looked up. "What did he swerve for?"

I smiled at her, no teeth. "A rabbit."

She watched me steadily and didn't reply.

The book I'd been reading lay across my chest. I put it aside and leaned toward her, stretching out a hand. Brow furrowed, like she suspected a trap, she reached back.

I caught her hand in mine. Touched a fingertip to a ridge of scar and looked at her questioningly.

She snatched it back. "Stop it."

"Mom," I said softly. An hour ago she'd spat another creature's tooth out of her own mouth. We'd watched her do it, watched her lie without even caring whether any of us believed her. It was like a game of pretend we never stopped playing.

I took a breath. "Who did you think I was when you walked in today?"

She flinched. Her face stayed smooth, but her shoulders jumped. "Ivy, you've got white hair and a fat lip. I didn't know *what* I was looking at."

There was a recklessness in me, rising. I lifted my hands, arranged them in the unnatural way she'd held hers in the front hall. It made my fingers prick. "What," I asked her, "does this mean?"

She lunged. Her knee came down on the bed and she was above me, squeezing my fingers in hers, forcing my arms to my sides.

"Don't," she said, her voice steady. "Do not."

Her right hand on my left was smooth and manicured, her left hand on my right patchworked with the scars she never talked about. And that was just the secret you could see. I made a sound in my throat, where bitterness burned like an aspirin pill. She heaved herself back off the bed.

"Ivy," she whispered. Her eyes were wet. I waited as her mouth worked itself over unsaid things, her expression shifting like a slots machine. And I watched as she went away from me, back inside herself, gone.

"Good night," she said, and closed the door.

After she left I tried to cry, but I couldn't. I stared at my windows instead. When they were bright black squares I sat up. The house was quiet, Hank off somewhere and my parents across the hall, sleeping or watching two different shows on two separate iPads. Midnight came and still I felt too hollow to sleep.

Downstairs I crouched in front of the open refrigerator, forking leftover noodles into my mouth. When I stood, swinging the door shut, something caught my eye through the window.

Someone was out there, among the herbs growing at the fence line. A stooped figure that stayed a while, troubling the dirt, and became my mother as it rose. She dusted her hands over the knees of her jeans before walking back toward the house.

Some instinct sent me swiftly across the kitchen, onto the basement stairs. Through the crack between door and frame I watched her pad softly to the sink. Her back was to me as she washed her hands, then filled and drained a water glass twice. She was still turned away when she collapsed, head dropping onto her folded arms, and let out a cry. Just one, pressed into her skin.

I stood on the step, the basement's cold breath on my neck, fear pricking at the backs of my knees. When my mother straightened it was with the sprung snap of a folding knife. Her face as she left the kitchen was set, her eyes a leaden blue. I waited behind the basement door until I was sure she was gone.

The backyard smelled wild, fermented crabapples and wet rosemary and the pungent soil my mom bought by the sackful. I took a trowel from a coil of hose and brushed through the mint plot, where black flies big as thumb joints hovered when the sun was out. When I reached the place I'd seen her brushing the dirt away, I got on my knees and started to dig.

The trowel hit metal a few inches down. It took a while to unearth it: a screw-top jam jar buried vertically in the dirt, empty but for an inch of sludge at the bottom. I held it to the moonlight. Earth, dried herbs, enough blood that I could identify it by the drops adhered to the glass. Stirred into the mess was a piece of broken mirror and a curl of white paper.

From a distance I observed the contents of the jar and the thudding of my own heart. Then I shoved the jar back into the ground and covered it, tramping over the soil until it looked the way she'd left it.

I went straight from the backyard to the shower, no idea what I'd say if she stepped out of her room and saw my dirty knees, my raw fingers.

I was breathing too fast. My vision sizzled, my head felt helium-light. Not because I was scared of what I'd dug up from the garden, but because I *wasn't*. The discovery should have felt alien, appalling. It didn't. It chimed in grim accord with the feeling I got when she arranged her hands just so, and the certainty I had glimpsing the rabbit's tooth in her palm.

There was a quiet place at the center of me. A pool of black water frozen to a sheen. It was made up of the questions it was easier not to ask, the mysteries I didn't bother prodding. I'd been letting it thicken as far back as I could recall. Something was moving beneath the ice now. Shifting, making the surface creak, turning it rotten.

You're so chill, Nate told me once, approvingly. *Nothing bothers you.*

My dad, indulgently: *What happened last night, that wasn't like you.*

And my mother. When she didn't like the question I asked she pushed me back on the bed, rearranging my hands like I was her doll, like my body didn't even belong to me. I hadn't fought back. I made it so *easy* for her; I didn't say a word.

I was done with that now. Even under the shower's spray I kept my eyes wide open, so suddenly sick of secrets I couldn't bear the dark.

CHAPTER FIVE

)

The city
Back then

I never really knew my mother. She died when I was two, and my dad wasn't the kind to keep a candle burning. When I asked questions, he'd send me to the kitchen drawer where he kept a stack of old photos and a rubber-banded lock of her red hair.

So. A mother can be a photograph.

My best friend lost her mother even earlier. Fee came into the world and the woman who'd carried her stepped out. Death transfigured her into a dark-eyed martyr, their apartment the reliquary where Fee's father tended to her traces.

A mother can be a saint, then. A ghost. A blessed outline that shows where she's gone missing.

Sometimes she's a stranger on a park bench, feeding her child from her fingers, the air between them so tender you could knead it like bread dough. Or a woman on the train, Coke in the sippy cup and yanking the kid's arm until it cries. I've always liked to watch bad mothers.

A mother can be a paring knife, a chisel. She can shape and destroy. I never really thought I would become one.

There are things a daughter should know about the woman who's raising her. If that woman had the courage. If she could say the words.

Let's say you lie in bed at night and rehearse the things you'd tell her, if you could. This daughter of yours, infinitely unreachable and just across the hall. This deep into the disaster, what could you still say?

Where would you begin?

When I was five my dad lost his keys in the dark between the bar and our apartment. I was up on his hip, his breath painting beery clouds over the frozen air. We'd walked half a mile in the cold blowing in from the lake, him in his unzipped chore coat because he ran hot, me shivering in a Rainbow Brite windbreaker because he never remembered kids grow. It was always late November by the time I got a winter coat that fit me.

My dad's good mood flipped like a card when we got to the street door and couldn't unlock it. While he stabbed at the superintendent's buzzer I wriggled out of his arms and started walking. Halfway back to the Green Man Tavern I swerved onto the black grass, plucking his keys from the hollow where they'd fallen.

When I was nine I put my fingers down a drain hole in the school washroom and got hold of a clasp I hadn't actually seen, attached to a charm bracelet I didn't know was there. Easel, candy cane, pointe shoe. I named each slimy charm before dropping the bracelet into the trash.

When I was twelve I walked home by myself one soft summer night. My dad was out and our apartment keys hung on a chain beneath my shirt. Up to the third floor, down the hall, then I stopped, staring at our closed apartment door. I heard nothing; there was nothing to hear. But quiet as I could I crept back to the street, then flew up the block to Fee and Uncle Nestor's place. So it was my dad, not me, who opened the door an hour later to find the man in the shadows with a kitchen knife, his jeans unzipped. It was my dad who broke a brown-paper-wrapped bottle over his head and scared him away, leaving a path of bloodstains over the carpet that never washed out.

There were stories like this about my mom, too, what my dad said she'd called her *guesses*. But the way I described it to my best friend, Fee, the only one who ever asked, was that I could just *feel* things. Objects, places, the contours of them and how the air moved through. Think about standing in the center of your own room. Closing your eyes. Now feel the saturated tug of your diary beneath the mattress. The photo of your crush pinned to the corkboard among postcards and magazine pictures. The hidden place where you spilled nail polish and it stained the floor, so you pulled your bed a foot to the right.

That's how I felt about the whole world. Or at least our little piece of it. We didn't think it was weird, Fee and I. We didn't even think it was special. Probably because she had her own thing: she always knew what people needed. Not their heads but their bodies. She was forever walking up to you with a glass of water, an apple, a bottle of Tylenol. She never stopped hassling my dad to eat a vegetable once in a while.

We were best friends who grew up like sisters, our world contained within the ten-block patch that spread like an oil stain around the street where we lived with our dads, two three-flats between our place and theirs. Our moms had been best friends, too, before dying a couple of years apart. We had this superstitious belief that the same thing would happen to us one day.

Our dads loved us, they tried, but they weren't all there. Uncle Nestor was a good man who couldn't look at his daughter without seeing his lost wife. And my dad ran like our bathroom faucet: wicked hot or freezing. I was his best girl or his heaviest burden, and I never could predict which it would be.

In a lot of ways we grew up fast—we were taking the train alone when we were eight, working part-time for our fathers at ten. I spent so much time haunting my dad's local that I couldn't actually remember when I had my first drink.

But in all the ways that counted, we were babies. We didn't know how to dress right or act cool or talk to people who weren't each other. My dad had told me, bluntly and early, why I should kick, scream, and run if a man ever tried to grab me, and I'd told Fee, so we had a cloudy understanding of sex. I wondered sometimes what our mothers would've wanted us to know, if they'd been around to teach us.

We made it all the way to fifteen this way. Who knows how much longer we might've gone if we hadn't met Marion.

CHAPTER SIX

)

The suburbs
Right now

I woke in the predawn hour to the sound of Aunt Fee's truck clearing its throat at the end of our drive. I listened for my mom's step in the downstairs hall, the creak and sigh of the front door, the resettling of the house around her absence. An hour of quiet passed, then the familiar unfolding of my dad's morning routine. Shower, NPR, coffee grinder. A band of thickening daylight crawled up my legs. When I heard the garage door close, I sat up.

Hank's bed was empty. He must not have come home last night. Still I crossed the hall on tiptoe, stopping in front of my parents' door. I tried to remember the last time I'd been inside. It gave me vertigo, straining to dredge up one memory of this room.

There, I had it. The feeling of my younger self lying between my parents. Eyes tracing a water stain on the ceiling, feet shoved beneath my dad's warm legs. My head propped on my mother's shoulder. The memory almost hurt.

Was it even real? Gingerly I pushed open the door, crossed

the threshold, and lay back on the bed. There, on the ceiling, the water stain.

I scrambled to the floor. Their bedroom looked like a college dorm shared by roommates with nothing in common. My dad's side was friendly, full of the kind of clutter you couldn't tidy: dog-eared books of poetry, cube-thick fantasy novels, a framed photo of me and Hank with blue Popsicle mouths. Hers was sparer. There was a spindly glass-fronted bookcase stocked with memoirs and biographies, an empty bedside table. An aggressively vivacious fern sprawled beneath the window, a clipping from Aunt Fee's garden.

I moved to the photos that marched along the master bathroom's vanity top. Here were my parents looking impossibly young on their wedding day, next to school pictures of my brother and me randomly stuck at thirteen and eleven. At the end of the row was a photo of Mom and Aunt Fee, taken when they were in high school. I picked it up.

The old paper had warped, bowing against the glass on one side. The camera's papery flash sheened over the fearsome curve of my aunt's brows, my mom's oxblood nails, the broken-heart necklaces glinting from their throats. They had poison-apple mouths and bad eyeliner, and this look on their faces like they knew they were the only girls in the world.

I was at least as old as they were in this picture, but still it made me feel like a child, forever locked out of their two-person circle. I started to set it down, but something made me pause. Scrubbing my shirt over the dusty glass, I peered closer.

It was their necklaces. Old-school cracked BFF hearts on chintzy chains, made of the same bendable metal used to cast diary keys. The hearts weren't broken halves, like I'd assumed. They were cut into thirds. My mom wore a jagged rim and Fee the middle piece, serrated on both sides. Someone must've had the other edge.

Still chewing on that thought, I moved to the closet. I ran an eye over my mother's tightly packed clothes, and sifted crinkled receipts and faded cookie fortunes out of the change tray. Stuck into the closet's doorframe was a photo booth strip of my mom as a child, squeezed in beside the dissolute mug of my long-gone granddad. He was rocking tinted newscaster glasses and too much visible chest hair, she a brick of bangs and no front teeth. Along the side of the strip ran the words TOPS OFF AND BOTTOMS UP AT SHENANIGANS BAR.

I kept going, but I had no idea what I was looking for. A journal that explained everything? More broken glass, more blood? There was a box of papers on an upper shelf, but it was all bone dry: birth certificates, tax forms, marriage license. I stared a while at the signatures on that last one, trying to imagine my parents—twenty and twenty-four, an unborn Hank already dreaming behind my mother's navel—standing shoulder to shoulder at the registry office.

There were small mysteries here. Tantalizing, but with meanings impossible to discern. In the bottom of a hideous backpack purse of flaking fake leather I found a sandwich baggie full of feathers, most of them brown or gray or mottled but a few the hot bright colors of Hi-C. I slid a tube of Rum Raisin from the pocket of an ancient pair of overalls and found the lipstick had been removed, replaced with an evil-looking clatter of needles and pins.

Beneath a shoe box holding a pair of high-heeled boots was a copy of Mary Oliver's *Dream Work*, an age-thinned receipt stuck into it like a bookmark. I pulled it out. A quarter century ago my mother bought CoverGirl eye shadow and a pack of Bubblicious at a Walgreens on Halsted Avenue, then wrote an address on the receipt in blue pen. A friend's apartment, probably, or a coffee shop. Something that meant a little bit back then and nothing now.

And yet. The thing was so carefully preserved, pressed like a flower in the pages of a book. I took a photo of the scrawled address before returning the receipt to its place.

I was setting the closet back to rights when I paused. In front of me was a soft wall of hanging clothes, black on black on the occasional blue. Following a rootless instinct I thrust my arms into their center like a diver, pushing hangers aside until I could see the closet wall.

Embedded into it was a safe the size of a cutting board.

I froze, more surprised by my hunch paying off than by the safe's existence. Then I ran out of the room and across the hall, to my dad's home office. I flipped over his chunky keyboard, freeing a scatter of everything bagel crumbs, and took a photo of the Post-it Notes stuck to its underside, scribbled with years' worth of passwords.

Back in front of the wall safe, I scanned the list: combinations of family birthdays, jersey numbers, strings of letters that seemed random but were probably mnemonics. Cutting out the passwords that wouldn't fit left me with a reasonable handful.

I cracked the lock on my third attempt. Dry-mouthed, ears chugging in the quiet, I opened the safe.

Inside it was an object the size and shape of a trade paperback, made entirely of gold.

I'd heard of people keeping their money in gold bars, but this seemed too big for that. And it was too beautiful to just be currency. It looked like something you'd find at a museum or an antique store, under glass.

When I lifted the object it felt hollow, but there was no seam I could see. Its surface was just a little warmer than my skin. Gently I tilted it from side to side, then shook it, taking in its burnished top, its expensive heft, the way its sides broke the light into a prismatic gleam. What was it *for*?

I pressed an ear to its top. Nothing. Of course, nothing. Again I turned it over. Impulsively, I touched it to my tongue.

My palms tingled with the struck vibration of a bat hitting a baseball. The metal tasted shocking, electric, *alive*.

I heard my mother speaking in my ear. I didn't imagine her, I *heard* her, low voice tip-tapping over a crooked bundle of syllables I couldn't quite discern. My eyes fell shut and I dropped into a memory of such startling clarity it felt like teleportation.

I smelled the wide cold fragrance of the lake at night. I saw the stars the way they look when hung over water, like they're checking their faces in a compact mirror. The vision was as palpable as a freshly painted canvas. I could've reached out to smear its colors if I wanted to. Though I couldn't turn to see her, I could feel my mother beside me, warm in the cool air.

When I opened my eyes I was sitting on the closet floor. I stared at but didn't see the rattan front of my parents' hamper, the frill of cobweb at its base. The gold object was inert again, whatever static charge I'd made with spit and metal fizzled out, died away.

A dream, I thought dizzily. A piece of wishful thinking, cooked with paranoia into ... whatever had just happened to me.

But I didn't really think so. It had stirred something up, something real. A memory so buried it didn't feel like it belonged to me.

I licked its shining side again. Nothing happened. I considered keeping it, but I didn't want to be on the hook for losing something priceless. So I returned it to the safe, for now. And as I did I saw something I'd missed, tucked into its very back.

It was a little box made of fragrant wood. A coat of arms was painted onto its top, its front read FLOR FINA. It fit familiarly into my hands, because it was *mine*. A cigar box I used to stash my treasures in when I was a kid. It had been lost years ago.

Not lost. Taken. Locked in a safe, in a closet wall, in a room I never entered. A stolen piece of me.

CHAPTER SEVEN

)

The city
Back then

I don't remember what I was doing the first time I saw Marion. Lifting fish fingers out of the fryer, probably. Rolling quarters, short-changing some biddy in a rain bonnet because she pissed me off paying for her four-piece plate in nickels. This was when our dads were running a fried-fish shop a couple blocks off the lake.

I was waiting around for the new part-timer. My dad's wrecked back was just then entering its final decline, and he could no longer handle fourteen-hour days. I was a snotty little brat, still my dad's princess whenever he wanted me to be, and I'd been looking forward to putting the new hire in her place. Someone else could clean the grease traps for once. But when she walked in, all the snark died in my throat.

Marion was older, seventeen. Ears chewed up with metal, wearing this cool green jacket that was too thin for the weather. But that wasn't why I was staring. Like a lost set of keys, like a hidden bracelet, something about this girl I'd never seen before drew me in. I could *feel* her standing there on the rubbed-out tile, denser and realer than anything else in the room.

She stared back. I had my dead mom's red hair, though hers was curly and mine the sort of watery-fine that folds into points when you pile it. It was winter out but sweltering over the fryer. I was wearing a T-shirt, little freckles of grease burn climbing my arms.

"Have we ever—" she started, at the same time I said, "Do you think we've—"

We stopped. A charged silence we could've broken with laughter, but didn't.

"I'm Marion," she said.

"Dana."

"Dana." She repeated the word like it was the name of some unmapped country, still unpacking me with her pale eyes. "We're gonna be friends."

Redheads blush easily. You don't need to be angry or embarrassed for it to happen, you just need to be pushed the slightest bit off center. I lifted my chin and thought of icebergs, of jumping into a cold white ocean. "You think?" I said, a little meanly.

"I know." Her voice was quiet but strangely commanding, so earnest I could've died. Right then I knew she was as maladjusted as I was.

I showed her where to hang her jacket and her black shoulder bag, all the time trying to figure out what it *was* about her. Her body was stocky, her cheeks ruddy, her ponytail tucked under a newsboy cap. She wasn't pretty, but there was something in her face that made you want to keep looking. She took a CD from her jacket and held it up. On its black-and-white cover a woman whipped her wet head, hair caught in a wild half-crown.

"Your dad said I could pick the music when I work," she said. "Where's your player?"

Fee and I grew up loving the music our dads loved. Cream, the Moody Blues, Led Zeppelin. Even the polka my dad was raised on, that they played in the Polish dance halls where his parents met. Fee and I used to spin around on bare feet while the record player *oompa*'ed and crackled and our dads got drunk on ferocious Ukrainian vodka, shouting us on.

The music Marion played was not that kind of music. It was jittery fistfuls of punk, working you over in ninety-second bursts. Heavy guitar rock where it was women who howled like Robert Plant, and glam stuff that glittered and cut like the shards of a colored lantern.

That first day we worked side by side without talking much, Marion picking up the repetitive rhythms of fast-food service while I soaked up the music. At closing time Fee was waiting for me on the curb, playing Tetris with her feet in the gutter. When she saw Marion her face went guarded, before softening the way it does when she's channeling her empathy thing.

"You're hungry," she said.

Marion fiddled with the zip of her jacket. Sometimes Fee's looks made people shy. "I ate already. In there."

"That doesn't count," Fee said dismissively. "You need *food*."

We went back to her place, where there was always a Pyrex

tray of something good in the fridge. That night it was picadillo, fragrant with the mint her dad grew on the back porch.

"I don't really like meat," Marion told us, before ripping like a Rottweiler through a plateful. Afterward she sighed, her smile changing the balance of her whole odd face.

"I can't believe your dad made that. All my dad makes is highballs. All my mom does is put SnackWell's on a plate."

I got a mental image of her parents from that. The mom doing Tae Bo in a sweat suit, portioning her Weight Watchers points across the days. The dad clinking his shot glass twice against the bar for luck, like mine did, before dropping it into a pint of Guinness. I'd feel stupid later, when I learned how wrong I had it.

But right then we were full and warm and we couldn't stop smiling. Marion handed Fee a CD and we lay on the uneven floor of her bedroom to listen, heads close and the music loud enough that we could feel it vibrating through the boards.

That was how it began. Food and music. The rest of it came later: the magic, the things that fueled it. We were angry before Marion came, even if we didn't know it. At our dads, at our dead moms, at ourselves for being fifteen years old with lives the size of a pinprick, and no idea how to change them. But it was Marion who gave our anger form.

It started with the music. That's not where it ended.

CHAPTER EIGHT

)

The suburbs
Right now

I sat on my bed, sifting through the cigar box.

There were familiar things, of course. A green-paste gemstone from my old paper dress-up crown, a ticket stub from the time my aunt took me—just me—to see *Hamilton*. A marbled guitar pick my dad had given me, strung on thin ribbon, and a fountain pen with a cobalt cartridge.

But I couldn't remember where I'd picked up the flat black stone, roughly circular with an eraser-width hole straight through its center. Or the four-leaf clover, dried and pressed beneath a piece of Scotch tape. I looked closer; it was a *five*-leaf clover. I must've taped the extra leaf in. There was a ring of tree branch the width and thickness of a dollar coin, a stump of white candle, a rubber-banded hank of red hair. Mine? My mother's? I ran a palm over my bleached head.

I was about to pack everything away when I saw the paper at the very bottom, folded to the size of the box's interior. Just its grain against my fingers was familiar. Even before I opened it I knew it was a sheet from one of my old sketchbooks.

It was a pencil drawing, a pretty good one. In it a boy in jeans and bare feet cradled an armful of white gardenias, smiling with closed eyes. His freckles were rendered as a smear of stars.

I touched a finger to the drawing. The ruffled Degas skirts of the flowers, the boy's dreamy smile. I'd captured that, somehow. But what had moved me to make—much less *save*—a drawing of Billy Paxton?

I checked the date. I'd drawn it the summer before seventh grade, just a few months before the Embarrassing Incident that marked the first and, until the other night, last time Billy and I ever spoke. His face in my sketchbook—distant, serene—clashed with my crystal-etched memory of the way he'd looked at me that day, hot-eyed and almost hateful.

I must have seen him from across the street before I drew this. Gotten his face caught in my head and exorcised it on a wave of white petals.

I studied the drawing, then each object I'd pulled out before it, panning for any clue as to why the box had been hidden. But there were no answers here. Just another mystery.

Why? While washing my face, getting dressed, eating a Pop-Tart from a box labeled HANK'S POP-TARTS, I asked myself the question. Why lock up a child's treasure box? I kept bouncing up, pacing, sitting down again. Until finally I got sick of yelling at my mother in my head.

I had to face her now, today. Because right *now* I could still feel her slender fingers squeezing mine, pressing me back onto the bed. I could taste the weird sizzle of the gold. There was a flame in my head, I couldn't let it burn out.

I set off through the heat feeling fragile as sugar glass. Biking across the back ends of parking lots, through dusty stands of Queen Anne's lace. Bathing in the shuffle of passing radios and teetering along the rims of retention ponds, hoping nobody winged a Big Gulp at me out a car window.

I was glazed in sweat by the time I hit Woodbine's downtown stretch. It was six blocks of stores and restaurants and coffee shops, plus a two-screen movie theater and the hilarious Lounge Le Bleu, where people who wanted to pretend they were in the city went to drink cocktails stuck with glow-in-the-dark swizzle sticks.

My mom and aunt's shop was sandwiched between two fancy candy stores and just below a dance studio, so there were always footfalls shaking the ceiling. As I rolled up I could hear the tinny sounds of a recorded symphony drifting from the studio's open windows.

But the Small Shop's window was dark. When I yanked the door, it didn't give.

The day was so bright I couldn't make out its interior, even when I cupped my hands to the glass. I scanned the posted hours, though I knew them by heart. The shop should've opened at ten.

A cobbled corridor ran between the Small Shop and Vanilla Fudge, decked with cast-iron lanterns. I hurried beneath them, glad for the first time that I was forced into service as a gift wrapper during the shop's holiday rush—I had a copy of its employee-door key.

I let myself into the cellar coolness of the back room. Nobody there, but the lights were on.

"Hello? Mom?"

No answer. It was cluttered back here, but organized. I scanned the shelves, the tidy piles of stock, the rolling mail crate where they kept unopened product samples—slivers of chocolate made beneath the harvest moon, minerals you rubbed on your face, magazines featuring Scandinavian women in recycled overalls telling you why you should feed your babies raw honey. All sorts of goofy shit.

The Small Shop was named for Aunt Fee's theory of small good things: everything they sold was meant to provide a small good, a slight adjustment that would make your life better. Usually it smelled like herbs and organic oolong, plus whatever aggressive candle they had going on the counter, but today the air was acrid, unpleasant. It coated my tongue. I looked around for something to rinse my mouth and found an iced coffee cup sweating atop a filing cabinet, Aunt Fee's dark lipstick ringing the straw. I touched a knuckle to its beading side. Still cold.

"Mom?" I said again. "Aunt Fee?"

I threw the rest of the lights and walked into the empty shop. Everything out here was mellow white or the wind-blasted gray of driftwood. Against it all the products stood out like art pieces. My eye went straight to the rust-colored smear in front of the counter.

Blood. Too big for a nosebleed, too small to start looking for a body. A tuft of hair was smeared into it. I moved closer and it became something else, with a distinctive ombre of brown and gray. Rabbit fur.

There was a pressure in my head, climbing. Not quite pain, not yet.

I turned, sped through the shop's back door, out onto the suburban concrete. Kneeling in the anemic shade of a lamppost, my lungs all clotted with sugared air, I called my mother.

The call went straight to voicemail. She was forever leaving her phone in the car, letting it die, allowing her voicemail box to fill up.

Aunt Fee, then. At least her phone rang. When that call, too, went to voicemail I cursed so loud and long the ponytailed fudge shop employee sucking on a vape a few sidewalk squares down said, "Whoa."

I flipped her off and got back on my bike. I could hear her laughing as I rode away.

Aunt Fee lived in a two-story cottage at the end of a street lined with them, suburban starter homes for one-kid families. Her driveway was empty. When I peeked in the windows of her garage, that was empty, too. I tried the bell, but no one answered.

I was standing on the step, considering whether to check for unlocked windows, when my phone chimed.

Sorry I missed your call. Talk soon okay?

Aunt Fee. The fist around my heart loosened as I dropped onto the steps.

I went to the shop, I replied. What's happening? Where are you?

The house was at my back. Empty, but as I waited for her reply my neck started to itch. The feeling pushed me off the stoop and onto the grass, turning to keep the house's windows in my sights.

Sorry, she texted. Dealing with something but we're fine. I'll call you soon, Ivy-girl.

I read and reread her words, trying to source my unease. I breathed out slow. Rubbed a hand over my prickling neck.

Does this something have to do with the rabbits?

This time she didn't reply. I stood another minute on the grass, waiting for her to get back to me, but she never did.

CHAPTER NINE

>

The city
Back then

By the time I was fifteen I'd learned how to be lots of different people. With my dad I was demanding and high-strung, a showoff. With the kids at school I was quiet. With Fee I never had to think about it, so who knows. On the train, in the world, I was a girl as hard as safety glass.

But Marion was one person. She wouldn't, she *couldn't*, shape-shift. Some days I was impressed by it, and on others her refusal to fake it pissed me off. Fee and I knew when to make ourselves small and when to pretend we felt big, but Marion refused to be anything other than who she was. She was too intense, she came on too strong, she could never take a joke unless she'd made it. She told off customers out loud instead of under her breath, and snapped like a twig at catcallers.

Her refusal to compromise made us braver. She coaxed us out of our neighborhood, down the long spine of the city. Together we slid through the crowds at all-ages shows, hands linked, pretending someone was waiting for us at the front. We walked under the viaduct at two in the morning, past sleeping bags and shopping carts. For the price of coffee and pie we rented out tables in all-night diners populated by men in work boots and gutter punks ashing into their eggs.

Marion started working at the fish shop in midwinter, when the city was half dead under a rock-salt overcoat. It was a night in late March, at the start of the thaw, that we sat on the beach at Farwell, fish grease breathing off our clothes, passing around a bottle of Malört.

This late the beach was a cruising ground. Nobody paid us any mind. It was warm for the season, Marion's boombox playing Yo La Tengo on low. She was relaxed for once, elbows in the sand. Fee's head was in my lap and I was furrowing her black hair into loose braids and out again, rhythmic as a rosary. Down by the water two men shuffled by. I saw one of them notice us, grabbing his friend's arm to reroute him.

I jostled my knee until Fee sat up.

The men, two white dudes, walked up the beach, their pin-striped shirts untucked from their Casual Friday khakis. The one who'd seen us first was ferret-skinny, his hair in bleached spikes. His friend was shorter, a young man with an old man's paunch. He'd managed to get himself a sunburn somewhere. They stopped a few yards away, cocking up our view of the lake.

"Evening, ladies," slurred the Ferret. He was so drunk he looked like he had pinkeye.

"Gentlemen," I said. "Nice night at the Admiral?"

The sunburnt one blinked. "We weren't at the Admiral."

"She's mocking us," said the Ferret, grinning. He had that slippery veneer of high good humor that generally conceals a black hole. He ticked a finger at each of us in turn—Marion,

Fee, me. "Lemme guess. You're the slutty one, you're the spicy one, and you're the sad emo chick."

"I like emo music," Sunburn said, beaming in from a different conversation. "I used to be in a band. In high school."

Ferret slung an arm around his friend. "Hear that? Which one of you wants to blow a rock star?"

"Huh?" Sunburn focused on us with difficulty. "Dude. They're kids."

"Not interested," Fee said, her voice ironed flat. "Keep walking."

Ferret plonked his ass down in the sand. "Keep walking! What are you, fuckin' . . . fuckin' Johnny Corleone? *Keep walking.*"

"Vito Corleone," said Sunburn. "Come on, Matt. Let's go."

I knew how to coat my disdain with enough sugar to get guys like this to back off. *Sorry, I have a boyfriend*, that kind of thing. But my mouth was wicked with wormwood and I was pissed at Marion's silence.

"Listen to your friend, Matt," I told him. "You're gross. Nobody here wants you."

Ferret's mask slipped. I think he wanted to haul back and hit me, but he was trapped in the grip of the nice-guy dilemma: if you're too good a dude to ever hit a girl, what do you do when some bitch disrespects you?

He settled on leaning over almost lazily and rapping his knuckles twice on my skull, hard. "Talk nicer to me, sweetheart."

Before I could react Fee was between us, shoving him away. "No way, motherfucker," she spat. "You don't *touch* her."

Then Marion surged to her feet. Shaking, fisted hands held out. Her lips were moving and her face looked possessed, one eye wandering off center.

"You sh-*shit*," she panted.

Ferret laughed, but it sounded nervous. I think all of us were spooked.

"What did you think would happen here?" Her voice still trembled. "What ugly things do you think about when you mess with girls who don't want you?"

His lip curled back. "You wanna talk about ugly, babe? I'd be doing you a favor."

Marion went still. No, she *steadied*, drawing herself up and in like a flame clapped under a hurricane glass. When she spoke, the words came low. A cadenced murmur that played havoc with my heart.

"Let all his thoughts be seen." Her voice gained volume, grew sure. "Let their dark matter touch the air. Let them trouble him from without."

The two men exchanged a look. "Yeah, I'm out," said Ferret, clapping his hands to his knees. "Fuckin' weirdos."

As he stood, something fluttered onto his cheek. It had the crunchy, iridescent heft of a cicada, with wings of red lace and a black carapace. He swiped it away.

A second insect landed on his temple. This time he slapped it, killing it in a messy crush that smeared over his eyebrow. "What the hell," he muttered, looking at his palm.

Now came a third, cutting itself out of the backlit night to settle onto his jaw.

And another.

And another.

Their wings a sickly whir, their tendril legs flexing over his forehead and cheeks and neck, and the V of skin showing above his button-up. He swept them away, skin reddening and pricking with sweat.

"What is . . . what are you . . ." An insect landed on his mouth. He dragged an arm across it, whimpering, then screamed as a fresh drift settled over him. "No," he said. "*No no no no—*"

Then he stopped talking, mouth seamed tight against the onslaught. He was down, he was screaming with his lips closed, he was mashing his face into the sand. I didn't know whether the insects were stinging or biting or just crawling over his skin, but they kept coming.

I hung back, horrified. Fee kicked sand at the guy, I think in an attempt to drive off the bugs. Marion stared. Her mouth was open, her face like a room someone had just walked out of, slamming the door.

"Help!" Sunburn screamed. "Help us!"

Down by the water a man in a backpack slowed down to watch. On the path a pair of cyclists swung off their bikes, peering across the sand.

"Time to go." Fee was gathering our stuff, her voice calm but rising. "Let's go now, now, *right now, Marion, mueve tu culo!*"

Marion snapped back to life. Her eyes were hot with shock, taking in the scene as if she were blameless. Then she ran.

"Wait!" yelled Sunburn, kneeling close but not too close to the man writhing on the ground. "Come back!"

We pounded over the sand. Marion's boombox was in my arms. My eyes were watering, my legs rubbery with shock, and by the time we hit Morse I could barely stand.

"Stop," I said, "*stop.*"

We held on to each other, we held each other up, the sounds

coming out of our mouths something like laughter. Marion cut out abruptly and turned, vomiting French fries and Malört over the grass. When she was done we held her up, rubbing her back while she cried.

What did you do?

"I don't know," Marion kept saying. "I don't know."

How did you do it?

There was vomit on the toes of her shoes. She scuffed them against a curb. "Please. Stop asking."

We could hear that she meant it. We were quiet for as long as we could stand it. Then:

Could we do it, too?

We were sitting at the edge of the Dominick's lot, empty snack bags sifting around our feet. Fee had run in to buy Marion water and came back with Bugles and Pop-Tarts and Cool Ranch Doritos. All of it tasted so *good*, so electric, blasted with fake flavor that singed my tongue. We kept laughing with fresh surprise, mouths full of sodium crumbs, remembering the way the Ferret had fallen to his knees, then farther, embracing the sand.

"Yes," Marion said. She said it so shyly. Like an old-fashioned bride. "If you want to. We could do it together."

If, she said. *If* we wanted to learn how to be ferocious, how to have *power*, how to bring shitheads to their knees. We'd never wanted anything as much as we wanted this.

CHAPTER TEN

)

The suburbs
Right now

I wheeled up the drive to find my brother sitting in the sun, rolling a joint. He squinted at me.

"Your mouth looks better. I thought you were grounded, though."

I dropped my bike by the garage. "Whatever. You get away with so much worse."

Hank shrugged, like *Yeah, I do.* "Dad told me what happened with your King Shit boyfriend. Need me to do something?"

"*Ex*-boyfriend. And definitely not."

"Just call me next time, dumbass. If you need a ride."

"Fine, but you better answer when I do." I sat beside him. "So. Hank."

"So. Ivy."

"I know you don't want to. Like, ever. But we need to talk about Mom."

He kept his eyes on his work. "That's actually the last thing we need to do."

"I'm serious," I persisted. "Something's going on with her. You haven't talked to her lately, have you?"

"Talked? To Mom? That's funny."

Their rocky relationship was a scab I tried not to pick. Usually. "Listen to me. Last night I saw her burying something in the backyard. So I dug it up."

He took a beat. "Yeah?"

"It was a jar of *blood*. And broken glass. And blood! I mean, what the hell?"

"Was it a full moon last night?"

My heart sped up. "I'm not sure. I don't think so. Why?"

"That's totally the kind of thing a New Age white lady does under a full moon. It's probably some prosperity thing she read in a book."

That was so annoyingly plausible I got out my phone and pulled up the dead rabbit. "Fine, except someone left *this* on our driveway the other day. And I was just at the shop. It's closed for no reason, and I'm pretty sure someone left another rabbit on the floor."

He glanced at my screen, then twisted away. "Ugh, who takes a *photo* of that? I know about the rabbit, I saw Dad hosing down the drive. That child of the corn probably left it, whatshisname who lives in the blue house."

"Peter."

"Right. Peter. But if you're worried, talk to Aunt Fee."

"I texted her. She's gonna call me later."

"Good." He watched me for a second, eyes clouded. Then he shook his head. "She'll tell you if things aren't okay. Mom wouldn't, but she will."

"I guess," I said, and hesitated. Tell him about the safe in the closet, yes or no?

Not yet, I decided. He'd want to break in again, see for himself. Or he'd underplay it completely. Either way I'd end up annoyed.

Hank held up the joint he'd finished rolling. "You want?"

"I'm good."

"Cool." He stashed it in an empty Altoids tin, swatting skunky flecks from his knees like he was about to stand. But I wasn't done talking, so I opened my mouth and said the first thing I thought of. One of the drain holes my thoughts had been swirling around.

"Do you remember Hattie Carter?"

"Oh, *god*." He laughed a little. "Everyone remembers Hattie Carter."

"Right, but did you know she was my bully?"

"You had a bully?"

"Everyone has one at some point. Unless they *are* the bully." I made my voice light, but it was bad. Cherry Coke poured into the slats of my locker bad. Rumors about my invented sluttiness bad. Aching stomach, Sunday-night dread *bad*. The worst part was, it was completely random. She was just some dick in my gym class who terrorized me for weeks, for no reason, until our teacher caught her texting a locker-room photo of me in my underwear to her friends. That skated close enough to lawsuit territory that the school got off its ass and did something about it.

Something: We were pulled from class one day, made to sit with our parents in the principal's office. The principal delivered a nonspecific lecture that seemed damning of me as well, about cliques and responsible phone use and accepting our differences. I thought my mom would laser her into pieces with her eyes. Hattie presented me with an apology letter written in green gel pen and covered with shiny puppy stickers, which the principal took as a sweet gesture but I knew to be the passive-aggressive act of an unrepentant monster who'd spent half our freshman year barking at me in the halls.

My dad blustered and brooded through it, one hand protective on my shoulder, while hers didn't even pretend not to be scrolling on his phone. Her mom wasn't there. Mine sat in a civilized rictus, nails in her knees and an odd little smile playing over her mouth. At the end she stood and smoothed herself down and with that same slight smile told the principal her intervention was a travesty and she'd be out of a job within the year, before transferring her nails into my upper arm and guiding me out the door.

My mom was right. A couple of months later the principal "resigned" on a wave of rumors having to do with inappropriate texts sent to a very recent graduate. Her departure was my mom's lucky guess, or maybe the texts had saved her from having to plant heroin in the woman's car. I wouldn't put a thing past Dana Nowak.

Hattie's downfall came sooner. The high school talent show fell on a balmy April night, just a week after she'd flashed her crocodile smile at me in the principal's office. Along with the rest of the choir I had a bit part backing up a cute tenth-grader's pitch-agnostic rendition of "You Can't Always Get What You

Want." I was back in the audience, covered in polyester-choir-robe sweat, when Hattie took the stage.

She was performing a lip synch of "bad guy," her blue eyes ringed like Saturn with glitter liner and her hair combed into a wet curtain. I knew how rotten she was inside. That she could look so pretty anyway made me want to cry.

Her performance was wooden and surprisingly graceless, though her friends whooped it up the entire time anyway. Until she stopped cold at center stage. The song went on, but her lips weren't moving. When she wrapped both arms around her middle, I thought she might throw up.

She didn't. She did this awkward, cowboy-legged run off stage left, her eyes panicked spotlights in their circles of liner. And it didn't matter that no one could actually tell what had happened then and there. By the start of the next school day, roughly every kid in every grade knew that cool Hattie Carter had shit her pants onstage.

After she'd run into the wings, when everyone was still shifting and looking around, the quiet broken here and there by peals of nervous laughter, I glanced over at my mother. I'd felt us united in our hatred of Hattie and thought she might look back and smile, or wink, or whisper *Serves her right.* But she was facing straight ahead, chin coolly cocked, still looking at the place Hattie had stood. Her mouth was curved into that same dangerous smile she'd worn in the principal's office.

I thought about all that now, held it up against Nate and our matching split lips. And the itchy sense I'd had for years, that the times my mother most felt like a *mom* was when she was furious on our behalf. Like a bad boyfriend. Like a little girl who didn't want anyone else playing with her dolls.

"That thing with Hattie at the talent show. It was right after Mom found out she was messing with me." I hesitated. "And remember Coach Keene?"

Hank made a disgusted sound. "That bigot. Of course I do."

"They never diagnosed him, right? And he got sick, what, a few days after what he said to you?" I looked at Hank, his big blue Mom eyes a little startling this close. "Do you think . . . have you ever thought that Mom . . ."

"Ivy!" He brought a fist down on his leg, then flattened it. "Stop. You're thinking too hard."

"I'm *thinking* too hard?" I flicked him in the temple. "Are you worried I'll break my lady brain?"

"I'm just saying, Mom is *Mom*. We know this. And you have nothing to do right now, so you're making it into a thing. Be grounded. Get it over with. Then move on. And just . . . don't worry, okay? There's no point."

Across the street a station wagon was pulling into the Paxtons' drive. I watched as Billy and three other kids spilled out, two girls and a guy I recognized from school. I wondered if one of them was Billy's girlfriend.

Hank knocked my shoulder so the elbow I was leaning on fell off my knee. "Having a good stare? Paxton got cute, didn't he?"

I scowled at him. "I'm staring into space! I'm resting my eyes on his house!"

"I *bet* you wanna rest your eyes on his house."

Billy was letting his friends through the front door. He

paused before stepping inside, looking back at me. I thought of the drawing I'd found in my cigar box, of his younger, star-flecked face, and dropped my gaze. "*Hank*. Shut up before he hears you."

"I didn't know he had supersonic bat hearing. That's hot."

When Billy was gone, Hank looked at me sidewise. "What ever happened with you guys, anyway?"

I let my head fall back and groaned. "I was *twelve*. Was I supposed to be an expert on letting people down gently at twelve? I was embarrassed!"

Because that was the thing, the seventh-grade incident that still made my body brace with remembered shame. Little Billy Paxton, the random sixth-grader who lived across the street, walked right up to me the second week of school. *Ivy*, he said, his face as sick and determined as if I were a firing squad. *Will you be my girlfriend?*

I'd stared at him in disbelief, both of us going redder and redder, other kids gumming up around us to watch the drama unfold. *No, thank you*, I'd finally said, robotically, before turning heel and fleeing for the bathroom. We hadn't spoken again until the other night, with Nate. Not one word.

Hank blinked at me. "Man, you are ice cold. Poor Billy."

I started to sputter, then his phone buzzed for maybe the tenth time since I'd sat down. Sighing gustily, he slid it out of his pocket. Its screen was lined with a one-way conversation, all incoming texts from his college boyfriend. Hank had a bit of a ghosting habit.

He held it up. "Go away now. I have to focus on breaking up with Jared."

I tilted my head to read the last unanswered text in the thread. Are you being weird or am I being paranoid?

"Oh, totally," I said. "You've got to pay attention when you're breaking up with someone by text. Otherwise it would be mean."

"For sure," he replied, either not getting it or not taking the bait. But as I stood he reached back, wrapping a hand around my ankle.

"Hey. Ivy. I wouldn't, like, get in Mom's way. If I were you."

I touched my arm, where goosebumps were rising. "What do you mean?"

He shifted, not quite looking at me. "Just let her do what she wants to do. We'll both be out of here soon enough."

His phone started to ring. "Now he's *calling* me?" he said incredulously, waving a hand at me to go.

I went to the kitchen to splash my face from the tap. All morning I'd been running around like a kid playing detective, and I had nothing to show for any of it but this drumbeat of dread. Hank's warning, blood on the Small Shop's floor. Shitty Nate and Hattie Carter and the puzzling contents of a closet safe. Aunt Fee still hadn't called.

Then I remembered the address, the one I'd found written on the old receipt. When I looked it up the most likely result was a store in a college town north of the city. A flower shop that sold books, it looked like. I called it.

"Petals and Prose," a woman said warmly, her voice turning up into a question at the end.

"Hi! My name is . . . uh, sorry. I was wondering, how long has your store been at this location?"

A pause as she took all that in. "It'll be eight years this fall."

"Do you happen to know what was there before you?"

"We used to be a record store. Oh, let me think. Dr. Wax, it was called."

"So that's what was at this address twenty-five years ago?"

"No . . . I'm sorry, can you hold on a sec?" When she spoke again, it was muffled, directed at someone else. I listened to her talking, laughing. After a few minutes she came back.

"You still there?"

"I'm here."

"Okay. The record store was actually next door. We were vacant for a long time. Twenty-something years ago this was a place called 'Twixt and 'Tween."

I pressed the phone to my ear. "Twicksintween? Could you spell that?"

"'Twixt and 'Tween," she enunciated. "Like betwixt and be-tween? You know what, I'm not the one who grew up around here. Let me pass you to the owner."

More rustling, and a new voice came on the line. Less friendly, older. "Hello? You're asking about store history?"

"Yeah. Yes."

"May I ask why?"

I didn't have a lie prepared, so I told the truth. "I think my mom used to go there. To whatever your store was when she was my age."

A brief silence. When she spoke again, her brusque voice was touched with something complex. "So she was one of Sharon's girls."

The house was very quiet. Just my window screen, creaking

against the breeze. "That's right," I said. "I'm trying to get in touch with Sharon."

Sharon's dead, I imagined her saying. Or, *Psych, you liar, I made her up!* Instead she told me, "Well, go ahead and give me your name and number. No guarantees, but I'll pass them along."

I did, and I gave her my mom's name, too. Then I flopped back on my bed and stared at the ceiling, letting my thoughts flicker like leaves.

CHAPTER ELEVEN

)

The city
Back then

Two days after the beach, we got on the bus heading north.

It was our first time going to Marion's place. I don't know what Fee thought, but I'd assumed Marion was the same as us. Not donation-box poor, not *eviction* poor, but no money, either. She dressed like we did, grotty thrift-store clothes. She inked rings on her fingers and liner around her eyes with the same blue rollerball, and made minimum wage under the table serving fried fish fingers to construction workers and surly neighborhood types. Nobody would've thought she had money.

It was one of those raw, unjust spring afternoons when the air is so bright and clean it focuses the whole world like a lens, but it's cold still and you're shivering. Just a half-hour trip, then we stepped off the bus like we'd landed in Oz. All the lawns were fat green pincushions, all the faces well fed. The sun sliced through the clouds in tempered golden bars, like even the light got expensive when you left the city.

The raw hems of Marion's jeans caught on her Cons as she led us through the streets of her cushy college town, past houses perched like sailboats on grassy swells. When she turned onto a slate path that led to a Craftsman cottage, Fee and I looked at each other behind her back. It was sharp as a box cutter, that look.

We moved like creepy crawlers through Marion's pristine house. Inspecting objects that had no function but to be pretty, opening the fridge to find fresh orange juice and hummus tubs instead of Old Style cans and irradiated deli meat. Marion was the klepto, but that place gave me itchy fingers. I nicked a Buffalo nickel from a wooden ashtray and a slim book titled *Dream Work* off the arm of a rocking chair. Fee watched me do it, mouth flat as the horizon.

That house was a confessional. Marion's sins laid before us: that she lived in a place with a piano and washed her hair with brand shampoo. That she went to sleep each night in a four-poster bed with a flowered canopy. Even the bed wore a skirt.

From the nightstand I picked up a photo in which an adolescent Marion beamed, sallow in a yellow satin dance costume and stripe of stage lipstick. My thumbs smudged its glass front, nails painted in chipped black Wet 'n Wild.

We'd been quiet all through the tour, but now I laughed. Inside that laugh was all my jealousy, all my betrayal, boiled down into disdain. Fee was reaching for a blown-glass unicorn caught mid-prance. Her voice when she turned was as harsh as I'd ever heard it.

"Why do you even need it?"

The magic, she meant. It had only been a couple of days that we'd known it was real, and already we sensed magic didn't grow in soft places.

Marion stood in the center of her little rich girl's room, planted like a weed in the yellow carpet. "If I tell you, will you listen?"

We shrugged. We were two skittish city mice, making bruises in the carpet's pile. But by the end, we were listening.

Marion was the surprise child of her parents' old age, born after their sons were grown and gone. Her mother and father were indulgent but distant, happy to trust her upkeep to a string of nannies.

Marion tried to be a dutiful daughter. She had the sense of owing it to her parents, of tiptoeing like a guest through their house. She believed the distance they kept was her fault alone, and something she still might fix. But the older she got, the more they withdrew.

She was twelve when she finally gave up on pleasing them. It took her that long to look around her life and see that not one piece of it was truly hers. Her younger self came to feel like a departed sister still haunting their house. Her photos covered the walls, but it was Marion who slept uneasily in her ruffled bed. Or maybe Marion had it wrong. Maybe *she* was the ghost.

When she wasn't at school she roamed the campus where her parents taught, sneaking into the backs of lecture halls and reading books on the green. There were two university libraries and she spent lots of time at the main one, a redbrick hive of student activity and brightly lit carrels. The other library—a scholar's haven, annexed sometime in the 1940s—Marion never bothered with. She wasn't even sure where it was.

On a frigid Monday evening, she found it.

She'd been wandering since school let out, killing time beneath a midwinter sky that was blue as a mood ring. It was almost dinner but there was no one waiting for her—her mom had office hours, her dad a late seminar. She was a mile from home and had forgotten her scarf and she felt like crying for no good reason. She was distracted enough to mistake an unfamiliar stretch of sidewalk for a shortcut.

The lamps on the path were old. They tinted her skin an ugly orange and gave off a teeth-itching hum. She figured out pretty quickly she was going the wrong way but kept moving anyway, until the path poured itself into a bowl of frozen lawn.

Beyond it was the weirdest building she'd ever seen. It was a multistory Frankenstein, afflicted with strangely shaped windows and unexpected outcroppings. It was, according to the brass sign on its front, the other library.

Marion checked her orchid-pink Swatch: 5:35. She let herself in through the carved wooden doors, and it took her fewer than the twenty-five minutes before closing to fall in love.

The library was eccentrically designed, as full of secrets as an advent calendar. There were hidden alcoves and dead doors, half-stairs and galleries and a third-floor reading nook Marion claimed as her own. Here and there you came upon stained glass: a girl holding a knife and an apple at the top of a staircase; a fox curled beneath a rosebush in a third-floor hall.

Only faculty and visiting researchers had browsing rights, but Marion was the brat of two tenured professors, her mother the fearsome chair of the anthropology department. And she was the right kind of quiet. Not shy, not cute, just hard to see, bobbing along below the float line of adults' notice. Soon the guard at the door just waved her through.

The library was always cold as a cathedral. Coldest was the basement, its warren of shelves studded like a Christmas cake with dank reading rooms. Its carpets ate sound, so you always thought you were alone until you came, suddenly, upon some old-fart prof who gawked at you like you were one of the *Shining* twins.

Marion didn't believe in hauntings, not really—her parents had a tendency to debunk her fears in chilly academic terms, and though annoying, it worked—but that floor of the library felt *layered*, let's say. You could feel the way history accreted there, laying its scaly paw over your neck. Mainly she stayed out of the basement.

For a long time Marion had been expecting—hoping—*praying* her life would change. But her life was a broken flip-book. She was twelve the night she discovered the library. And she was fourteen—taller, lonelier, angrier at being alone—the day she ducked in to wait out a September storm. It hadn't happened yet but you could smell it coming, sizzled pavement and green mulch.

The guard wasn't at his usual place when Marion rushed in. The front desk, too, was empty. She hadn't been here in a while. Books had always felt like the cure to her loneliness, but lately she'd wondered whether they were the cause of it, too. Ninth grade had just begun and already her classmates had closed ranks. They passed around tubes of Dr Pepper lip gloss and stories about who got to third base and a dog-eared copy of *My Sweet Audrina*, which Marion had already read. Nobody was outright mean to her, but they didn't let her borrow their Lip Smackers, either.

She had the right clothes, her mother still made sure of it. She wasn't *ugly*. Her voice sounded normal and she smelled fine and plenty of kids were way weirder and they had friends. Why, then, was she always alone? *Why?*

She was motoring up the main staircase, tripping over her high-tops, when she saw the bird. Felt it: a winged bullet that zipped past her shoulder, so close her hair moved. Then it was perched on the top step, watching her. A cardinal, of all things, bright and uncanny as an elf.

Marion swiped at her wet eyes. "Hi," she said.

The bird took off. She followed it down the stairs, hoping to scoot it out the front door, but it went left, wheeling around the grape-leaf cornices and through the basement doorway.

Marion stopped. It was just a stupid bird. She could pretend she hadn't seen it. Then she realized the only person she'd be pretending to was herself, and that thought was so pathetic she followed the creature into the dark.

Not that it was *dark*. The staircase was murky and the lights too green, but it wasn't like you couldn't see. Marion shoved her hands into her jacket pockets, among the soft grit of old Kleenex and Nature Valley crumbs, and set out to find the bird.

It twittered showily up ahead. Resentfully she followed it through Medieval War History, Epic Poetry, past sub-

subcategories that only occupied a fraction of shelf, scholarly tastes whittled down to unreadable pencil points. There was the little asshole, probably crapping on something valuable, and there, it was gone again. She saw a streak of red feathers swooping beneath a marble archway and hustled after it, eyes pointed up. No cardinal. When she turned her gaze down again, she sucked in a breath.

But she didn't scream. And it didn't take long for her heart to slow, her shock to cool into curiosity. She would wonder, later, whether this quick regaining of equilibrium was admirable or wicked. She never could decide.

There was a table in the room's center, dark wood inlaid with a repeating design of paler wood fruit. In the table's only chair was a scholar Marion had seen before, a fortyish woman with a Modernist bowl cut. She was slumped far over, forehead nearly touching the table's surface. From the doorway Marion could see the dull glass of her open right eye.

The library was a place where you could, conceivably, lie dead and unlooked-for for days. But this woman hadn't been dead long. For one thing, she didn't smell. Or, she did, but it was of human things. Stale coffee and coconut shampoo and the cloying rasp of Swisher Sweets. Marion's breath as she hovered over the woman displaced her satiny hair. The ripple made it seem, briefly, as if she might lift her head.

Her blackberry lipstick looked so fresh you could picture her sliding it on in one of the library's wobbly antique mirrors. She would've looked like a ghost already. Her skin was neither warm nor cold. The tea in her thermos was still hot, though. Marion tasted it, scenting the cosmetic odor of lipstick on the mouthpiece.

There was a book pressed beneath the woman's right arm. *Howlett House: A History*. That was the library's name in its first life; now it was Howlett House Library. Marion frowned, because it seemed an unremarkable book to die on. But that was before she'd read the pages it was open to—and before she realized the woman's left hand, hidden beneath the table, was curled around a second book. The book and the hand were stowed in the capacious black purse slouched in her lap, as if she were a kid in class trying to hide it from a teacher.

A book worth hiding is a book worth tugging from a dead woman's cooling fingers, especially once you've seen that its rippled, no-color cover is enticingly blank, and too ancient-looking to be the woman's own notebook.

From elsewhere in the basement, Marion heard voices. Not quite panicked, but quick and numerous enough that she knew she hadn't been the first to find the body.

Swiftly she straightened. The volume of history and the unlabeled book went into her backpack. There was a gold lipstick tube glinting from the dead scholar's purse. Marion took that, too.

Then she slipped from the room. She walked a circuitous path to the stairs, peering through shelves as two librarians and a pair of uniformed paramedics sped past. When they were gone she moved stealthily up the stairs.

The uncracked storm pressed its nose to every window, slippery dark and static-charged. But the tempest had gone out of her. Death was the only thing she'd ever seen that was big enough, hungry enough, to swallow all her anxieties and leave her quiet.

Up in her nook Marion read the chapter the dead scholar had been reading. It was a thumbnail history of the library's first inhabitant—John Howlett, an eccentric munitions heir who built a dizzying chimera of a house, then died at thirty—and the female servant to whom he'd left everything. Her stint as mistress of the house was brief and ended with her murder, likely by the rich man's nephew, who inherited once she was gone.

It was probable, the book conceded, that she deserved it: it was generally believed she'd killed her master and altered his will. His former servants claimed they were lovers, or, more shockingly, an occultist and his apprentice. The full truth, claimed the historian, was stranger: Howlett was the apprentice, she a fugitive occultist who'd fled the death penalty in Baltimore and worked from an infamous spell book bound in skin.

If that profane book ever existed—unlikely, per the historian—it would have been burned long ago. But some believed the occultist had hidden it in the house. Servants, other historians, guests of Howlett House, all had searched for it without luck.

Marion read in a state of rising fever. The sounds of voices below, heavy footsteps, the crackle of police radios, none of it reached her. When she was done she turned to the older book, pressing her fingers into its mottled cover. Vision speckling, lips bitten red and white, she opened it.

Outside the windows, the rain began.

She'd walked into the library a lonesome girl fleeing a storm. She walked out with the seeds of her new, true self planted, and an occultist's skin-bound book tucked into her pack.

Marion clung jealously to its promise of a different kind of life. The thrift-store clothes and the musical taste and the hand-punched piercings running up her ears were expressions of who she'd become, between that day and this one, but they were more than that: they were a lure, baited and cocked. Because what fun was magic if you were alone?

Three years later she walked into her first shift at the fish shop, a job she took in secret to save up for the noncollegiate life her parents would never approve. And she knew as soon as she saw Dana. Just looking at her, she knew she was no longer alone.

"You found a dead body," said Fee.

"Professor of occult studies," Marion replied primly. "Aneurysm."

"You're a *witch*," I said.

"An occultist. Practitioner. There are lots of names for it. I want to be. I *will* be." Her face was vivid. You could almost see the coal of her hungry heart.

"Show us," I told her.

"Show you the book? Or show you magic?"

"Just . . . all of it. Fucking *all* of it."

"Yeah," Fee said, grinning now. "Let us in."

CHAPTER TWELVE

>

The suburbs
Right now

It was nighttime now, and I was laying out the pieces.

A buried jar, a closet safe. Migraines and dead rabbits and the fate of Hattie Carter. And this: *So she was one of Sharon's girls.* I'd googled 'Twixt and 'Tween, of course, and *sharon twixt and tween*, but there were some things even the internet doesn't know.

There was a word I kept thinking, kept prodding at like a seed caught in my teeth. A word for what it might mean when you *do* something—something that might involve a jar of blood, let's say—with the expectation that, somewhere else in the world, you've made something *happen*.

Hank's derisive words came back to me. *That's the kind of thing a New Age white lady does under a full moon.*

Okay, yes. But what if—for argument's sake—what if, in my mother's case, the moon *listened*?

It was ridiculous. If I believed that, I was as bad as the Small Shop's most codependent customers, those questing souls who poured money into herbs and crystals and my aunt's remedies, like shiny objects could stave off the dark.

Except: I pressed my lips together to feel the place where my skin had closed. I'd used Aunt Fee's salve once and wiped it right off. Still I'd healed up like Wolverine. Even arnica can't do *that*. Which meant, if this was real, it was both of them.

Maybe I was an idiot if I *didn't* believe it. If I didn't accept what was right in front of me, what could very well be the reason behind the scars and the silences and the secretive bullshit I'd learned to live with: my mother was capable of unnatural things.

I was alone with my spiraling thoughts. Hank was out, my dad off pretending to be an orc or whatever at game night with his grad school friends. He'd texted around eight to let me know he was crashing in the city. I reread the last text Aunt Fee sent me.

Sorry. Dealing with something but we're fine. I'll call you soon, Ivy-girl.

I microwaved a plate of Chips Ahoy! and sat at the kitchen table. The AC cycled off with a sigh and the house was too quiet. At my back was the basement door, across from me the windows. With the sun down and the lights on they'd become a one-way mirror. Inside it a platinum-haired stranger picked at a plate of cookies.

Someone could be standing right there. On the other side of the glass, watching me. They could be yards away and I wouldn't even know it.

I heard a rubbery *thump*. Faint but definite, not from the windows but the other side of the house, where the sliding door opened onto the backyard.

The cookie turned to sand on my tongue. That was the sound of something bumping up against glass.

I stood slowly, clutching my phone. As I moved through the house I turned off every light, so I could see out but no one else could see in. The backyard was dark. The light out there had a sensor and turned on if anyone came as close as the patio. That gave me the courage to charge across the carpet, past the black mouth of the laundry room, and throw open the sliding door.

I hung there a while breathing in the summer air, laced with flowers and smoke from somebody's barbecue. The moon was very high and very far, glowing like a halogen bulb in its cowl of cloud. Nothing moved but the wind through the garden. I was about to go back inside when I heard the smallest sound: the fairy-tale whisper of breeze over broken glass.

There, nearly lost beneath the picnic table, lay a scatter of glinting pieces. Beside it, bisected between shadow and moonlight, an arc of spilled blood. My breath went ragged, but I didn't understand what I was looking at until I saw the shard of mirror.

Someone had dug up the jar my mom buried and smashed it over the concrete.

There'd been a piece of white paper curled inside that jar. I couldn't see it from where I stood, but I knew it was there. It took all the courage I had to make myself walk down the steps in search of it. The light clicked on and my mother's blood was sickening beneath its glow. I found the curl of paper, stained and stuck to the leg of a deck chair, and plucked it free with two fingertips. Breathing through my teeth, I unrolled it. My mom's handwriting spooled across the scrap in an unbroken line.

If it be unfriendly let it go if it be unwilling make it go if it be a poison may it go if it be a threat I will it go

A breeze slid over me like staticky silk. The night wasn't so silent after all. It ticked and scratched with creatures and weather and sleepy suburban machines. I ran back into the house and locked the door behind me.

The word I'd been avoiding came back like a scream. The one I was too practical to say, too stupid, maybe, a poppy seed that crunched, releasing poison, as I finally bit in. *Magic.* The words on the piece of paper, the blood in the jar—the pins and feathers in her closet, even. All pointed toward the same impossible probability.

It wasn't surprise I felt. Or even relief, to finally have a label for the thing that made my mother so unreachable. I was flooded instead with a strangling fury. Because what the *fuck?* What did my mom think she was doing? Where did she get the nerve to think reality should bend to her, of all people?

And what the hell did it say about reality that it might actually have *worked?*

Beneath the anger something else squirmed, rolling its bright green eyes. *Jealousy.* I jerked away from the thought. Leaving the lights off, I batted around the first floor, checking the doors and windows. All were locked, all was quiet except for the clamor in my head. In the kitchen I peered out at nothing more sinister than lilac bushes and the next house's yellow siding. When I turned my eye fell on the cookies left on my plate.

I'd eaten two, left three untouched. Now, by the light coming through the window, I saw that each remaining cookie had a bite taken out of it, in three perfect cartoon curves.

Nimbly I strode from the kitchen, to the front door. I turned the lock, then the knob, and flung myself onto the porch.

Mosquitoes threw themselves at my skin as I sprinted down the drive. The house was dark and still, all its windows pitch-colored or glazed with silver. When I reached for my phone, I realized I'd left it inside. I swore and dropped into a crouch, hands over my face.

"Ivy?"

I turned. The Paxtons' house was belted in the shadows of its long country-style porch. Inside them floated the orange cherry of Billy's cigarette, fading and brightening like a signal at sea. "Did something happen?" he called.

"I think there's someone inside my house."

"Seriously?" He dropped his cigarette and jogged down the drive. "Are you okay? Did you call the police?"

Even by streetlight he was sunny, charged up like a solar battery. I could see every freckle on his skin. My cheeks heated remembering the sketch I'd found, in which my younger self drew those freckles as stars. "I didn't."

"Oh." He looked mistrustfully at my house. "Should I?"

"Not yet. Can you just . . . sit with me a sec?"

He dropped obediently to the concrete. "Yeah. Of course. So—what happened?"

I didn't know what I looked like. Like I'd just stepped away from an explosion, probably, my eyes all wide with revelation. I couldn't bear to start blathering about cookies. "Nothing. Nothing actually happened, I just . . . I'm home alone. I thought someone was in the backyard. Then I went back inside and I thought maybe they were in the house."

"Holy shit. Were they?"

"I don't know," I said slowly. Maybe I'd bitten the cookies myself. Had I? *Hadn't* I? I could still taste chocolate on my tongue. When I tried to picture an intruder, all I could see was my mother moving through the house in horror-film jump cuts. I shuddered. "I don't know what's going on."

He pressed his toes into a strip of soft tar. "But you don't want to call the cops."

"No."

I thought he'd push me on that, but he only nodded. It was oddly intense sitting so close to him. Billy Paxton, with that lanky body in jeans stained with paint and oil and pizza sauce, because he had three part-time jobs. I only knew that because I'd seen him in his blue jumpsuit at the Jiffy Lube, and rolling down the drive with a Pepino's delivery light on his hood, and climbing in and out of his dad's truck, its bed laden with primer cans. I had the strangest urge to tell him the whole and actual truth. I didn't, of course. I told him one sliced-down, shined-up piece of it.

"The weirdest things have been happening," I said. "And it's all—it's all making me think I don't really know my mother."

For the briefest moment, he seemed to stiffen. But right away he relaxed, and spoke in such an even tone I figured I'd imagined it. "Oh, yeah?"

"Yeah." My fear was abating now. In its place came a kind of recklessness. For years I'd avoided looking at this boy, but out here, in the late and the quiet, I finally could. Tea-colored eyes, dark brows that made him look kinda wicked. His bottom teeth were crooked. I got a flash of him as a kid, lisping around a retainer, and blinked.

"I see you sometimes on your porch," I said. "When I'm awake too late and I look out the window. Even in winter I see you there."

"Spying on me?"

"I'm just wondering when you sleep."

"Who needs sleep?" Billy said lightly, then sighed. "Nightmares, you know? Not often, but sometimes."

I didn't know, but I nodded. "That sucks. I can never remember my dreams."

Now I knew I wasn't imagining the odd expression that skidded over his face, like a hard wind across water. He looked down, pulled a pack of cigarettes from his pocket, smacked them against the heel of his hand. Then he shook his head. "Look, would you throw these away for me? I quit."

"In the last five minutes, you quit?"

"Yeah. I was out here having my last one."

"So just . . . for your health?"

He mopped a hand over his hair. There was a dent in his curls where a hat had been. "No, for Amy. She vowed not to speak to me till I quit, and she actually did it. It's been two weeks of total silence."

Amy was his little sister. She had to be about twelve. "Really? That's awesome. She must really love you."

"I mean, probably. But no, she's just pissed I left a pack out and Gremlin ate it. Don't worry, he's completely fine."

Gremlin was their pit mix, infamous in the neighborhood

for all the things he'd eaten and somehow survived: channel changers, a bag of sugar, part of a laptop. "That's good. Poor Gremlin."

"Poor *Gremlin*? He'll be running around eating garbage when we're all in the ground. Sometimes after he eats my shoes or whatever he leaves the pieces in my *bed*. Like he's the Godfather."

I laughed and Billy smiled a little shyly, raising his brows.

"You ready to call the cops yet?"

"Not yet."

"You ready to go to sleep?"

"Who needs sleep?"

"Do you wanna go do something instead?"

I paused, mouth half open, and did a split-second audit of myself. Chapped lips, stretched-out tank top, my freshly bleached hair pushed back with a headband. It felt freeing to look so crap.

"What's there to do in Woodbine in the middle of the night?"

He lifted a shoulder. "Go to Denny's? Walk around the Super Walmart, eating baked goods?"

I looked up at him, at his freckles like stars. I didn't want to be alone. And no part of me wanted to go back inside my house.

"Okay," I told him. "Let's go."

CHAPTER THIRTEEN

)

The city
Back then

What Marion did on the beach was the first real thing she'd ever done. A flare of wicked intent, shaped by words she hadn't known she possessed.

"It's you," she said. "It's *us*. The three of us together, that's why it worked."

Alone, she told us, she'd almost done lots of things. With the three of us combined, all those *almost*s could become ways of remaking the world.

But first we had to wake ourselves up.

You couldn't look for things in the occultist's book, couldn't read it cover to cover. If you tried, it would show you blank pages, or black ones. Lines of tangled characters, rhymes that scratched at your ears. Densely inked images, sometimes, that left purple aftereffects on your vision. The way it worked, she told us, was like a tarot deck, delivering the pages you needed to see. And since the beach it kept showing her a single spell, opaquely titled and built for three practitioners. *To turn your hand toward working.*

It began with a purification ritual. For three days we stayed inside, playing sick so we could avoid mirrors, direct sunlight, and human touch. We drank herbs steeped in spring water, briny with rock salt, and performed ablutions once an hour between sundown and sunup. By the end of it I felt so fragile I wondered if that was part of the spell. You could've told me anything right then, and I'd have believed you. Including that I could do magic.

At sundown on the fourth day we gathered the spell's ingredients—some at the store, the rest harvested from Loyola Park—and went to my empty apartment, our fingers resinous with growing things.

Marion was edgy, withdrawn, her unwashed hair skimmed back into a ponytail. She wouldn't let either of us touch the book. She kept checking our work, again and again, until there was nothing left to prepare.

I can still close my eyes and summon up the shy, hallucinatory feeling of sitting down with Fee and Marion to perform that first spell. Shallow breaths syncing, hearts up high, nobody sure where to look. Marion was tight as a tuning peg, Fee rippling with nervous laughter. We moved haltingly through the steps, and I was sure it wouldn't work.

Until Marion completed the final incantation and the air clarified like butter in a pan. Inside that flue of vivid air we fell back, hands entangled, heads thumping hard to the floorboards.

I didn't feel it. I felt nothing, because my consciousness was rising up, up, and away.

I saw my own body and the bodies of my friends laid out like starfish. I saw the roof of my building and the flat scatter of our street and still I rose higher, until the whole city sprawled beneath me like a spider's web, like a dragnet of white gold, black water lapping at its eastern rim and the suburbs biting down its ribs to the west and the downtown a hard metal knot so dazzling you could weep.

From up here I could see we were small, we were specks, we were cosmic dust off a god's left shoulder, and the discovery filled me with an electric joy. The air was thin and the stars sang their elliptical star song and didn't care that I heard it. I was less to them than the drifting exhalation of a seed head.

At the apex of my flight—Venus burning at my left hand, Mercury to my right—I felt the very beginnings of fear. It was heavy and it drew me down again, whistling through the black and the silver, through layers of untouched sky, then the man-made haze of pollution and light, the dizzying Escher entanglements of radio waves, until I hung over my body again.

I felt such tenderness for its flawed skin and tangled hair, its angry geometry. But I wasn't ready to be human again, to breathe and sweat and ache and thirst. So I left it there on the boards.

I coasted through the city on the backs of breezes: a gust hissed out of a bus's hydraulic lift. The sigh of a woman fixing her bangs in the dirty glass of a convenience store fridge. An old man's cracked cough, expelled through the gap below a newspaper-covered window.

The city opened its doors to me, tapped out its secrets like cigarettes. It was a street-corner flock of lean and hungry men, work shirts and hard hands. Girls with their elbows set on chrome countertops, eating sugar packets grain by grain. A sticky-buttoned jukebox at the back of a shotgun bar, full of songs about an America that never existed. Powdery paperbacks sold from blankets spread across the sidewalk and mildew-scented Legion halls clicking with the sounds of a bingo cage. Hot wet rooms full of dancers with helpless faces and music amplified until it was fuzzy as peaches, sharp as grapefruit spoons.

Craving silence, I whistled to the water's edge. I sped like a skater over its rippling top, hissing around the heads of night sailors and diving down to witness a conquest of zebra mussels, their slow invading sway.

Back to dry land, where I slid between the mouths of a couple on a bench, gaunt and pierced but folded into each other with the perfect courtliness of a Victorian cameo. The bench was at the edge of a graveyard, overgrown. If my soul had hands I'd have reached them out to skim the waving tops of butterfly weed and bellflower, blazing star and mountain mint and the dainty fireworks of golden alexanders.

Rising up from among the sounds of the city—bad brakes and sharp laughter, the furious yowling of unspayed cats—came the rhythm of a slowing heartbeat. My own. The kite string that tethered me to the body on my bedroom floor was calling me home. I took hold of it like a zip line, shinning over El tracks and headlights and the minnow dart of bicyclists.

The candles we'd lit were flickering wax coins and my room was gray as a mourning dove. Before the sun could rise and my tether could break I slipped back inside myself, braced for the magnetized click of body and soul.

It didn't come. Maybe, I thought, that was part of the transformation. Maybe it was within the slipstream drag of spirit moving within form that magic could play.

Fee was back from her own journey. I could feel her beside me, hand warm in mine. But on the other side of me, Marion lay still. Her hand was corn-husk light and her pulse too slow. I tried to sit up, to check on her.

I couldn't. I couldn't move at all, beyond a twitch of my fingers.

Just the realization made my throat tighten. The tightness slid sideways into panic. Not because the spell had gone wrong. It was working as it was meant to: we had entered this state together. We would come out that way, too. Until Marion returned, Fee and I would stay just like this.

I'd thought I'd felt fear before but it was nothing to what I felt then, still as waking death and listening to her pulse tick down, down, down. Caught in endless suspension, not breathing enough but not dying of it either. Waiting, in agony. Waiting.

Then, with a glittering rush and the scent of woodfire, she was back.

My relief was so great and instant it swallowed the fear. And I almost—almost—forgot how it felt to lie captive to magic's rules, waiting on Marion to release us.

We opened our eyes. And with them our *eyes*, the ones we hadn't known we had. In the moment before joy came in, I shuddered. Because we'd gained something, but we'd lost something, too. It would take a long time for me to work out what that was.

We sat up, looking at each other, and started helplessly to laugh—Fee and I did. Marion, though, she cried. Still crying, she put her arms out and pulled us into a rare hug. Her mouth was in my hair but I think what she said was, *Thank you*.

When I looked back on that night I wondered whether that stretch of frozen abandonment was our first true glimpse of what magic would make of Marion. Later, when my head was filled with the odor of witching and my left hand bloodied on broken glass, it was one of the things I thought about. Our first neon sign that her hunger had a double edge.

It took time for the effects of our awakening to fade. For a handful of disorienting days, everyone we looked at wore a halo of colored light. Soft, mystical, unmistakably there, unmistakably *magic*. Fee was limned in fresh green like an elf princess. Marion's aura was the color of brick dust. A lonesome, hard-road color. Fee told me mine was blue, that I looked gift-wrapped in sky.

Twice I tried taking the train and had to step right off, the car such a riot of overlapping colors I could almost hear it. By the end the feeling was like a high that went on too long. Even after it was gone I received occasional flashes of useful sight: the good-looking man smiling at me from across the train, his aura the color of dried blood. The girl dancing at the show, crackling with the contagious, brushfire shade of damage.

I'd always had that extra ounce of perception, always moved through a world in which I knew by instinct which streets not to turn down, and where small treasures hid. But the spell in the occultist's book caught like a fishhook on that quiet part of me, reeling it up until it bobbed against my skin.

"Your wedding ring is stuck in your pocket lining," I told a woman ordering food at the fish shop. She didn't look grateful. Fee, too, had to readjust. It was uncomfortable, she said, to stand in crowds. "Everyone's thirsty all the time. I'm drinking gallons 'cause it's hard to convince myself it isn't *me*."

But these were small prices to pay. The spells the book served us were small, too, at first. They pointed inward, spells for good luck and good sleep and good skin. We boiled herbs to sludge on Uncle Nestor's gas stove, we etched incantations into candles with a safety pin. We chalked complicated shapes onto Fee's bedroom floor and whispered into a mirror unwrapped from a length of white linen. We learned the many uses of moonlight. Every piece of magic the book gave us worked like a gateway drug, until we couldn't imagine our lives without that thrill, that bend, that shock of the world giving way beneath our hands.

We didn't wonder where the magic came from, or why it worked. We never asked ourselves, *Is this ours to take?* We were three damp ducklings, green as leaves, believing with all our crooked hearts that *we* were the ones writing this story. Even as a dead woman's book paved the road beneath our feet.

CHAPTER FOURTEEN

)

The suburbs
Right now

Billy's car was a low-slung box that smelled like blue car tree.
I climbed in feeling low-level giddy. It felt surreal to go from
bloody concrete and swirling thoughts to here, in this car, next
to this boy I knew but didn't *know*.

Back when we rode the same school bus Billy wore T-shirts
with howling wolves or leaping whales screen-printed on them,
and colored rubber bands on his braces. Now he was wearing a
Pepino's T-shirt under a faded button-up, and his Adam's apple
stood out like a peach pit. He drove like a dad, putting an arm
behind my seat as he backed out then taking the wheel one-
handed, elbow perched on the open window.

We rolled through corridors of quiet houses, the stale warmth
of the car mixing like water with the breeze. When he turned
onto the main road his arm flexed beneath a patch of streetlight.
I stared, then turned away.

"I like your hair," he said abruptly. "I mean, I already liked it.
But I like the blonde, too."

I touched my fingers to my cheek. "Thanks."

Billy kept his eyes on the road. "So. You and Nate King broke up."

"Big-time."

"What happened?"

"Aside from finding out that he smokes cigarillos?" I let my head fall back. "I think the real problem was neither of us was actually dating the other person. I was dating, like, Poet Boy. He was dating, I don't know, Aloof Redhead. I should've just gone out with a fountain pen. He could've carried around a sexy wig. Everyone would've been much happier."

Billy laughed. "I can see Nate King and a wig."

"How about you?" I watched streetlights slide past through the moonroof. "Who are you dating?"

A pause. "To be honest, I'm holding out for King's hot wig."

My heart was speeding up, because this felt like an opening. If I didn't say something now, I probably never would. Billy pulled into a spot at the back of the lot, and before he could unbuckle his seat belt I grabbed his arm. "Hey."

He looked at my hand, then at me, smiling.

"Seventh grade," I said.

The smile dropped. His face went utterly neutral.

"Seventh grade was brutal," I told him. "Honestly, it felt embarrassing just to be alive. So, that day. That thing when . . . that thing when you . . ."

I trailed off. He looked so pained I couldn't finish my thought.

"It's in the past," he said abruptly, and opened his door.

I followed him out of the car, the space between us suddenly flat as old Coke. I thought it'd make it *better* to acknowledge his having asked me out back then. I thought, stupidly, that we might laugh about it.

Apparently not. Neither of us spoke as we walked over the humid concrete and into the ice-age chill of the Super Walmart.

I blinked against the fluorescents. At midnight the store was deserted and carnival-bright, the song of some distant summer bleeding through bad speakers. Billy glanced at my goosebumpy arms and walked over to a carousel of grandma hoodies, tossing me one in teal.

"Zip up, Myrtle," he said.

I raised a brow and slipped it on, sticking my hands in the shallow pockets. "No room for my Kools."

He held up a cheetah-print fanny pack. "Here. Now you can steal all the sugar packets from the IHOP."

After clipping it around my waist I passed him a navy windbreaker with tacky nautical epaulets. "In case it gets breezy on the deck of your murder yacht."

"Ah, yes. I'm a wealthy murderer who shops at Walmart."

"You're a gentleman *and* an enigma."

"And now I'm cruising bingo halls for my next victim." He held out a hand. "Myrtle?"

His fingers in mine were warm and dry and as soon as our palms touched it stopped feeling like a joke. I dropped his hand and shot toward a display of hideous caftans, as thin and rippable as craft paper. "Big prom possibilities, yeah?"

"Only if you want to be dressed like every other person there."

By the time we reached the end of Apparel, we were layers deep in the worst clothes we could find. We shucked them off and wended our way to Grocery for a box of Lofthouse cookies. In Toys we took turns riding a kids' dirt bike, then carried a hula hoop to the broader aisles of Lawn Care.

"Amateur hour," he said after I let it fall for the third time. He took the hoop, flipped it over his head, and set it spinning around his waist in mesmerizing slow motion. He spun it up to his chest, then down to his knees. He took out his phone and pretended to make an important call. It was so compelling I started tossing pieces of cookie into his mouth to break his concentration. He leapt for one and the hoop clattered to the floor.

"But we both know I could've gone all night," he said, then looked away, a flush crawling up his neck.

"Hey," I said, too loud. "Did I tell you I have a fake ID?"

His face brightened. "Yeah? Lemme see."

I dug out the ID Emily's older brother helped me get. While Billy studied it I took the opportunity to stare at him. He was extra freckled over his nose and the tops of his cheeks, like the sun had swiped a paintbrush across his skin.

He exploded into laughter. "Oh, my god," he said. "It's too good. First off, you look about eleven. How did a fake ID make you look younger? Secondly, *Mary Jenkins*? That's the fakest fake name of all time! Wait wait wait, *420 High Street*? That can't be an actual address." He looked a little longer and cracked up again. "Your birthday! They made your birthday sixty-nine!"

I snatched it back. "They made it June ninth! There's nothing wrong with June ninth!"

He put his hands on my shoulders, his face solemn. The crinkles by his eyes were paler than his skin, like he spent a lot of time squinting into the sun. "That is the worst fake ID of all time."

"Then how come it works every time?"

"Bullshit. You couldn't get served a beer out of a fridge with that thing."

"I'll prove it."

I marched him over to the liquor aisle and considered what I could afford, settling on a bottle of strawberry Wild Vines.

"Whoa." He put his hands up. "Party at 420 High Street."

From Liquor we cruised through Baking Supplies, then over to Personal Care. By the end I'd added a box of tampons, a roll of toilet paper, and yellow cake mix to our haul.

"This is where my genius comes in," I told him. "The ID is amazing, yes, but it's not perfect. Maybe I do look slightly young and the name couldn't possibly be real. So what you do is distract them with something wholesome"—I held up the cake mix—"and something personal." I raised the tampons and the toilet paper.

"And this has worked for you?"

It had. Once. Despite Nate loudly talking about his nonexistent office job as I paid, like that would convince the cashier we were in our twenties. Emily and I had gotten the IDs a month ago, and we'd spent way more time since then planning the perfect distracting shopping list than actually buying alcohol.

"It's worked every time," I said firmly.

There was one cashier on duty, a matronly woman with high sprayed bangs that seemed like a bad omen. She rang up the empty cookie box, the cake mix, the tampons. I'd put the wine down fourth in line, like somebody trying to sneak into a club in the middle of a crowd.

"I'm baking a cake tonight," I told her brightly as she scanned the bottle. "Yellow cake. And I'm on my period, so, you know. Chocolate frosting."

"Need a bag?" she asked flatly.

"No, thanks!" I piled everything into Billy's arms. "Have a nice night!"

I could feel him laughing silently beside me as we walked away slowly, then faster, finally bursting out into the heat.

"See?" I said. "It worked!"

"No, it didn't! She didn't even make you show it!"

"That's because my tampon and cake mix plan was so good."

"You know she's coming to your house later for proof you made that cake. You're gonna get arrested for baking lies."

"So we'll make the cake." I lifted a shoulder. "You wanna?"

We smiled at each other. "I do," he said.

It was past two when we let ourselves into Billy's place. The front hall smelled like pasta sauce and hewn wood and dog fur, but in a good, comforting way. Gremlin surged around our legs as we crept over the creaky floor, both of us laughing at nothing.

"Bill?" His dad's voice came down from the dark.

Shit, Billy mouthed, and guided me gently into the kitchen. We stopped against the wall, looking up, his hands still on my shoulders. "Hey, Dad," he called. His breath was sweet with cheap sugar.

"You've been out on the porch all this time?"

"Couldn't sleep." He didn't quite lie, I noted. "I'll be quiet."

"All right." A pause, then his dad started walking down

the stairs. We widened our eyes at each other but Mr. Paxton stopped halfway, feet creaking at the level of our heads. "Don't wake your sister when you come up. And try to go to bed a little earlier, this is getting ridiculous."

"Okay," Billy said. "Good night."

We stood there for another small eternity, until we heard his dad's door close. Billy took my hand and pressed it to his heart, so I could feel it racing. "Close," he whispered.

We were standing face-to-face, the air snapping giddy between us. I felt this welling in my chest, like laughter but bigger, more painful. It felt momentous just lifting my eyes to meet his. Like an act of bravery. But I did it.

He hesitated, his saturated eyes on mine. Then he said my name.

And when he did it I got this flash. It was as swift and disorienting as the vision I'd had in my parents' closet. In my ears his voice became *two* voices—one his own, one high and rough, a little boy's; and his face was *two* faces—the one in front of me, and the one he'd worn when he was younger. The feeling it gave me was sweet and sharp and terrible and I jerked back, hitting the wall.

"What is it?" he said. Not bothering now to whisper.

"Nothing."

"You just jumped a mile."

I was frantic suddenly to be alone, to think. "Yeah, no. I'm fine. I just. I've gotta go."

He was on some precipice. I could see it. "Ivy," he said again, so soft. "Please don't do this."

"Do what?" For no reason his words sent an ice cube down

my spine. "What are you talking about? Why are you being weird?"

He stepped away from me, his face shocked clean. "Why am *I* being weird. Wow. That's messed up. Actually, *all* of this is messed up. Why did I even try?"

Panic made me speak too sharply. "Is this still about me turning you down in junior high?"

"Turning me down," Billy said, voice rising. "Is that how you'd describe it?"

Then he checked himself, glancing at the ceiling. "Look," he said quietly. "I know we were kids. I know I should be over it. I *am*. But pretending none of it ever happened? That's just so *mean*."

I gaped at him. "Are you talking about the— Are you still talking about the—"

Billy glared at me, jaw ticked forward like he was trying not to cry. "You broke my heart, Ivy. You broke my fucking heart. And the worst part is you made your *mom* do it for you."

The tile floor was dropping away from me. Smoky bites were being taken from the edges of my sight. "No," I said, shaking my head. "*No.*"

He pressed his hands to his eyes, like he couldn't stand to look at me. "Please just go. Okay? Just go."

)

CHAPTER FIFTEEN

The city
Back then

Summer came and school let out and the city was our candy box. We bought mangoes on Devon and ate them by the lake. We swam in deep water off the ledge at Ohio Street, our mouths all sticky with coconut paletas. We went to so many shows our ears never had time to stop humming, so we walked around all the time in a mellow cocoon of damage.

And all that long, heat-sick season, we were magic.

When I remembered that summer later it was bright and dark, all my memories sun-drenched or cast in hard shadow. I was in love, with Fee and Marion and our city and the possibilities that hissed under our hands every time we gathered in a circle of three.

But in the other half of my life was my dad. His spine a column of crumbling discs, his bedside table a cache of orange pill bottles. By summer's end I'd understand he was never going to be okay again. I think I knew I'd be an orphan soon. The knowledge was the black-eyed dog that followed me, nipping at my bike tires and curling up in the corners of my room. Magic was joy and power and control. It was the thunderclap that chased away, at least for a little while, that slinking dog.

Through everything Fee and I kept telling ourselves it was all just *fun*. Even as the spells we worked stained steadily darker. Even as the riskier magic we found in the occultist's book—spells to distract, to mislead, to punish—rebounded on us with strobing headaches and a wrung-out famishment, and Fee started brewing a fermented tea that helped with the pain of blowback. Even then we told ourselves this drug we were living on, whose costs we couldn't begin to reckon, was within our control.

Not Marion. She was a liar, but she didn't lie to herself. From the very start she came to magic as an acolyte. Of the book, of the craft, and, most of all, of the dead occultist whose book it had been. Her name was Astrid Washington, and Marion talked about her like a girl with a crush.

"Astrid was *amazing*. She wasn't just an occultist, she was a healer. She charged society people loads of money for love charms and pennyroyal tea, then took care of poor people for free.

"In Baltimore they called her the Widow's Nursemaid—she'd off abusive husbands on the cheap, with poisons that weren't traceable.

"Six days after Astrid was killed, John Howlett's nephew—her murderer—died in his sleep. He was twenty-five, completely healthy. No apparent cause."

She told us that one night in a sticky booth at the Pick Me Up, eating brownie sundae off a silver spoon.

Fee looked fascinated. "So her *ghost* killed him?"

Marion smiled a glassy little smile. "That's one theory."

"You told us Astrid was supposed to be executed," I said. "What'd she do? Kill the wrong shitty husband?"

She shrugged, her gaze going murky, inward. "People blame powerful women for everything."

I looked at the place where the occultist's book was hidden in her bag. It was always with her. Neither Fee nor I had ever actually held it, and that was fine by me. I preferred to think of our magic as being drawn from a faceless place, a store of power accessible to brave girls with bright hearts. I didn't understand Marion's obsession with constantly reminding us Astrid had been an actual woman. Not a figure but a *person*, and maybe not a very good one.

I shivered. Somewhere in the future, someone was walking over my grave. Or maybe I was remembering, just for a moment, that magic was a thing with teeth, and a history as old as the world.

I try to remember how it began, the beginning of the end.

There was an evening I was riding my bike under the El, grocery bags swinging off my handlebars, and almost got clipped by a Ford Fairlane. I swerved to avoid it, food shaking out over the pavement. "Hey, asshole!" I screamed. "You broke my eggs!"

The driver flipped me the bird. "Ah, go fuck your boyfriend!" he bawled out his open window.

The chain had come off my bike. I chucked it onto the sidewalk and took off running, head empty but for a bright white rage. I threw an arm out and his back tire popped like a smashed pumpkin, sending his car fishtailing across Glenwood Avenue.

I hadn't said anything. I hadn't thought I'd *done* anything.

But my body was quaking with expelled magic, a headache already filing its nails on my brain. Shithead regained control of his car and went sailing on but I couldn't stop picturing crumpled metal, blood on the pavement.

Right then I didn't feel like a girl with a gift. I felt like a child carrying around a crate of leaky dynamite.

Then there was the night of the love spell.

Fee had a loose trigger for falling in love. She liked dirty-mouthed girls, girls with shaved heads, girls on bikes who darted like fish through traffic. But it wasn't until we were magic that she got up the guts to actually *talk* to any of them.

She had her first kiss, then her second, with a bartender at the Rainbo Club, pink pixie cut and a collar of tattooed hyacinths. Then the bartender found out how young Fee really was and stopped talking to her.

For the first time, the occultist's book showed us a love spell. Its ingredients were fit for a wedding bouquet: ribbons, roses, lavender. You could almost believe it was good magic.

"I don't know," Fee said, finger-combing the ends of her hair. "How does a love spell even work? Does it *trick* her into thinking she loves me? Does it tweak her brain so she does? I don't want someone to love me if it doesn't count."

Marion's voice was icy. "How does magic not *count*? Love is chemicals. It's your own brain making you drunk. Magic is a hundred times realer than love. Anyway"—she narrowed her eyes at the book—"Astrid won't show us anything else till it's done."

So we gathered our rosebuds, our pretty scented things. I

lurked at the Rainbo until I saw the inconstant bartender sip soda through a straw, then I grabbed the straw and bolted.

It was the first time the three of us weren't of one mind, and you could feel it in the magic. There was a resistance there, a sulfur-scented headwind that kicked our balance askew.

In the middle of the spell, Fee screamed. She reached under her shirt for the necklace that always nestled just below her throat's hollow: her mother's crucifix. She yanked until its thin chain snapped and sent it skidding across the floor.

"Gimme a mirror," she said, voice wretched.

When she pulled her shirt up to look, there was a fine cross-shaped mark where the crucifix had lain. Not a fresh wound, but a pale scar. It was so pretty, positioned like a charm beside her remaining necklace: a cheap gold-colored chain strung with a slice of broken heart, part of the Best Friends set she'd bought for the three of us on Maxwell Street.

As I hugged her, smoothing back her hair, Marion scooted to the fallen cross and wrapped it in a square of black paper pulled from her bottomless bag.

"There," she said, placing the parcel in a drawer. "Let's start again."

"Marion, no," I said over Fee's shoulder.

Her face tightened. "No?"

"It was a bad idea," I told her pointedly. "Let's do something else."

"What else is there to do?" She put her arms out to encompass the room, the whole twilit city, nothing out there worth doing unless the first-drag burn of magic was in it. "Seriously, *what*?"

Fee pulled away, fixing Marion with a look. "That was my mother's. She died wearing that crucifix."

Marion was all ready to push back, you could see it. Then she made some calculation, and changed course. "Yeah, okay," she said, and dropped it.

Things were fine after that. We listened to music and read one-card tarot and it was all just fine. But when Marion left the next morning Fee looked at me, and I nodded back, and we both knew something had changed.

We were done with the occultist's book. Done with Marion's jealous doling out of its darkening gifts, like ghostly footprints leading us deeper into a fog.

Astrid Washington wasn't the only teacher. Her magic wasn't the only kind.

Without a word to Marion, we started looking elsewhere. We combed through witchery handbooks and herbalists' guides and one-off necronomicons dug out of bookshops the size of a closet. We picked up smudgy xeroxed witchcraft zines from Quimby's and Myopic. We met some people that way who invited us to gatherings in parks and basements and daytime bars, where we hovered together at the edges. We found plenty of dead ends, but flickers of true magic, too.

And it felt so *good* to work without Marion watching. Fee discovered she had a keen herb-sense. Under her hands her dad's potted kitchen garden grew preternaturally lush, carpeting the wooden porch that overlooked a weedy back lot. She spoke with curanderas in Pilsen, coming away with herb bundles and recipes written on squares of butcher paper.

Magic was a rougher, cheaper currency than we'd thought, the city a great living library of secret mystics, civilians with ancient knowledge embedded in their bones. We riffled their pages in search of information: tantalizing scraps of shtetl magic gleaned from a Rogers Park stoop sitter; a cracklingly uncanny Norwegian jumping rhyme recited by a waitress in Andersonville; a hair-raising anecdote about effigy magic teased out of a West African cabbie. It was good to be reminded magic had denser, older thickets than the occultist's book.

We pulled away from Marion. But she was pulling away from us, too. There was no blowup, just a slackening. After the love spell we heard from her less and less, then not at all for days. She started skipping fish-shop shifts. We'd made up our minds to go to her house to check on her when she came to find us first.

She showed up at the shop in a faded black dress and a copper cuff stuck with a hunk of raw citrine. There was a new edge to her, a bad radiance. Something had changed since we'd seen her last, and she looked all at once like the witch she wanted to be: famished and startling.

We thought she'd ask what we'd been up to, but instead she went on and on about a ritual given to her by the occultist's book, meant to increase the body's magical potency: the strength of your blood, urine, spit, nails, all the cheap ingredients you can harvest from yourself. Her bag clanked with hellish-looking roots steeped in dirty city rain, the teas she fed herself in place of food. Her skin smelled piney and metallic.

And there was something else, she said. Something she had to show us.

Neither of us wanted to go. We'd been up late the night before, dealing with my dad, and were brittle with exhaustion. But when we got off work we trailed her to the bus stop anyway.

It was late August and the vibe among us was as suffocating as the weather. When we got off the bus we didn't go to her parents' house. She led us through campus instead, past university buildings and green spaces so verdant they felt sinister, to a Disneyland downtown of shops.

We stopped in front of one of those Clark and Belmont–type places where wannabe witches shopped: blown glass pipes and cheap fetishwear, jewelry embedded with fake lapis or mother of pearl. It had the dorkiest name—'Twixt and 'Tween—and I felt embarrassed going inside, because the cool record shop boys from next door were on the pavement having a cigarette.

The shop smelled like sandalwood and was stuffed with *stuff*, one-hitters and hesher tees and tie-dyed wall hangings. Then a woman came out from the back and wrapped Marion in her arms. "Hey, pretty girl."

She was a white woman in her late twenties, I'd guess, but she vibed like an old punk. Her skin was sunbaked hardpan, her eyes a quartz blue. She had a dandelion of black hair and triangles and stars tattooed over the backs of her hands. She didn't look at Fee or me. Still holding Marion, she said, "Did you bring the book?"

Fee and I glanced narrowly at each other as Marion fished around in her bag, then took out the occultist's book. The woman laughed softly, hands up like Marion might give it to her. When she didn't, the woman finally looked at me and Fee.

"So this is your coven."

I ticked my chin at her. "Who's she? Why are we in her crappy store?"

The woman laughed again, but Marion tensed. The cords in her neck were unnerving. "This is Sharon. She's another practitioner."

"You can say witch, honey." Sharon tongued her lip ring. "It's not a bad word."

"It's limiting, though," Marion said earnestly. Always so humorless around magic, all her borders down. "We're more than that. I want to be *more* than that. Don't you?"

"Sure," Sharon replied after a pause. "For sure I do."

Marion was nodding. "Yeah. So. Sharon's shop is kind of a meeting place for . . . for practitioners. I came in to buy supplies the other day and we ended up talking for, what, two hours?"

"That's right," Sharon said, looking at me.

Marion cradled the book, her voice dropping into a reverent register. "Something happened the night after I met Sharon. The book gave me a spell for *four* workers. It's never done that before." She looked at us solemnly. "I think Astrid wants us to work with Sharon."

I scoffed. "What, is she our pimp? I'm not working with someone I don't know."

"I like this one." Sharon's eyes were hard with liking's opposite. "I like you, honey."

"Your admiration and a nickel, *honey*."

Sharon pursed her lips and breathed out. An impossibly

long *whoosh* that filled my nose with licorice and made the lights flicker and broke the room's tension into mosaic pieces. Fee's eyes widened, fingertips pressed to the place her crucifix had scarred her.

"We've got time." Sharon seemed happier now that she'd impressed us. "Let's talk. Let's drink some tea. I'll send somebody out for Jimmy John's."

I got one of my occasional flashes of clarity then. A glimpse of Sharon's aura. It was ultraviolet and an orange that was hard to look at, striated like a tiger's fur. The only dual-toned aura I'd ever seen. I had no idea what it meant.

I looked at Fee. She raised a brow.

"Yeah, all right. We can talk."

CHAPTER SIXTEEN

)

The suburbs
Right now

I walked back to my haunted house, holding my haunted head. When I saw Hank's car in the drive I broke into a run. I flew up the stairs and into his room, breathing out when I found him asleep. His face was slack, bathed in the light of the movie playing on his open laptop.

I closed it and jostled his shoulder. "Hank. Hanky Hank Hank. *Henry.*"

He woke up as he always did, complete unconsciousness to loud confusion, like an old man who fell asleep on a roller coaster. "Ivy? What time is it? Why are you in here? Where'd my computer go? Did it fall on the floor?"

"Settle," I said. "Breathe."

He fell back dramatically. "Oh, my god. It's the middle of the night!"

"Did you just get home?"

"I don't know. I was *sleeping.*"

"Did you see anything weird when you came in?"

"Weird like what? Never mind, I don't care. No. Go to bed."

My breathing slowed a little. "I will. In a minute. But, Hank. What did you mean earlier, when you said that thing about Billy? That thing about, *what happened with you guys?*"

"*This* is why you woke me up?" He caterpillared up his headboard, squinting at me through one eye. "I just meant that you used to be friends. Till you dropped him."

"No," I said firmly. "That never happened."

"It did, though."

"*Listen* to me. I barely know Billy Paxton. Aside from his being our neighbor. I've never had a full conversation with him before tonight."

My brother blinked at me, the moon carving his face into the high angles of an Anonymous mask. Then he threw back his sheets. "Get the light."

When Hank was a kid, Aunt Fee gave him her old Polaroid camera. He was immediately obsessed, and started keeping a photo record of every person who entered his room. Eight years later the wall between closet and door was given over entirely to photo squares in various stages of fade. He stood before them in sleep hair and pajama pants, searching.

I was there, of course, at different ages. The one where I had a triangular haircut, freshly grown-in beaver teeth, and crooked red glasses was suspiciously prominent. There were boys in baseball jerseys and girls caught with their eyes closed, holding phones and jackets and joints, bleached with flash. The photos were stuck up with pushpins, collaging over each other, some of the older ones perforated multiple times along their rims.

"Here." Hank detached one that hung at the level of our

knees, mostly hidden behind a picture of him and his friend Jada dressed as Magenta and Riff Raff, and pushed it into my hand.

I looked, but for a moment I didn't *see*.

In the photo Billy and I stood side by side, aged about nine and ten. It must've been summer because we were both wearing shorts, and, for some reason, oversized sport coats. Billy was talking, this expression on his face like he was in the middle of telling me a joke, and my eyes were squeezed shut with laughter. It was a silly, happy photo. I started to smile. Then the unreality of it hit.

I shoved it against Hank's chest with trembling fingers. "I don't remember this."

"Ivy." His voice was almost pleading. "How could you not?"

"I'm telling you, this *never happened*. How are we . . . what even *is* this?"

He swallowed. "It's that dorky game you used to play, where you dressed up in Dad's work clothes and spied on people. You called yourselves the Detective Twins."

I put a hand to my neck. "The *Detector* Twins?" It was the name of a cheesy kids' mystery series I used to love.

My brother looked relieved. "See, you do remember."

"No." I was cold and prickling with sweat. "Why have you never said anything to me before, about Billy?"

His shoulders twitched up, like he was bracing himself. "Mom."

"What about her?"

"She told me not to."

I didn't know what I looked like when he said that. But going by the way his expression changed, I'd say dangerous. "When was this?"

"Summer before I started high school," he said immediately. "So you were going into seventh grade. I remember because it was right before I came out. You were acting weird for a while, but my mind was on my own shit."

"What *exactly* did she say to you?"

"She said—she told me you and Billy had a falling-out and I should leave you alone about it, I shouldn't tease you. I assumed he'd done something. But then he was so obviously lovesick, I figured it must've been you."

"But you never asked."

"Like I said." He looked miserable. "I was distracted."

"She was lying," I told him. "I remember none of this. *Nothing.*"

"That's . . ." Hank trailed off, mouth twisting.

"I saw Billy tonight. He told me I broke his heart when we were kids, and that I made *Mom* do it for me. Whatever is happening here, she did it."

"Made you forget an entire *person*? How? Why?"

"Oh, come on, Hank," I said. "We both know she can do stuff."

I thought he'd argue with me, but he didn't. "Yeah," he said quietly.

We looked at each other for a while, neither of us talking.

"What about Dad?" I said. "How much does he know?"

"Ivy, *stop*." Hank flopped back onto his bed and covered his face. "Three in the morning is not the time to get into it. Also I may have eaten mushrooms with Jada today and I *cannot* talk any more about this right now. Obviously you need to talk to Mom. And Billy."

"Right, except Mom is *hiding* from us, and Billy hates me."

"Billy's been in love with you since he was seven," he said faintly, laying a pillow over his face. "And Mom'll be home eventually."

"Billy *what?*"

He moved the pillow. "If you let me sleep now, I promise I'll talk to her with you. Okay? I'm not promising I'll *talk*, but I'll be in the room. I'll be, like, your lieutenant. But right now you have to let me go to bed."

I did. I went to the bathroom and stared at my reflection like I might see straight through to my brain, to the traces she'd left when she broke into my head.

Then I remembered standing outside my aunt's house feeling the subtle weight of being watched, reading the texts Aunt Fee just happened to send right after I rang her bell. What if they were there? Hiding out, taking care of the mysterious "something" that had started with that first dead rabbit. My dad was staying in the city, which meant his car was at the train station less than a mile away. There were spare keys in the junk drawer, and a key to my aunt's house. This time, if she didn't answer, I'd let myself in.

Billy's car was gone from his drive when I stepped outside. I guessed he couldn't sleep, either.

CHAPTER SEVENTEEN

)

The city
Back then

Sharon turned the CLOSED sign over and led us into the shop's back room. Boxes were stacked against one wall, bookshelves lined another. There was a hot plate and an electric kettle and a *Lost Boys* poster pinned up on the whitewash. Beside it hung a molting bulletin board layered in postcards and flyers and a few bright oddities: dried flowers, lengths of woven thread, a plait of hair so shiny it had to be synthetic.

In the room's center was a chipped mint Formica table. An East Asian girl in a Mickey Mouse T-shirt sat in one of its two chairs looking at Sharon with the hungriest eyes I'd ever seen. A wooden ruler and a piece of knotted rope lay on the tabletop in front of her. When she saw me looking she swept both into her lap.

"Who are they?" she demanded, her voice a deep-dish wedge of South Side.

Sharon smiled at her perfunctorily. "Sweet Jane. This is Marion and her friends." We didn't rate names, apparently. "Honey, would you run out and grab us some sandwiches? Four, make 'em turkey."

"I'm not hungry," Marion said colorlessly.

"Right. You're fasting. Three, then."

Jane looked at her unhappily. "I'm hungry."

Sharon squeezed her shoulder, kissed her cheek. It was motherly, I was pretty sure. "Just three, okay?"

Jane avoided looking at us as she tucked her ruler and her rope into a purple JanSport. Watching her reminded me we'd be back in school soon, surrounded by girls her age. *Our* age. But it was sundown in summer and I was standing in a head shop's back room, my temples aching with last night's magic. High school couldn't have felt further away.

Sharon pulled limp greenery from her mini-fridge and stuffed it into a plug-in kettle. Soon the room smelled like hot cilantro. When she handed me a mug I noticed, among the silver and the topaz and the black ink, a ring of pale hair on her right middle finger.

"Mourning ring," she said, catching me looking. "I cut it from my half-brother's head when he was lying in his casket. I spent most of my teens on a compound out in Arizona. He saved me when nobody else could be fucked to try."

"Compound?" Fee said.

"Cult. Went in when I was fifteen, came out again at twenty. I've got lots of souvenirs, though." She shook her bracelets away to reveal a row of pale hatch scars, the marks of someone counting off the days on a prison wall. "These are mine. Not these, though." Three circular burn scars clustered in the hollow of her elbow. "The C-section scar is even better. I should've died. But the midwife snuck me off the ranch and got me to a hospital. The ranch—that's what we called his compound."

Just like that, Sharon clicked into focus. She was one of those people who wielded her own history like a knife. Spend enough time with career alcoholics and you can spot this kind from an avenue block away: threading their conversation with terrible, intimate revelations, designed to make you believe they're telling you their secrets. Making you think you had to pay them back in kind. Sharon was magically gifted, but I'd bet her true talent was an eye for damage.

Well, mine wasn't the right kind. I glared at her. Freshly sixteen, a virgin in an X T-shirt and combat boots. "Why are you telling us this?"

"Because it's not a costume." Her smoked voice hardened and she planted her legs wide, daring us to look at her. The Robert Smith hair, the jailhouse tattoos. "My body is a *battery*. I will never burn through everything that's been done to me. Where does your power come from? Watching *The Craft?*"

My eyelid spasmed. Last night my dad couldn't sleep for the grinding agony in his back. Last night he found the pain-relief charm I'd kicked under his bed and made me flush it. *What hairball voodoo shit are you onto.* His words damp with vomit because pills make a bad mixer. Fee came over and we stayed up until dawn cobbling together something to numb him, something to make him quiet, and I must've brewed my resentment into it too, because all morning I was fragile with blowback.

"There it is," Sharon said softly. "Let your blood up, honey, it's good for you. Anger is good for you. Hurt lets you work. Can we work together? I want to."

"What about me?" Fee said. "I'm here, too."

Fee was prettier than me. Taller, thicker. But even across those messed-up months there was a bedrock solidity to her that I never had. It allowed people to feel safe enough to look away.

With a finger hovering just shy of touch Sharon traced a lowercase *t* over Fee's shirt, above the place where its fabric hid her cross-shaped scar. "Lost faith is a powerful engine. Frustrated faith is even better. I want to work with you, too."

Marion just sat there sipping her tea, the cat with the cream.

I took a swig from my cup. It had been sitting a while but it was still wicked hot. "What's the spell?"

Marion's real smiles had become rare. Nothing with her seemed spontaneous anymore, you could always see her *thinking,* sense the ticking behind her eyes. But she smiled now, bright and tremulous. "It's a power-up."

"A what?"

"Listen to this." Marion pinned the page with her finger and read aloud. "'A blessing of power, for those bold enough to take it. That my gifts may not stagnate. That I may not die but live in you. A spell for eight hands.'" Her cheeks were flushed, her voice unsteady. "Increased magical force. *That's* the spell."

"'For those bold enough,'" I repeated. "It sounds like a dare. Like she's calling us chicken."

"Have some respect," Marion hissed. "This spell is a promise. A *reward*. A piece of Astrid's power."

"A reward for what, though?"

She brushed the question away. "We knew she was teaching us with the book. But all along she's been *testing* us, too. Making sure we're worthy. And we've proven ourselves." Her eyes shone. "She's chosen us."

"How long does it last?" I asked.

"Forever."

"No way," I said dismissively. Fee frowned.

"*Forever?* Plus, what, we die of blowback?"

Marion's mouth twisted. "This isn't about give and take and *balance* and whatever you're on about. This is a gift. Could you seriously say no to this?"

"Hey, come on." Fee took her hand. "It just . . . Mar, doesn't it seem a little too good to be true?"

Marion squeezed back, face softening. "Don't we deserve something good?"

Sharon was looking between Fee and me with mild eyes. "I thought you two were workers," she said. "But it sounds like you don't want to work."

"Nobody's talking to you," I snapped.

"Stop," said Marion. "*Listen.*"

The word had weight to it. Texture. I almost wondered if it was a spell. When we met Marion, she'd been soft and ruddy, no grace to her but gravity. Now her color was rinsed out, her curves filed down to bone. The changes gave her the unsettling authority of an ascetic.

"I've done my homework. Since I found Astrid's book I've read everything I could find about practitioners, occultists, witchcraft, all of it. No one could do what Astrid Washington could do. If we had just a sliver of her power, just a *crumb* . . ." She closed her eyes, as if the idea was a light too bright to look at.

When she opened them, her face was lit with the questing cartographer's fervor that had made it so *fun* to let her obsession become our own.

"Just think," she said. "Think of what we could do."

My skin prickled with goosebumps. I thought about juiced-up healing charms, my dad's face free of pain. I didn't quite allow myself to picture the unimaginable: a cure. When I looked at Fee her expression had gone inward. I wondered what was passing behind her eyes.

"What goes into it?"

I spoke coolly, but Marion knew she had me. She hefted her bag onto the table, an oversize artist's tote from which she slid a massive disk of mirror wrapped in deer leather, a fat red candle, and the empty lipstick tube she used to hold pins and needles.

"That's it?" asked Fee.

"And this." Marion put a palm to the book's rough cover. "And the right moon—tonight's moon. And the right place."

"So it has to be tonight. What if we're busy?"

"I know your work schedules. You're free."

"Fine, but we have lives."

Marion spun her finger in a circle, encompassing Fee and me. "You are each other's lives."

At the start of summer she might've sounded jealous, but her eyes weren't really on us now. They were pointed toward some other horizon. Fee and I proved her point by looking at each other, conferring in silence.

I don't like it, her face told me.

Me, neither.

But . . .

Inside our hesitation was all sorts of things. Curiosity and guilt and desire. Optimism, even. And beside them all the ugliest, most vivid parts of ourselves. The pieces magic had sharpened into blades we could use to skin the world. Think of it: sixteen and brimming with power, after being told all your life you were powerless.

Even now, when I try in memory to make my long-lost self say *No*, to imagine taking Fee's hand and walking away forever—from Marion, from magic—I can't do it. There is no version of me that was ever going to refuse.

CHAPTER EIGHTEEN

)

The suburbs
Right now

I never knew the streetlights let off a pale buzz until I walked beneath them, alone, at half past three in the morning. Across the street between subdivisions, past the old playground, its rusted merry-go-round glinting septically in the moonlight. A breeze came up and set all the trees to sighing, like old women coming in from the heat.

Walk long enough through the snow-globe world of the middle of the night and even familiar things get corrupted. The houses where porchlights shone seemed like friendly liars, the unlit ones like lockboxes for secrets. I felt an obscure relief as I escaped the suburban grid, breaking onto the road that rolled past the elementary school and the park district and the strip mall with the all-night 7-Eleven, its clean corporate lights looming against a sky the color of grape candy.

The store's insides were lit like a stage set, empty except for a clerk leaning over the counter. I swayed at the lot's edge, feeling around in my pocket for change. I was about to step onto the pavement when a girl slid into view from the side, down the row of closed storefronts. As she pushed through the 7-Eleven's door I shivered, imagining the chill of its AC, its odor of mop water and soda syrup and liquid cheese. I stared after her, but I didn't feel true surprise. It didn't seem so unlikely that I should find her again in the dark.

She was the stranger Nate and I had followed to the water in the woods. I knew by her bunker-white skin, her certainty of step. Her face that, even in profile, made me think of an ancient flaking painting done on wood, its subjects blunt-featured and arresting. Also, she was still wearing my shirt.

I dropped to a crouch behind a Subaru. I had a line on the door, so I could see it when the girl came out holding a two-liter of Mountain Dew and a hot dog. A goddamned 7-Eleven hot dog! Even Hank wouldn't eat one of those. Amina and I liked to joke that it was always the *same* hot dog, spinning in its little tanning bed, begging people to eat it in an Oliver Twist voice.

Queasily I watched the girl uncap the pop bottle and start to drink, head dropping back and back, throat working like a python's until it was drained. When she was done she ate the hot dog in three bites and dropped all her garbage on the ground, even though a trash can was right there. She cut left at the end of the lot, walking in the direction I'd come from.

"What in the actual fuck," I whispered, and followed her.

Her pale hair fell to the middle of her back. She was wearing faded, badly fitting jeans and the light blue button-up I'd tossed to her by the creek. She should've shone in the dark like a white-furred dog, but right away I lost her. I made a lucky guess at a turning and saw her again.

I kept losing and finding her, block by block. The shadows she walked through seemed sticky, fond of her skin. I stayed well back but she never turned nor hesitated. We walked past the playground, across the arterial road that ran through the neighborhoods, into my own subdivision. The closer we got to home the farther back I hung.

She turned onto my street. I held my breath, thinking *walk, walk, keep going, don't turn*, right up until she stopped at the end of our drive. Dead still, arms at her sides, looking at my house.

I tucked myself into the shadows alongside Billy's place. "Pick up, Hank, you jackass," I muttered, phone pressed to my ear, but my call went to voicemail. Then the girl came sharply unstuck, striding up the drive and around the side of the house.

"Hey!" Panic ripped the word right out of me. I sprinted across the street, through the weird violet air. The side of our house was a wilderness of raspberry canes, their fruit boiled jammy by the heat. I almost expected to find her trapped among them like a fairy-tale prince, but they were empty.

The backyard was empty, too. I kept going, tongue running sour, darting toward the fence on Barbie toes, then over it. Past the kitchen windows, the room behind them the indistinct color of lake water. I circled back to the driveway, but the girl was gone.

Or—I thought of the cookies I'd left on my plate, a neat bite taken from each—or maybe she'd let herself in.

I stepped into the front hall and listened. I didn't think I was imagining the unfriendly texture to the quiet, the feeling of wrongness as palpable as a smell. I circled the first floor, then went upstairs. Hank was in bed, safe and snoring, one hand up under his chin. My room was empty, the bathroom, too. I saved my parents' room for last.

Nothing inside it looked out of place. But the air itself felt ruffled and staticky. I checked the closet and the bathroom, then dropped to my hands and knees to check beneath the bed. As I scanned the dust, my phone lit up with an unfamiliar number.

I shot upright. No one stood in the doorway. Across the room, the window was a box of empty sky. Still I imagined the strange girl could see me, that she was waiting for me to pick up the phone. I clattered swiftly down the stairs and back out to the driveway, answering after the fourth ring.

"Hello?"

A long silence with a rushing sound beneath it. Like traffic, or the ocean. Something about it made me grip the phone in sudden hope. "Mom?"

"Christ, no," the voice said. "This is Sharon. You left a message for me."

CHAPTER NINETEEN

)

The city
Back then

The spell had to happen at midnight. Because while some supernatural clichés turned out to be crap, plenty were true.

We left the shop just after eleven. The lake had pursed its
cool blue lips and blown the humidity away. It wasn't late for the
city, but it felt late in this sleepy summer town.

The people who were out kept an eye on us as we passed, or
looked away fast. Together we'd become fearsome, a bouquet
of night-blooming flowers. Fee was a plum-mouthed goddess,
Marion a shattered-glass witch. Sharon was a barely reformed
Manson girl, and then there was me. You can't ever really see
yourself, but I liked the feel of my red hair down my back, the
afterparty ache of my insomniac's eyes.

Marion led us into the campus's heart, through shadows cast
by ugly cement buildings named for dead men. Down a tricky
pathway lit orange with old lights, over a fairy bowl of lush clover, and up to the steps of a baroque fever dream of a house.

"Is that . . ." Fee began.

Marion faced the library that had been the occultist's house. "We're going inside."

"What?" I glared at her. "You didn't tell us we'd be breaking and entering."

"We're not breaking. We're just gonna enter."

You could easily miss the little gangway in the lake-facing wall, unless you were Marion and you'd already cased the place. It was an architectural quirk I'd never seen before: a winding interior corridor so narrow we walked single file. One sharp turn, and another, and another, then it ended in a garden that smelled of basil and tomatoes and rampaging mint, bleached gray by the moon. Under sunlight it must've looked like something found on the grounds of a medieval nunnery. Fat bees, syrupy herbs, nodding flowers. Fee ran a gentle hand over a sage plant, releasing its scent.

Marion waded into one of the beds. From between the wall and the rhubarb she lifted a gridded metal box. A cage, one of those rat traps you see in alleyways. Inside it blinked a rabbit, a domesticated creature the colors of valentines on snow.

"Oh, come on," Fee said plaintively.

Handing the cage to Sharon, Marion dropped to her elbows and knees before an arched wooden door in the old stone wall. From her bag she pulled out a flashlight and a bent wire hanger, a magnet banded to its end. There was a gap beneath the door where the wood had warped. She set her flashlight in front of it, shoved her magnet stick through, and went fishing.

"*Yes,*" she breathed, slowly extracting a key.

Sharon whistled. "Nice work, MacGyver."

Marion had been planning this for a long time. Longer than she'd let on. I bit my thumbnail as I watched her unlock the door, bumping it with her hip to dislodge the swollen wood from the frame. She'd done that before, too. Pleased with herself, she beckoned us in.

Just a step over the threshold and the temperature dropped. The sweet bakery funk of deteriorating paper and old ink blotted out the green clamor of the garden. Even with your eyes closed you'd know were inside a library. When the door had shut behind us we stood in the silence, an unwieldy circle of four. Five. The rabbit's eye shone like a dime in the dark.

"Join hands," Marion said in a slumber-party whisper. "I'll lead us. We can't risk the flashlight." She reached a hand to Sharon, who reached back for Fee. I took Fee's hand and became the tail of the comet streaking through the quiet library.

It was beautiful. There had to be fifty kinds of magic waiting to be woken in a place this stuffed with old books and history. We shuffled past a carved wooden screen that tossed geometric cutouts onto our skin and up a sweeping staircase. At its top a stained-glass window depicted a picnic party of well-dressed foxes, casting the landing in light the colors of fallen fruit. A recollection hit me with an ice-water charge: Marion had once found a body in this place.

We cut right, through an unlit passageway and up another stair, Marion cursing as the rabbit's cage banged against her knees. On the third floor the ceilings were lower, the windows fewer. For rubbery stretches of time we had to rely on Marion's memory and our daisy chain of interlocked hands to pull us through the dark.

Midway between two pools of moonlight, she stopped and set down the cage.

"Gimme a boost."

Sharon dropped, weaving her hands into a step. I could just see their outlines, one kneeling like a cavalier and the other straining upward, arms over her head to fiddle with something on the ceiling. Whatever it was came undone, and she caught it as it fell.

"Ouch," she said, full volume, guiding the wooden ladder toward the floor. It came from an open hatch through which more moonlight fell. The same light from the same moon but up there it had an astringency to it, a thinness like lemon juice.

Marion climbed up first, disappearing in neat pieces before reaching back for the rabbit. Then Sharon, then Fee. As soon as I was alone the dark grew teeth and bad intentions, sending me scurrying up after them. Once I'd pulled my legs in and the ladder up, Marion pulled the trapdoor shut, locking us inside a tart bubble of light.

The room was circular, a snow globe filled with moon. We were above the tree line and the windows were placed in some tricky way that rendered the whole place shadowless. There was a stain in the center of the floor the size of a curled-up mastiff.

Marion dropped her bag beside it and pulled out a compass. Consulting it, she placed us in a fan along the room's southern curve.

"Take off your shoes." Her spine was a reptilian ridge as she bent over the laces of her boots. "We don't need northeast for this, throw them there."

The floor was the same neutral temperature as the air. If it wasn't for the dust I'd have barely felt it. I was southwest, Sharon was south, standing taut with her hands folded behind her. Fee stood motionless at southeast, just the tip of her nose showing behind her fall of hair. I willed her to look back at me but for once she didn't feel it.

Marion took out a wooden box the size of a matchbook, sliding it open and dusting her hands with white powder. When she blew the excess away it swirled up into a cloud, settling slowly on her shoulders and hair as she unwrapped the mirror, laying it on the stain before arranging a candle and the caged rabbit to her right. To her left she placed a cereal bowl full of salt poured from a Ziploc and the occultist's book.

Usually spellwork made Marion stiffen up, like she was bracing for a blow. But tonight she moved nimbly on bare feet, chalking lines over the floor and adjusting our placement with impersonal hands before giving each of us a needle. I pinched mine tight.

"I'll do most of the work." Her voice broke the hush, sudden as a slap. "Stay where I put you, and when I tell you, you're gonna draw the needle over your left hand from here to here." She pointed at the bend of her thumb, then the base of her life line. "Deep enough that the blood comes up. When I say so, you'll press your palm to the floor."

My bare toes rubbed half-moons in the dust. Blood magic equals big blowback. But I knew there'd be a cost. Maybe Marion would pay for a hotel room where we could dry out after. Cheesy TV and takeout and Fee's vinegar brew. It could be fun.

There are scenes in your life you replay like a movie, sitting in some darkened room inside yourself yelling, *Get out, you idiot, run!* The person in the movie looks like you, sounds like you. Like you, she does the things she shouldn't, failing every time to save herself. Over time you can almost convince yourself she's some anarchic stranger, malevolent in her ignorance.

Here's a scene that still plays in my head. Not daily like it used to, not weekly anymore, but often enough, stealing over me at random like a carbon monoxide cloud.

Four figures stand barefoot in a circular room. The light is such that their shapes appear hazy, insubstantial. They vary in age but all are young, their hair red or black or pale, their posture predatorial and prepared. Who knows what lies in their hearts.

The girl with pale hair crouches before a stain on the floor. Beside her is a bowl of coarse salt, a book, a red candle, and a panting rabbit. A circle of mirror lies over the stain, its glass reflecting not the ceiling but a dirty sheep's-wool circle of sky, unrelated to the night outside the windows.

Some spells are finicky down to the last detail. Some have small gaps inside them, left open to interpretation. The pale-haired witch lights her candle with a Bic shellacked in cutout magazine mouths, because the spell doesn't care how the fire starts, just that it does. It's a steady orange tongue of ordinary candlelight until she holds a hand over it and speaks the first words of the incantation. The flame crackles, then expands into a mellow blue globe.

The spell is stronger than the witch working it. This first success makes her bite her cheek against a triumphant smile.

The blue flame eats through the wax in triple time, melting

the candle into a thin-sided saucer. Carefully the girl pours the wax onto the mirror, spiraling from center to edges like she's making a crepe. She speaks in a language no one knows, not in this room or any other. Moving rapidly now, she unlatches the catch of the cage and drags out the rabbit. Placid to this point, now it's kicking frantically, born to be a house pet but the fight it puts up is worthy of a wild thing. You want it to *win*, anyone would, but with the flash of a blade and a scream as pagan as anything else in that room it gives up the fight, its life dropping in a red rush over the swirled wax.

The witch doesn't just slice its throat but beheads it completely, with a blade pulled from her clothes. See the enameled horses on its handle and remember a day at the beach when she used it to slice mangoes, handing them around on the blade like a mother with a paring knife.

She sets the dead animal down and takes a needle to the bloodied wax, inscribing letters in it from right to left, bottom to top. How she can still hold it, how she can see anything around the blood, isn't clear. The other figures in the room are so still you might think it part of the magic, but there: the flicker of eyes, the flick of a tongue catching sweat.

The room is hot now and getting hotter.

When her inscription is done the witch stands, bowl in her bloody hands. She pours the salt in a circle that seals her in with the candle and the mirror and the stain, leaving the other three without. She moves with careful speed. Still incanting, she cracks the candle's sides away, so the blue firelight rides atop a thin wax circle. This she holds over the mirror, tilting until the globe of fire rolls like a shooter marble onto the coated glass.

The inscribed wax lights up all at once, turning the mirror into a porthole to Hell.

At this moment the witch is sure she's done it. Her voice is victorious, her throat ripe with iron and smoke. Outside the circle the heat is receding. Inside it the pale witch sweats, hair lifted by a sudden wind. She puts up a hand.

"Now," she says.

The faces of the three outside the circle are sluggish, featureless, as if watching through a scrim of sleep. In perfect somnambulists' tandem they lift their silver needles and paint beading red lines over their palms, pressing them to the floor.

Two of them do. The third, black-haired, purple lips trembling, hesitates with her hand upheld. She stares at the flaming mirror.

"*Now!*" the pale witch repeats, face prickling all over with sweat.

"Qué carajo," whispers the black-haired witch.

"Do it," hisses the woman beside her, whose black hair is the bottled kind. "Are you *trying* to get us killed?"

Then the other worker sees what her friend has seen.

I see it. I can't stop myself now, I'm poured back into my body and I'm *there*. Seeing what's inside the circle of mirror, its wax burned away and its glass hazed with blue fire.

A woman's face. Her face and her hands, pressed to the glass from below, as if she's standing under the floor looking up. Nails sharp and fingertips callused, her forehead high as a child's. Her hands pushed against the glass's underside. They pushed *through*.

The surface of the memory is eroded now, taffy soft and crimped with overuse. Sometimes I think I heard the occultist's laughter. Sometimes I think I *smelled* her, Florida Water and a bilious tang. But always I remember this:

One reaching hand rising from the fiery circle, then the other, pressing into the stained wooden floor. Nails curved to grip, Astrid Washington dragged her body over the mirror's edge.

First her head, crowned by a wet-looking cap of blonde hair. Then her face rose inch by merciless inch. The eyes that might've been brown once, tarnished by time to an unholy gold, the mouth too lush and red as a warning. She had her elbows up, she was out to the middle of her rib cage. Panting, determined, each gasp making ripples in the pooling blood. She hoisted herself higher.

That's when Fee charged forward, shoes smudging the salt. As soon as she was over the line she pulled back, crying out. The moonlight was so bright I could see her reddened skin. Marion must've been *roasting* inside that circle.

I stood frozen as Fee stuck a hand into her pocket, digging out a black-paper bundle. She shook free from it her mother's crucifix.

Marion had been watching Astrid's rise with shining eyes. Now she looked up. "Don't," she shrieked, too late, as Fee tossed the gold cross underhand at the mirror.

The occultist might have been stronger than whatever was in that necklace. But it startled her enough to lose her grip.

She fell back. Below the flames, below the glass. Her body went down but something else went up, some grainy exhalation of spit or spirit. The cross hit the mirror just after her fingertips went through and the glass cracked, four perfect lines blooming into an asterisk.

A rushing sound rose as the flames went out. A burning wind plucked at our hair, the salt circle's hellish heat spilling into the rest of the room. Something interrupted the moonlight, casting the walls in reaching, fast-flickering shadows, like we were moving at speed through a naked wood.

"We have to end it," Sharon said tightly. "Forget the spell, the spell is broken, we need to end the *magic*. Clasp hands. *Now*."

We did, flinching from each other's scorching touch even as our fingers tightened. When we were a circle of four Sharon began to chant.

I dropped my pail into your well
From your well I drew
With blood for thanks and a strand for luck
My gratitude I'll shew.
Until we meet on a blood-moon night
Or on a silver shore
I'll thank the Devil once, twice, thrice
Before I ask for more.

She let go of us to rip a few hairs from her head, pressing them and her bleeding hand to the floorboards. My scalp freckled with heat as I yanked my own strands free.

Our hair and blood joined the mess on the ground and the wind snapped off. The writhing shadows withdrew, the temperature dropped to the middling warmth of an ordinary attic room. Our bare feet shifted over boards slicked with salt and chalk and blood and the remains of a rabbit. It was done.

Marion's flat blue eyes came alive with rage. "You *bitch*," she said to Fee, and charged her.

But Fee and I were two bodies with one heart, and one fighter with eight limbs, and her dad had taught us how to throw a punch and mine taught us how to make it dirty. I pulled Marion off my best friend by her hair. She twisted like a cat, sinking her teeth into my upper arm. Fee socked her in the gut to make her let go. Marion went at her again and I caught her around the stomach, hauling her down and pressing an arm to her throat the way I'd seen my dad do, breaking up fights on the block. By then the will had gone out of her. I scrambled back, sickened and ashamed, as she started to cry.

"That was her," Marion said, her voice bitter with broken hope, her face red and naked. The circle's heat had fizzed her eyebrows down and her lashes away. "That was *her*."

"You lied." Fee sat ramrod-straight, looking at the mirror. Her mother's cross had bled into the cracks, sealing them with gold. "You lied to us."

"I didn't."

Fee's cheeks flushed hotter. "That was a *summoning*! We were dragging Astrid Washington out of, what, Hell? Mother of God, Marion!"

Sharon stirred. She'd watched in silence as we fought; now she pushed herself off the wall. "Are you three done? Because we have bigger problems."

Sharon was not okay. Her fingers quivered as she pulled

out a squashed pack of Camel Reds, patting manically at her pockets until Marion tossed her lighter across. The room felt flammable with enchantment, but nothing blew when she lit up.

"You broke a prime fucking rule here," Sharon said. "You lied to your fellow workers. You withheld some *crucial information*. I don't know *how* you pulled that off, how far it would've gone . . ." She trailed off. "But at least she was contained. Until *you*"—she nodded at Fee—"let her out of the circle."

"Hey," I said sharply. "Marion did this. Fee was trying to stop her."

"That's great. Magic definitely gives a red shit what you *meant* to do."

I felt dizzy, my temples burbling like a kettle with the approach of blowback. "But she did. She did stop her. And you stopped the magic. So now what? We clean up. We bury the rabbit."

"How are you bitches not dead yet?" Sharon said scornfully. "She didn't stop shit. She broke the circle mid-summoning. Yeah, okay, Marion's girlfriend isn't embodied, but she's not tucked up safe in witches' Valhalla either. You let her *out*. She's, oh, man. Having some fun. Or maybe she's right here. Waiting for us to find another rabbit."

I cast my eyes around the room, searching for places where the moonlight hung funny. I didn't see or sense anything amiss.

Marion had stopped sniveling. Her lashless eyes were wide. "Wait. Are you saying it worked?"

Sharon stared at her. Then she flicked her smoldering butt in Marion's face, lip curling as she skittered back, her ass drawing a contrail through the blood.

"My fault for working with schoolgirls," Sharon said. "If I end up dying because of you I'll haunt you in Hell."

We crept down the ladder, through the halls, beneath the picnicking foxes. It seemed a year had passed since I'd first seen them. I was aching and terrified and thirsty as a desert wanderer for the sky, the garden, the world outside the nightmare. I hadn't grasped yet that the nightmare was *us*, that it clung like wet denim to our skin.

Through the years I'd find myself back there, retracing our path through the library's nighttime corridors. Walking the hall in the middle of the night, past the bedrooms where my children lay asleep, my foot would rise off bland suburban carpet and come down on age-stained parquet. My heart would seize, my blood burn with warning. Then I'd close my eyes and stand very still, waiting for the flashback to pass.

Here, now, back in the garden. Marion locked the door behind us and nudged the key through the crack. Sharon had done something to take care of the mess in the attic.

"What now?" It was Sharon I looked at when I asked it. She was older, her body scarred with bad knowledge. I thought she would be the one to save us.

She shrugged, thumb *zip-zip*ping over the wheel of Marion's lighter. "I don't know what you're gonna do, but I have to get home to my kid."

"You have a kid?"

"Yeah," she said shortly. "Look, come to the shop tomorrow

morning, we'll start trying to fix this. Till then, you know. Stay alive."

She disappeared into the tunnel, leaving the three of us alone. Fee watching Marion, Marion watching the garden, fingertips pressing white indents into her scalded skin.

"You completely fucked us," I told her.

She twitched her head. "Okay."

I took a step closer. "Were we ever even friends? Were you always just planning to use us?"

"Oh, stop it," she said raggedly, looking up. "If you'd let me finish we'd all have what we want. I wasn't lying. She *would* have increased our power."

"You've seen that spell before." Fee spoke with cold certainty. "Before you met us, even. *That's* why you pulled us in. You've been hating us, haven't you? Because magic makes us happy, and you're still fucking miserable."

Marion was quiet a minute. "Yeah, well. Nobody's gonna be happy now, are they?"

She slipped off after Sharon.

We went home to Fee's. Nobody on the bus at that time of night cared that we were covered in blood. We took showers and drank 7 and 7s and walked over to Jarvis Beach.

The lake was the same color as the sky. We stripped off our clothes and walked in. It was August but the water was so cold and thin it felt like swimming in chilled gin. We bobbed and gasped, looking back at the surreal curve of the city. The attic room and Sharon's dark warnings felt too far to touch us.

Maybe it would be okay. Maybe this—Seagram's and the small hours and the scouring cold—were as good as a banishing charm. Magic had always been good to us, fluid beneath our fingers. Why should that stop now?

I thought these arrogant thoughts right up until the fish bobbed to the surface beside me. Long and skinny as an eel, its teeth wicked and its eyes bone white. I splashed back, gulping dirty water as another fish joined it. Then another.

We stroked clumsily to shore, fish bodies boiling up around us. Our knees scraped sand and we dragged our bodies out, looking back at the spreading arrow point of silver corpses. Like Astrid had dipped one misty finger into the water and stirred.

CHAPTER TWENTY

)

The suburbs
Right now

"This is Sharon. You left a message for me."

"Sharon." My brain whirred, placing the name. "*Sharon.* Hi."

No reply.

"Thanks for calling. Sorry. It's just . . ." I gathered myself, trying to banish, briefly, visions of the pale-haired stranger. "It's really early."

"Where I am, it's late." Her words bumped against each other belligerently. "What do you want?"

"I think you knew my mom. Dana Nowak. From 'Twixt and 'Tween, a long time ago. That was your shop, right?"

"I haven't talked to Dana Nowak in over twenty years, honey. I've got nothing to tell you."

She was drunk. I tried to picture the stranger attached to the voice, tried to imagine what it was about this call that made her want to drink before she made it.

"You called me back. If you've got nothing to say, why bother?"

No reply.

"I just want to know what she was like," I told her, before she could decide to hang up. "Anything you can remember."

"Dana's dead," she said abruptly, and my head filled with white noise. Then I figured out she wasn't telling me, she was asking.

"God, no, that's not what I— Why would you think she was dead?"

"Some kinds of girl don't have a long life span."

I cupped a hand to my eyes. "I don't know what that means."

"What *do* you know?" Less aggressive now, but still wary.

"I know you called me back for a reason. And I know . . ." I hesitated. Even in my brain the word felt unwieldy. Standing alone on the drive, talking to a stranger, I finally said it. "I know she's a witch. I'm thinking you might be one, too."

"Worker." The word had a sarcastic edge. "But I'm out of work."

I dropped to the concrete, my head flooding with questions. "What does it mean, though—to be a witch, or a worker? What can you do? Do you learn it? Are you *born* with it?"

I could hear her loosening up. Liking to be asked questions she actually wanted to answer. "Some workers have aptitude, sure. But more have . . . other things. Hunger, ambition, nerve. The arrogance to look at reality and say, 'Here's how *I* would've done it.' Guess which one I am." She laughed, an unhealthy, rock-tumbler sound.

"What about my mom?"

"Aptitude," she said. "Arrogance, too."

"What could she do? When you knew her, could she—do you think she could've made a person forget something? Something really big?"

A pause. "Why don't you ask *her* all this? Seeing as she's not dead."

My laugh hurt coming up, its edges sharpened on broken glass and the bones of dead rabbits. "She's hard to talk to."

"I'll bet," Sharon said dryly, and sighed. "I only knew her a little while. I was glad to see the back of her. Thought she was tough, but she was nothing but underbelly. Her friend, Felicita, she was the strong one. There, that's something I know about your mom: she's a one-owner dog. She still hang around with a girl named Felicita Guzman?"

"Yeah."

"I figured. Fee was a good girl, but she and your mom were a package deal. Well, them and—"

She cut off so hard I might've thought the call had dropped, but I could still hear that ocean sound down the line. I edited my guess: it was the hiss of wind through trees. I pictured her standing at the rim of some lonely place.

"Them and who?"

"Them, Dana and Felicita. A matched set."

She said it with a note of hard finality. I paused before I spoke again.

"The woman at Petals and Prose said my mom was one of your *girls*. 'One of Sharon's girls,' she said. What does that mean?"

Sharon made a bitter sound. "Look, I don't like the person I was back then. There are people I hurt, people who probably wish they'd never met me. But your mom wasn't one of them. Not by a long shot. I wish—I wish and I fucking wish—that I had never met *her*." Her voice gained fervency as she spoke. By the end it was venomous.

I swallowed, struggling to keep myself steady. "Why's that?"

"Ah," she said softly. "Now we get to the point. But if you have to ask, then I've got nothing else to say to you."

The sky was lightening. Wherever Sharon was, it was still dark.

"Someone's been hanging around our house," I said. "Letting herself in, leaving my mom dead rabbits. So now I'm sitting here trying to figure out what the hell my mom did in her life to earn that kind of stalker."

The silence stretched like a body on a rack. "Did you say *rabbits*?"

My head pulsed. "You know. You know what that means."

"When?"

"When what?"

"The rabbits!"

"Um. Last few days. I've seen her, the person who did it. She's blonde, young. I have no idea how my mom even knows her."

"Blonde girl? Would you say—eighteenish?"

"I think so. Yeah."

Sharon let loose a string of profanity, long and bright as a birthday streamer. "Was she . . . Oh, sweet lord." Her voice bubbled with so many things. Horror and hope and a kind of raw wonder. "Did you get her name?"

"How would I get her name?"

"What did she look like?"

I rose on trembling legs, turning, running my eyes over the trees, the houses, the windows stained with reflected sky. "Pale. Never-sees-the-sun pale. Hair down her back, light-colored eyes."

"Where's your mom? Where's Dana right now?"

My hand was at my throat, each word came shriller. "I don't know. I can't reach her."

"You're alone. She left you *alone*. Do you at least know how to protect yourself?"

"Like, self-defense?"

A stunned pause, then I think she put the phone down. I could make her out at a distance, muttering.

"Okay," she said, putting her mouth back where I could hear it. "Felicita Guzman, your mom's old friend. Can you get in touch with her?"

"Aunt Fee is with my mom right now."

"Oh, that's cute," she said scornfully. "Here's my advice, since your mom and *Aunt Fee* couldn't be bothered: you lock yourself in, you sit tight till your mom gets home. Get some pepper spray if it makes you feel better, maybe a pocketknife. And you know what, stay away from mirrors. Better safe than sorry." A beat. "Not to say you'll be *safe*."

"Who *is* she?" My voice was stained with hysteria. "Is she another—worker? Is she trying to hurt my mom? What's happening?"

"I'm sorry, honey," Sharon said. "I really am. But I'm not a good person, and I can barely help myself. Take care, if you can. I've gotta go check my property for dead rabbits."

CHAPTER TWENTY-ONE

)

The city
Back then

The occultist sits beside you on a green bench, beneath a stained-glass window shaped like a compass rose. In the glass is a girl, an apple in one palm and a knife in the other. Her smile is hungry.

The occultist is hungry, too. In life she loved the rare, pink-fleshed apples that grew in her garden, bone broth slippery with marrow, bloody sweetmeats, and eggs barely cooked. Food that slid and coated and crunched. In her half-death she longs for few things more.

This is what she whispers to you, in the dream.

The work is not yet done, she says. Why did you stop the working? Finish what you started and until you do I will speak to you at all hours, you will never not hear me, you will see my hand in all your workings and my face in your own face and my heartbeat nested in your heartbeat and my—

I sat up gasping, mouth thick with pennies and salt. I ran my tongue over my teeth but couldn't find anyplace where I was bleeding.

Fee sat on the floor surrounded by open books. "Bad dream?"

I pressed a hand to my chest, where my heart moved with an eerie double-time flutter. "I can't remember."

"Same."

"Do you feel . . . how do you feel?"

"About as good as you look."

"Hah." I moved my hand from heart to head. "I feel weird, though. Almost like . . ." I sat up, reaching for the feeling, then lay back fast. My brain sloshed in its pan, every part of me singing with blowback.

"On the table," Fee said, running her finger down a page.

There were two mugs waiting, vinegar tea and lukewarm coffee. I downed the one and sipped at the other. "Find anything promising?"

"Not really."

The clock read 8:06. "Are we going to the shop?"

Now she focused on me. "What do you think?"

I lifted a shoulder. Even that hurt. "We can't trust either of them, but at least we know it. And we could fix this faster with four."

"Maybe. Maybe not. Marion is . . . I think Marion's pretty much gone, you know?" She sounded wistful. "The person she was before."

"I don't know that there was a before. I think we never actually knew her."

"It wasn't all fake," Fee said definitely. "But it doesn't matter now. At this point she'd eat our hearts if she thought it would make her stronger."

I was hit with a slippery, split-second vision of a woman

holding something ripe and terrible to her lips. The occultist. She'd been in the dream I was struggling to remember.

"Sharon, though," Fee went on. "She didn't know any more than we did. Plus she has a *kid*. Good reason to want to fix this quick, right?"

"You'd think." When I blinked I saw fish bodies, cracked mirrors, smudged-out circles of salt. The occultist's face. It took me too long to notice Fee swiping tears away.

"Hey," I said softly.

"I know," she told me, raising a hand. "But if I hadn't broken the circle . . ."

"*Stop.* Marion's not that strong. She was gonna lose control no matter what. At least this way the occultist isn't walking around on two feet. Doing god knows what."

"Devil knows what. God's not looking." Fee pressed two fingers into her temple. "Fucking Marion."

"Fucking Marion," I repeated, with feeling.

Fee stepped out the street door first. Promptly she stepped back, fist to her mouth. I slipped past her to see.

On the step lay a dead rabbit. Paws curled, belly to the summer sky. I knew what it was by the tail and the back legs: its head was gone. "Oh, god," Fee said, pointing. The head was a few steps down, where the stoop met the sidewalk.

I used a stick to scoop the remains into a section of last week's *Reader* and ran it to the dumpster. On the way to the bus stop my eye was drawn to every dead thing. Broken-necked birds, the cracked shell of a robin's egg. The roadkill carcass of an outdoor cat, pounded to leather by passing cars. Flies were everywhere; my sneakers squished over the remains of heat-stricken flowers.

We rolled into the shop around ten, nursing milk-white, sugar-blitzed Dunkin' Donuts coffees. Henry Rollins was screaming through fuzzy speakers and the air was dense with nag champa. The off-kilter feeling I'd woken up with was spiking, sharpening. I was taking in too much information, too much texture and color and sound. It carried me back to that very first spell, to my trip through a shining city I still longed for and would never see again. Right now it just made me want to curl up tightly and block out the light.

I caught myself on a jewelry case stuffed full of low-rent trinkets. Cheap mood rings, their stones the red-black color of anxiety. Leather cords strung with yin-yangs and peace signs and psychedelic mushrooms, and those silver claddaghs the shiny girls wore.

Fee put a hand between my shoulder blades. "I feel it, too."

"Hey. Are you who Sharon's waiting for?"

The girl behind the counter—hoodie pinned with punk-band patches, inflamed piercing in one blonde brow—looked us over shrewdly. We nodded and she jerked her chin toward the back.

The music was quieter there, the EXIT door propped open to the alley. There was a cot pushed against one wall and a pup tent on the floor, blankets spilling out of it. Beside it a little boy in a Spider-Man T-shirt sat cross-legged reading a comic book, hair wisping into a rattail that stopped between his shoulder blades.

"Morning," Sharon said without turning. She was heating SpaghettiOs on a hotplate. She tasted one, then scraped them into a plastic bowl and handed it to the kid.

Fee watched this nervously. I could feel her clocking the kid, sensing the nourishment he actually needed. I didn't think it came from a can.

"Morning," I said, before Fee could say something off topic. "Where's Marion?"

Sharon sat at the mint-colored table. "Marion's your girl, I figured she'd be coming with you."

"Nope." We'd called her twice that morning and gotten her parents' answering machine. "Did you figure anything out?"

"Since I last saw you I showered, slept, and woke up screaming. Then I spent the morning dealing with *this* one."

The kid flicked a mistrustful gaze our way. His eyes were the same space-age blue as his mother's.

"Hi," Fee said softly. "What's your name?"

He rolled those pretty eyes and went back to his X-Men.

"Don't bother," Sharon said dismissively. "He barely even talks to me."

The room was claustrophobic, even with the open door. I wanted to leave this place and never see Sharon again, never again breathe the hopeless tin-and-tomatoes scent of canned spaghetti. But we were stuck with each other for now.

"Right," Fee said after a pause. "So I've been looking into banishing spells. I've got some ideas, places to start."

"Not sure an off-the-shelf banishing would work." Sharon

folded tattooed hands over her stomach, rocking her chair to its tipping point.

"Okay. So what might?"

"We need Marion here to figure that out. She's a weak witch, but she's the only one who knows what we're unpicking."

Marion's voice came from the doorway. "Weak witch, reporting for duty."

She looked even worse than I did. Baggy dress and scarecrow limbs, and massive sunglasses that looked new. "I know what we have to do," she said.

"Oh yeah?" Sharon let the legs of her chair drop. "What's that?"

Marion slopped her bag onto the table. "Redo the spell. This time, we finish it."

"Not a chance," I said. "No way."

"It's the only way." She pulled off her sunglasses. The room went so quiet Sharon's kid looked up.

"*Gross*," he said. "What's wrong with her face?"

All around Marion's eyes, over her temples and the tops of her cheeks, were little bruises. She was speckled with them like a piece of bad fruit. "Astrid won't let me sleep until it's done," she said dreamily. Not crush-dreamily, but like a person talking in their sleep. "She pinches me awake each time I try." Her eyes cleared, went suspicious. "Did she let *you* guys sleep?"

"Like a baby," Sharon said. "Till I woke up with blood in my ear and my kid's hamster dead on my pillow."

"What?" the boy squeaked. "You said she ran away!"

Sharon closed her eyes. "Oh. I'm sorry, baby. Here, take this."

She rummaged in her pocket, then held out a crumpled bill. "Get an ice cream, okay? Take yourself to the movies. Just be gone for a couple hours. We'll get you a new pet next week."

He rose slowly, shoulders clenched, leaving his comic book propped beside the untouched SpaghettiOs. He looked too young to go anywhere by himself, but I'd been about that age when my dad stopped keeping tabs.

"Kids," Sharon muttered, after he'd snatched the money from her fingers and stomped off into the sun.

"Vengeful spirits," I said. "To get back to the matter at hand. She killed your *hamster?*"

"Beheaded it." Sharon made a guillotine of her hands to demonstrate.

Marion dropped heavily into a chair. "I was wrong. About the spell and what it would cost. There's more to it than I realized."

"Oh, well spotted," Sharon said caustically.

"Let her talk," Fee murmured.

Marion took out the occultist's book and lay beside it a thicker volume, stamped in gold lettering. *Howlett House: A History.*

"Last night I reread all the parts about Astrid. Lots of slanderous stuff and old wives' tales, but information, too. She—" Marion shook her head sharply, started again. "In Baltimore she was accused of killing four men. It was this massive story, probably because of the way she looked. She got all these marriage proposals, she was basically a celebrity. Right up to her escape she denied doing it. But one of the servants at Howlett House claimed she'd overheard Astrid talking about the killings with John Howlett. She said Astrid told him she'd used the men to test a theory she had: that there was a way to beat death."

Marion massaged one bruised temple. Black Flag melted into My Bloody Valentine on the other side of the door.

"This is secondhand, the word of a woman who also claimed Astrid turned into a white cat at night to ride the devil. But Astrid and Howlett were definitely obsessed with immortality, and this servant claimed Astrid had figured out a way to keep her spirit intact when she died. Intact, and close."

"Like a haunting?" I tried to say it coldly, but it came out in a whisper.

"Like a dam." Even now, Marion spoke of it with wonder. "A stopping place for her spirit between life and death, attached to the house itself. She figured out a way to *catch* herself, to build a place where she could wait to be summoned. Then she hid the spell where she knew it would be found."

Sharon was raking her nails through her hair as she listened. Sparks gathered in their wake, sizzling on her fingertips and scenting the air with cordite.

"Whoops." She shook the sparks to the floor. "Okay. Let's recap. What we're dealing with is a dead occultist who has spent the last however many years in magical solitary, losing her undead mind, and who will now be haunting us till we give her what she wants. Which is another go at the spell that will *reanimate her.* Is that everything?"

Marion jerked to her feet and pushed open the door to the shop, gesturing at us to follow. She stopped right below the speaker and drew us in, draping our four heads in a crimson throw.

Her breath was warm and sour and barely there. I almost couldn't hear her over the wall of dreaming sound. "Everything I said—it's true, but it's not the point. Astrid's *here*. She's *listening*."

Our hair crackled against the cotton. Everyone looked seedy in the red-dyed light.

"We have to be very careful now," Marion said. "We have to do just as I say. We're gonna do the spell again, to draw her out—but this time we'll end it with a banishing."

"You think we're gonna trust you again just like that?" I hissed. I wished I had a new penny to hold between my thumb and my left ring finger. *Penny bright, penny true, tell the lies that are told to you.* If the copper tarnishes, you know you're being taken for a ride.

"Look at me." Astrid's marks stood out on Marion's face like grains of black rice. "She's gonna *hunt* me till this is through."

Then the cloth was ripped away, trailing constellations of static shocks. It hovered over our heads before being flung to the floor with force.

The punk girl goggled at us from behind the register, hands up. "Holy shit."

"So we're agreed," Marion said, bruised and beady. "We do the spell again."

Fee wrapped her fingers in mine. She squeezed. I heard what she didn't say. *Astrid is listening. Tread carefully.*

"Right," I said, voice raspy.

Sharon rolled her neck. "Tonight? Get it over with?"

"Not the right kinda moon," Marion said shortly. "Next Friday's will work. Okay?"

Five days away. Five days to figure out a fix that didn't involve trusting Marion. I held onto Fee's hand and nodded my assent, for now.

Marion looked at the air over our heads. "Hear that?" she said. "We won't abandon you, Astrid."

CHAPTER TWENTY-TWO

)

The suburbs
Right now

I checked the locks on the doors again, because Sharon had told me to. But I knew it didn't matter. The girl stalking my mother had found her way in twice; she could do it again.

I'd been awake too long. In my bed, behind a locked door, I watched the dawn sky shade from purple jelly to pre-storm green, the atmosphere fattening like a wallet with unspent rain. Then the weather broke. A pause and a sizzle, the heat giving way. I closed my eyes.

While I slept the storm flooded the fields and pulled down branches and made the creeks swell up like black eyes. Rain leaked through the window seams and humidity tangled its fingers in my hair. When I woke my brain was beautifully blank. Then it caught hold of everything I'd gone to sleep to escape.

Nausea scratched at the back of my throat. I snatched up my phone, but its screen was empty. I tossed it aside, crossed the hall, and flung open my parents' door. I wanted so badly for her to be lying there, back safely from wherever she'd been, that for a moment I saw her shape beneath the sheets, her face against the pillow. But the illusion faded. No one was there.

It was half past three in the afternoon and it felt like the end of the world. Rain was still falling and the house was as dark as if it were underwater. I went to the kitchen and ate cereal from the box. When I drifted to the window I could see Billy out there, jogging between car and house, carrying disintegrating bags of groceries. His T-shirt was plastered to his skin, his hair water-dark and running.

I walked outside to meet him. All the storm's electricity had played out, leaving behind a saturating, paper-soft rain. Halfway down the drive I was soaked to my skin. Billy saw me coming and I watched him consider hurrying inside. But he stopped, swung his car door shut, and waited for me. I got right up close and still I didn't know what I was going to say. The rain hissed around us and the world was submarine green.

"Wait," I said, when it seemed like he was about to speak. His eyes widened as I came a step closer, too close, dropping my head back to see him. I took in air like a Channel swimmer and began.

"I've had one conversation with you in my life. Last night. I've seen you around, I remember what happened in junior high. But last night, that's the first time we really talked."

He said nothing, just watched me.

"Except that's not true, is it," I said quietly. "I know that now, but I swear I didn't know it yesterday. And the thing is, it doesn't even feel that strange. Because all these years I've been ignoring the way I *notice* you. The feeling I get when I look at you. The way you are, the way you move through the world, it's all so familiar to me." I looked at him, freckles and villainous eyebrows and hair swept back in wet waves. "I *know* you. How do I know you?"

He breathed in. Then he wrapped his arms around me, pulling me against him. My head filled with honey and I rose to my toes and we held each other inside the green rain. His head dipped low, his mouth pressed into my shoulder. I could feel the relief that ran through him in a long shudder.

He lifted his head, just a little, so his lips were at my ear.

"When I kiss you," he whispered, "it won't be our first kiss. I need you to know—before you can let me, I need to tell you about the first time."

I nodded. And I listened with a hurricane heart as he spoke with total certainty of an alternate past.

"Five years ago," he began, his voice a little shaky, "I was eleven, you were twelve. It was the summer before you started junior high, and I was so worried everything was about to change. We were always neighborhood friends, you know? Summer friends, weekend friends. And in junior high there's *dances*. I figured you'd get some mall cologne boyfriend and never talk to me again."

"I would never get a mall cologne boyfriend," I said, then flushed, thinking of Nate. Though he was more of a discontinued French cologne boyfriend.

Billy laughed. "So what I decided was, *I* would become your boyfriend. Except I had no idea how to do it. I honest to god looked up, like, *how to become someone's boyfriend* and *how to be more than friends*, and I'm reading all this horrible pickup artist stuff thinking, *that can't be right*, and I'm getting nowhere because I'm eleven years old and I don't know my ass from a hole in the ground—according to my dad, when I got desperate enough to talk to him about it. Never ask for love advice from John Paxton, by the way.

"It was the very end of summer and the sun was going down. We were playing by that part of the creek we called the saucer, where we found all those teeny frogspawn after the flood, remember?" His brows knit. "No, wait, you don't.

"We had our feet in the water and the sun was almost gone and I wanted to kiss you so badly. But I knew I'd look like a turtle even trying to reach your lips. Then you slid all the way into the water, right over your head, and when you came up you pulled me in, too. Then *you* kissed *me*. And I was . . ." He moved his hand in the arc of a paper plane. "Gone."

I could see it. Looking at him now, soaked through with rain, I could picture a younger Billy standing in the bowl of the creek, grinning at me.

"That was a Monday," he said. "The week before school started. The next day your mom had to go to the hospital—it was her appendix, I think—and for a while you couldn't see me. Then I started to worry you didn't *want* to see me. I came over on Saturday and your mom said you couldn't come to the door. I tried twice on Sunday. The second time . . ."

I leaned back to see him. His face, this close, was almost blinding. "She broke your heart."

"She told me you'd . . . I can't believe this is still so hard to say. She told me you'd outgrown me. You were my best friend since I was seven. You were my first kiss. I thought you were my first *girlfriend*. Then it all just stopped." He winced. "So I decided to make a grand gesture."

"Oh, no," I said, putting my hand to my mouth. "When you asked me to be your girlfriend . . . oh, *no*. You must've thought I was awful."

He didn't deny it. "After that I was too mad and embarrassed to talk to you. But eventually I got over it. I guess. And that was that, until last night." Gently he moved my hand from my mouth and laced his fingers in mine, tentatively. Like he wasn't sure he was allowed to. "You remember none of that?"

I shook my head. "I'm so sorry. My mother was lying to you, I would *never*—all of this was her. I can't fully explain it, I know it sounds impossible, but she did this."

Billy blinked the rain from his lashes, his face filling with a slow-breaking light. He brought his hands up to cup my face. His skin was warmer than the air, our lips so close I could feel it when he spoke. "Oh, my god," he breathed. "I should've known."

I smiled at him, confused. "How could you possibly have known?"

"Ivy? Ivy, what's going on?"

My dad's voice, sudden and strangely severe. His car was in our drive and he was slamming its door. I started to step away from Billy, but he took my hand and held it tightly. Together we watched my father hustling across the street to meet us.

"Dad." My voice wasn't quite steady. "You're home early."

His work clothes were streaming, the hip glasses Hank and I picked out for him fogging over. He kept pinching the condensation away. "I should've come home last night. Your mom's not back, is she?"

"Not yet."

"Ah. How are you, Billy?"

Billy gripped my hand like it was an anchor. His face was expressionless. "All good, Mr. Chase."

My dad kept looking between us, then down at our clasped hands. I couldn't tell if it was the rain on his lenses that made him look so off-balance. "What were you two talking about?"

That was when my heart dropped low. Because he *knew*. Whatever my mom had done to me to make me forget Billy, my dad was in on it, too.

"Come into the house." His eyes were unreadable. "I need to talk to you. Now."

I watched, chest aching, as he hurried away. When I looked back at Billy his face was almost afraid.

"Ivy," he said. "Don't forget about this."

I nodded, but I didn't say the words. It wasn't a promise I was sure I could make.

CHAPTER TWENTY-THREE

)

The city
Back then

I had a shift that afternoon. Dipping fry baskets, making change, wishing I knew a spell that could make my mind sleep while my body kept trucking.

Something was happening to me. I was sure of it now. It wasn't blowback or hangover or the scum of bad dreams. It was in my body, growing like a virus, making a home for itself inside my skin. What was it the spell had said? I heard Marion's voice again, reading the occultist's promises. *That I may not die but live in you.*

I looked at my hand on the counter and felt the raw red terror of not recognizing it as my own. Not knowing what exactly it might do.

"Dana. *Dana.*"

One of the shop's full-timers, Lorna, was snapping her fingers in my face. I didn't know how she managed it with her nails. *Church nails,* she called them, long as Elvira's but painted a pearlescent Sunday color. When I kept staring she clapped her hands for emphasis. "Go. *Home.* I can't keep looking at your miserable face."

She was fifty and one of my dad's first hires. She got to talk to me like that. On the way out I peed and washed my hands and sprayed down the closet-sized employee bathroom with watered bleach. Then I glanced at myself in the pitted camp mirror stuck to the wall and screamed.

Astrid was there, looking back at me. Pretty face, pretty dolly hair, bottomless golden eyes. I shoved a hand in my pocket. There was a toothpick in there, birchwood. I snapped it and spat a quick curse, the first piece of magic I'd tried since the summoning.

Undo unmake
shatter break.

As the back of my tongue kissed off the final *k*, the bathroom light burst. Glass rained over my hair in the dark, but the sound of breakage was bigger than a bulb. I clawed the door open and recoiled from an eye-watering vinegar slap.

Brine and glass covered the floor. The spell I'd reached for—a small thing, good for, say, turning a drink that might be dosed to slivers in a bad man's hand—had swept through the back room, smashing a shelf of pickle jars. I thanked the gods and saints for plastic condiment containers. Then I saw that the safety-glass pane in the swinging door had cracked.

Lorna gaped at me as I charged out to the counter, her penciled brows climbing toward the burgundy floss of her wig. "What was that? What'd you do?"

I ignored her, scanning the shop. The spell hadn't reached the shop's plate-glass front. Nobody was screaming, no one was red with broken pieces, singing a song of lawsuit. "Stay up here," I said harshly.

When I ducked back into the bathroom, Astrid was gone. The camp mirror was still intact. Of course it was, it was made of stainless steel. The spell was just a panicked miscast that had gone bizarrely wide. Probably. Right?

Before going for the mop, I called Fee.

"Don't try any magic," I told her. "Don't do anything till I'm there."

We'd ended the summoning midstream. But what if we'd still gotten what we were after? What if Astrid Washington, however grudgingly, had granted us a piece of her power?

We tested my theory using the breaking spell's opposite. A simple mending charm, white wax poured over the halves of a broken pencil. Do it right and the wax disappears like syrup in tea, sealing the break.

Fee's room smelled like birthday cake. Scented candles work fine for lots of things, and we'd found a pack of vanilla tealights cheap at the Family Dollar. I spoke the incantation as she poured. The wax disappeared, the pieces merged back into a dull No. 2 pencil.

But the spell didn't stop. The pencil's grade-school yellow casing evanesced, revealing the wood below. It roughened, thickened, bark crawling over its planes and sending up a breath of incense cedar. The twig gave a shiver, as with the memory of a breeze, and in a Chia-pet time lapse sprouted a sickening coat of fungus. Out of it wriggled a trio of dull-backed beetles, like little licorice Tic Tacs.

Fee smashed them to jelly with a book.

"Fuck's *sake*," I said, holding my heart.

"'Finish the job,'" she said in an odd voice, "'and until you do you will see my hand in all your workings.'"

"What?"

"It's from my dream. It's been hanging over me all day, that I couldn't remember it. But I remember now. I remember Astrid saying that."

I let my eyelids fall, reaching again for my dream. This time it came.

Finish what you started and until you do I will speak to you at all hours, you will never not hear me, you will see my hand in all your workings and my face in your own face and my heartbeat nested in your heartbeat and my—

Hungry smiles, glass apples. "'My heartbeat nested in your heartbeat,'" I said. I pressed a hand to Fee's chest, feeling the same wrong ripple I felt in my own.

Five days until the summoning. They ran together like candies in a pocket.

The hours flickered past, or crawled in an endless dream. We avoided mirrors but Astrid found us anyway: in the rinse sink at work, the oily surface of a cup of black coffee. Her fingers curled in the steam of our showers and turned them cold. We played music to drown out her seashell sounds. My peripheral vision swam with mist, my footsteps crunched over fallen bluebottles.

And everywhere, dead rabbits. On the fire escape outside my window, curled inside Fee's rosemary pot. A fresh and bleeding rabbit foot stuffed into my knockoff One Star, squishing beneath my bare arch when I put it on without looking.

We couldn't sleep, we didn't dare cast, but we could still *search*, spending every minute we could muster looking for a way out that wasn't Marion's. Fee combed through her books and I visited everyone I could think of, all the practitioners and magical layfolk who might talk to me.

I started with a clairvoyant on Clark Street, who practically broke my fingers slamming the door in my face. "Over you hovers a darkness," he called through it, above the sound of a deadbolt hitting home.

"Why do you think I'm here?" I hollered, driving my fist into the door.

I let myself into a Cramps show at the Metro because I wanted to talk to this girl, Linh, who tended bar there. She had an affinity with the dead and a sideline helping the recently bereaved find things their departed left hidden—wedding rings, wills, car keys. If she knew how to open her mind to the dead, maybe she could help me close mine. Even before she saw me she had her face screwed up, looking around like she was trying to find a gas leak.

"That's coming from *you*?" she said when I bellied up. "Oof, babe, you look bad. What happened?"

"Long story, not good." I put a bill down on the bar. "Any advice on how to make a spirit *stop* talking to you?"

Linh moved her head back and forth like a radio dial. "Not really. I mean . . . *ugh*." She drew her chin down like a turtle. "That's like bleach poured into my ears. My *other* ears. Nuh-uh, no way." She flicked my twenty off the bar. "Keep your money. And stay away from me until you've got this resolved."

That was Wednesday night. Forty-eight hours to go.

CHAPTER TWENTY-FOUR

)

The suburbs
Right now

I stepped inside, dripping. When I walked into the kitchen there was a pop can and a sweating bottle of vodka on the counter, and my dad leaning against the sink gripping one of our dishwasher-scarred plastic tumblers. His face was so tense he looked like a stranger.

"What's going on with you and Billy?"

I stayed on my side of the room, as far from him as I could get. "Why are you asking me that?"

"Answer me."

"No," I said. Starting soft, then rising. "You answer *me*. What are you and Mom keeping from me?"

He eyed me, head at a tilt. "What are you talking about?"

I heard what he was really asking: What do you *know*? "I found the safe," I told him recklessly. "You should hide your passwords better."

My father crossed the room in two predatory strides, his posture so altered I flinched back against the wall. He saw it and checked himself, freezing in place.

"You opened it?" His voice was strained but steady.

I bobbed my chin. "And you know what I found? Stuff that belonged to *me*."

He blinked at me. Then he breathed out slowly.

"Your cigar box," he said, a little shaky. "Right. Right. We can talk about that. But I need to know why you went snooping in the first place."

"I've got a better question. Where is she, Dad?" My voice wobbled, broke. "Where the hell is Mom?"

His Adam's apple rose and fell. "I don't know."

"This isn't okay." I spoke with conviction. "The way she is, the way she just took off like this, it's not *normal*."

"Don't get hung up on normal. Everyone makes their own normal."

"We have no *fucking normal*." My voice spiraled to a shriek, each inhale was sharp as a pin. He moved in to hold me, but I threw up an arm. "Dad, I need her." The words burned. I hadn't meant to say them. "I'm so sick of pretending I don't need her."

"I need her, too," he said levelly. "But she can only do what she can do."

"That is not acceptable. That is *messed up*."

His eyes brightened with tears, but his voice didn't change. "Your mom is an extraordinary person. She has unusual boundaries. That's something that predates you. It's got nothing to do with you."

"*Unusual boundaries?* Dad, please. She's a witch."

He put a hand over his eyes. When he pulled it away he was older.

"Oh, my god." I drew back. "Oh, *shit*."

Even after everything, I guess I'd still believed he would deny it. The reality of it sank into my skin, scribbled like scrimshaw over my bones.

"She was going to tell you."

I laughed. "Right."

He moved closer and this time I let him hold me, keeping my arms at my sides but resting a cheek on his shirt. "I'm worried about her," I whispered.

"I know, sweetheart. I worry, too. But I promise she can take care of herself."

"What about us?" I pulled away to look at him. "Someone's been hanging around the house, looking for her. Messing with her. *You* saw the rabbit. And they . . ." I paused, the look on his face making me falter, hedge. "What if they could've broken in?"

"What *if?*" All his quiet sympathy evaporated. "What are you saying? Was someone in the house?"

His alarm infected me, dialing my anxiety up into something frantic. "Not in the house. Near it. This girl, about my age. Blonde hair, really pale."

"Your age?" he said, almost to himself. "Someone she fired from the shop, maybe?"

"I doubt that's it," I said. "She's the same person who—"

I cut myself off, remembering I hadn't told him about seeing a girl the night Nate drove off the road.

"The same person who what?"

"Who left the rabbit." I grabbed his hand, with its flattened nails and dinged-up wedding band. "Mom's in trouble, Dad. I know she is."

He squeezed back. "Oh, sweetheart," he said helplessly. I could see him making his own calculations, trying to hide his own fears.

"Did she tell you *anything* before she left?"

"She said she had to take care of something. That's all she said." His face showed a fleeting stab of fury. "If I'd known she wasn't coming home last night, I never would've left you and your brother alone."

"What are we supposed to do? Just *wait* for her?"

"We stay here, together, and we try to trust her. Take her at her word that she's handling this."

"Trust her," I said bitterly, and dropped his hand. "I know about Billy, okay? I know she did something to make me forget him."

The look on his face was unbearable. If I'd been at all unsure whether he knew, I wasn't now. "Why, Dad? Why would you do that to me?"

His eyes circled my face. I'd inherited their color, but not their gentleness. There was so little of him in Hank and me, he had to see my mother every time we walked in the room.

"We have so much to talk about," he said. "But I promised your mom this conversation wouldn't happen without her."

"What conversation?" I asked sharply.

"Not until she's here."

"Make an exception? Make a 'we've got a stalker, Mom's run off' exception?"

"No," he said with surprising vehemence. "This has gotta come from her. I can't even make myself say the words she owes you."

I started to fathom, then, the *size* of what he wasn't saying. And suddenly I wasn't sure I was ready to know. He must've seen my hesitation, because he grabbed my shoulder.

"Hey. Look at me. I'm not telling you to back off," he said fiercely. "I'm *proud* of you. I *love* seeing you ask questions this way."

I shook him off. "Here's another one for you, Dad. Why did you marry her?"

The softness in his face compacted. "Ivy."

"I mean, I know why you married her. Because of Hank. But why did you *stay* married?"

"Because I love her," he said dangerously. "She's my wife. We have two wonderful kids together, we have a home. We have a history that started long before you came along."

"How is that enough for you?" The question burst out of me. "Do you two even talk anymore? Did you ever? Don't you get sick of being lied to? Of the way your wife looks right past you?"

My dad's temper lived way down deep. When it did surface, it was with the vast inevitability of a leviathan.

"It's time for you to stop talking about what you don't understand," he said through gritted teeth. "She's your mother. You got me? You're seventeen now, well. She was an orphan by seventeen. She was a mother at twenty. She didn't have the luxury of a childhood, parents dragging her toward college, giving her a bedtime. She's been working since she was ten years old. Ten! There are things you should ask for and information you are owed, but an accounting of my marriage is not one of them. *Christ*, Ivy. You need to know when to *stop*."

Eyes down, quiet as I could, I fled the room.

"Ivy. Ivy, come back here."

I ignored him, sprinting up the stairs.

"Do not leave this house!" he shouted at my back.

I didn't start crying until I'd slammed my bedroom door.

CHAPTER TWENTY-FIVE

)

The city
Back then

I slumped across the plastic seats of the Blue Line, my skin feeling as thin and chitinous as butterfly wings. It was Thursday morning. We were almost out of time.

An hour ago I'd poured myself a bowl of Marshmallow Mateys and a dead bunny kit thumped out of the box, membranous eyelids shut tight. Any sleep I'd gotten was hole-punched to tatters by dreams in which I was falling, waking all night in a panic, body bouncing against the mattress. My heartbeats clicked against each other like billiard balls.

I got off the train at Halsted, the smell of my skin intensifying in the heat coming up from the tracks. I twisted my hair into a knot, tucking it beneath my ball cap.

There was this old guy Fee had introduced me to who kept a table at the market on Maxwell Street. Mr. Lazar sold enough worthless junk that you had to have a particular kind of eye to notice what he was *really* selling, overpriced but far from worthless. When I rolled up on him he was sitting in a sun-faded folding chair, doing the crossword.

He looked at me over his glasses. "By yourself today, brat? Where's the beauty?"

There was a possibility he could help me, so I bit my tongue. "Fee's busy."

"No window shopping today. If you're not here to buy, go bother Andy. He's got nothing worth paying for."

The guy at the next table flipped him the bird.

"I'm buying," I told him, "if you've got what I need."

Lazar's mouth stayed flat, but his eyes went keen. "I see. Step into my office."

Over his plot lay a balding carpet as dirty as the ground beneath it, stretching a few feet past the edges of his table. I stepped onto it and the world around us went vague. We could talk in privacy now, just yards away from hagglers and passersby who could no longer make out exactly what we said. I hoped that went for hovering spirits as well.

"We're being haunted," I said. "Bad summoning, ghost who won't go. I don't trust the person who says she can banish it. I wanna see if there's something else we can do."

Lazar considered me like I was a thorny crossword clue. Then he stood and shuffled around to the far side of his hoard.

"I've been thinking you'd be back," he said, his Algerian accent flattened by years spent in this city. "First time I met you, I knew I had something that was yours."

From between a limp stack of old newspapers and what I was pretty sure was a gramophone, he extracted a boxy black suitcase. It looked like the kind of thing a magician would use to carry around pieces of his assistant. Lazar settled the case over his knees and opened it with a toothy snap, revealing another, smaller suitcase. He went on like this for a while. I couldn't tell whether the matryoshka bit was pure showman's theater or something real, until he lifted the seventh box into the light.

Something real.

It was just over sandwich-size, made of what looked to be pure gold. Its leonine color made my heart drop. I had a pocket filled up from one of my dad's emergency cash stashes, the one I'd known about longest and judged most likely to have been forgotten. But if the box was actual gold I would never be able to afford it.

My throat dried at the thought. I *wanted* it. Badly enough that I guessed the wanting was part of how it worked.

I cleared my throat. "What is it?"

He knocked gently on the box's top. Or its bottom, maybe. The thing had no apparent lid. "It has a very long name. I call it the forgetting box."

"Forgetting box?" I acted skeptical, hoping that might make it come cheaper. "Doesn't sound like what I'm looking for."

"It's not about what you're looking for, it's about what you'll need. Tomorrow or next year or in fifty years. You know me, I'm a matchmaker."

I didn't really know him, not well, but Fee had told me as much. She'd heard about Lazar from a curandera to whom he'd sold a length of white lace. The woman used the lace to trim two christening gowns, completing them in secret just before her daughter learned she was pregnant with twins following years of infertility struggles. Though I doubted all the stories about him were so sweet.

"I've got a problem right now," I told him, still staring at the box. "Not in a year or fifty years."

"That hand is dealt. There's nothing I can sell you that will change it. All I can tell you is, one day you'll want *this*."

I found my fingers drifting toward my box. "What's it for?"

He eyed me up. "That red hair, I thought Irish. But you're Polish?"

"I'm both." I frowned. "Why do you know that?"

"I told you, I'm a matchmaker. The forgetting box is from Poland. Like you." He smirked. "What did you think, I'd sell a Polish-Irish girl a juju? A vial of Kvasir's blood? No. You children like to swim around in other people's waters, but you'll never go that deep. And there are things in the water that'll get you if you do. Blood, that's thicker. Stick with the magic that's in your blood."

I could feel his words sinking into me, where I didn't want them to go. I thought about the three of us working our shallow way through the grimoire of a dead occultist, a woman I preferred not to think about at all. As if every spell was a fresh-forged thing, devoid of fingerprints or history.

Lazar watched me, smiling faintly. "When it's hard to hear, that's how you know. Anyway. The box. There's a Polish folk story, goes by a few names. 'Agnes and the Lonely Prince,' 'The Little Hut in the Woods.' A girl falls in love with a prince, but a jealous fairy steals his memories and hides them in a golden box. The girl goes through many trials to find and unlock it, so her love will remember her."

"Uh-huh. And you're saying this is the box from that fairy tale?"

He inclined his head.

I could almost believe it. The thing would've looked at home in the chapped hands of some winter queen, faraway, long ago. Or maybe he was just jiggering up the price. "Why would I even want this?"

Lazar pursed his lips in that irritating French way. "I'm supposed to know?"

I asked the question I'd been putting off. "How much?"

Lazar snorted. "How much is it worth? More than you've got. How much will I take for it? That's another question."

I pulled out my wad of cash. "This is what I've got. This is *all* I've got. I don't even know if I want that thing."

"It's yours either way. You think I'm happy something worth this much belongs to a little girl who doesn't even clean her hair? No. I wish it was a rich man's treasure. Oh, well." He picked ten twenties off my pile. Considered the two that remained, and took one more. "A girl shouldn't walk around with empty pockets. It's still not enough, but how's this for a deal: if you tell the beauty to bring me a few more bottles of that stomach settler, we'll call it even."

"Just, she's got a name," I said, rubbing my forehead. "Call her Felicita, alright? And I don't know what you're talking about with *stomach settler.*"

"She's an herbalist, your friend. A good one. My wife is receiving chemotherapy, and nothing else works so well for the nausea. I take your money now, and Felicita brings me five big bottles of stomach settler. Do we have a deal?"

Still I hesitated, trying to imagine why I'd need the box. How would it feel to carry it around like a self-fulfilling prophecy, an empty place where stolen memories would one day reside? But whose—my father's? My own? Someone's I hadn't even met yet?

It didn't matter. Whether it was power of suggestion or true enchantment or my dad's Polish blood in my veins, I wanted it. It was meant to be mine. And right then it was comforting to be told I had a future coming at all.

"Okay," I told Mr. Lazar. "If telling me how it works is part of the asking price, then yes. We've got a deal."

I caught Fee up on my visit with Lazar. When I showed her the box she said, "Huh."

"What do you mean, *huh?*"

Delicately she placed a palm over its top. Bottom, whatever. It didn't matter, I knew how to open it when the time came. "I'm wondering if he's right about like calling to like. I look at this and I don't feel anything. It's pretty, but I wouldn't necessarily know it was even magic. What does it feel like to you?"

I took it back, sandwiched it between my hands. The metal was the same temperature as my skin, its grain so softly burnished it felt like fur. "It makes me hungry," I said. "I hope I never have to use it. The idea creeps me out, honestly. But I couldn't *not* take it. It makes me hungry just to hold."

"That's sort of how I feel in a garden," she said. Then, abruptly, "My mom's grandmother was a yerbera. My dad just told me. And I've been thinking. When all this Marion stuff is done, I want to be better. I want to use magic to help, you know? No more selfish shit. There's this practitioner in Pilsen, I know she'd take me on as her apprentice if I asked. When I'm done with school, or maybe before, even. Lazar is right, I think. About working stronger if you work with what's in your blood."

"Wow. That's so cool. That's . . . you'll be amazing." I bit the inside of my cheek. "It's just, I'll miss you. I'll miss working with you."

Under any other circumstance she would've reminded me we were sisters. Now she sighed. "Let's just get through tomorrow, okay? Let's get that over with."

"You think it'll be over after tomorrow?"

"Not really," she said. "You?"

I held the golden box to my chest. There was a slight vibration to it, like a purring cat turned down to its lowest setting. It made me feel braver about the shadows gathering in the upper corners of Fee's room, that would turn into breezes and whispers as soon as we turned off the lights.

"Personally, I think we're fucked."

CHAPTER TWENTY-SIX

)

The suburbs
Right now

When I closed my eyes I could feel it, the way your body remembers roller coasters. Billy's arm around me, pulling me in, and the whole warm dreaming world gone underwater.

When I kiss you, it won't be our first kiss.

I opened my eyes and the rest of it tumbled in.

I peeked out of my room around dinnertime, the house so quiet I got scared my dad had gone somewhere. Then I heard him talking behind his bedroom door. My heart leapt before I realized he was calling into the void of her voicemail.

"Where are you?" The pleading in his voice made me prickle all over with cold. "I need you. Your daughter needs you. We had a deal, goddammit, and I've kept it. Now *you* keep it. I swear to God, if you leave me alone with this . . ."

I leaned into the quiet that followed the threat, then lurched back from the sound of his fist meeting wood. Four blistering bangs, then silence.

That's when I stopped being angry at my dad. There was only one person to blame, and even he couldn't reach her.

I retreated to my room. I was scrolling through texts from Amina, trying to figure out how the hell I could respond—the last one, from an hour ago: Either your dad took your phone or you're dead—when I heard my parents' bedroom door fly open and hit the wall.

I jerked upright. My dad pounded across the hall and my heart clawed its way to my throat and when he threw the door open I saw right away he wasn't angry. He was *terrified*.

"Where's the box?" he said.

"The box?"

"The box you took from the safe." He was breathing too fast. "Give it to me."

I reached under my bed, to where I'd stashed the cigar box, and held it out.

"Jesus H., Ivy, not that one—the *golden box*!"

"The gold—" I shook my head. "I left that in the safe. I didn't even know it was a box. What's in it?"

Something was balled up in his hand. He dropped it on the bed, fingers trembling. "Are you sure you didn't take it out? You're absolutely certain?"

"*Yes.* All I did was pick it up and put it back. I couldn't even tell what it was, I thought it was solid metal . . ."

The longer I babbled, the eerier his silence. He was too pale, his skin drawn too tightly over his bones.

"The person you thought could've broken in. Describe her again."

I did, watching his face for recognition and seeing none.

"Okay," he said, when I was through. "I'll keep—trying to reach your mother. And if Hank gets in touch, can you please tell him to call me back, for god's sake?"

I didn't reply. I was looking at what he'd dropped on the foot of my bed. Slowly I leaned forward to pick it up: the button-up work shirt I'd given to the pale stranger, by the creek. The one she was wearing when I tailed her home from the 7-Eleven.

"Where did you find this?"

My voice must've sounded normal enough, because a fractional smile skated over his face. "Floor of our closet. You must've dropped it when you were snooping. I don't think you're cut out for a life of crime, kid."

The shirt smelled like sweat and fried food and, oddly, my mother's perfume. I squeezed it in bloodless fingers. "Dad," I whispered.

He was studying the cigar box sitting on the bed. "Ivy, do you mind if I . . . ?"

I shook my head, more shudder than assent. Carefully he lifted the lid, laughing softly at what lay inside. The ring of wood, the faded theater ticket, the guitar pick. He touched a finger to the lock of red hair. Then he closed the box and clicked its latch back into place.

"You're a good kid," he told me. "This is all gonna be fine."

That's when I truly understood he couldn't protect me. He wouldn't even know how to try. His only defense against the darkness was comforting lies.

"Thanks, Dad," I said.

So the girl was here for me.

That was the conclusion I'd reached. Knees drawn up, thumbnail in my mouth, staring at nothing until my eyes felt like swollen plum pits. She stole something from their closet, but she left *my* shirt. She broke into our house when I was alone, only to creep around taking bites out of my cookies. Like what she really wanted was to show me how close she could get.

Stay away from mirrors, Sharon had said. My belly bottomed out as I remembered that flash I'd seen after bleaching my hair, the girl's pale face in the bathroom mirror instead of my own reflection. What if I hadn't imagined it?

My dad came in one more time, around ten, to kiss me good night. He was still pretending everything would be fine, and I complied with a solid imitation of a person who wasn't losing her mind. When he slipped away my brain returned to its obsessive loop, leaping from one discovery to the next, gliding over the darkness between. It all felt like puzzle pieces from different boxes.

There was something that wanted to break through. A question, maybe, or a memory, slithering along the edges of conscious thought. I fell asleep still reaching for it, and in dreams it tiptoed from its hiding place.

I woke up.

It was the middle of the night but it could've been high noon. My brain switched on like a lamp. I climbed from bed holding delicately to the thought I'd had.

My bare soles on the carpet felt nervy, strangely tender, my vision scalloped at the edges with light. I crossed the hall and eased open my parents' bedroom door. My dad was facing away from me, keeping neatly to his half of the bed. I crept past him to the vanity and picked up the old framed photo of my mom and Aunt Fee at sixteen.

I moved to the light coming through the window to confirm the hazy recollection that had come clear to me in dreaming:

one half of the photo lay flat. But the other bulged outward, against the glass.

And the best friend hearts around their necks, broken into thirds.

I unclasped the back of the frame and flipped the photo out.

I was right. The photo pushed against the glass because one third of it had been folded under, tucked away, by someone who didn't want to look at it anymore but couldn't bring themselves to scissor it free. A wave of queasy revelation broke over me as I saw what had been hidden.

My mother and aunt leaned into each other, but the third girl stood straight as a fingerbone. Heavy eyeliner, naked mouth, a length of green ribbon tied around her throat like an urban legend. Hanging below it, the other edge of the Best Friends heart. You could have daubed her face into an old painting— something Dutch, maybe, with peasants or saints—and aside from the eyeliner nobody would've blinked.

She was less raw-boned here. Less leached and furtive. But she was absolutely the girl who'd appeared on the road in front of Nate's car. The specter who'd paced ahead of me through Woodbine's night-lit streets, all the way to our door. Twenty-five years after this photo was taken, her face as untouched as a time traveler's.

CHAPTER TWENTY-SEVEN

〉

The city
Back then

Friday morning. We hadn't talked to Marion or Sharon since the shop. But we knew they'd be waiting at the occultist's house tonight, Marion all fairy-pinched with bruises.

"At least we'll get to sleep again," Fee said. It was just past eight in the morning and we were walking back from the Mc-Donald's. "Whatever happens tonight, tomorrow we *sleep*."

Warily I slid my apple pie from its sleeve. Nothing gross came with it, or at least nothing grosser than a McDonald's apple pie. "So true. I hear you get the best sleep ever when you're dead."

"Don't be fucking funny, Dana," she said. "Can you imagine what would happen to our dads if we were dead?"

"Mine would sell my shit and buy a Trans Am."

"What do you have that's worth anything? He'd buy a Trans Am decal."

"Who's being funny now?"

She wrung her hands. "I don't want to be another one of my dad's saints. I don't want to be on his sad wall between my mother and the Virgin for the rest of my dead life."

"All soft focus. Velvet hair bow, crucifix on."

"He asked about the crucifix, by the way. I told him you were borrowing it. I told him you needed it to pray for your dad."

"Uncle Nestor! He believed that?"

She pressed her palms together and looked up. "Perdóname, Padre."

"Oh, my love," I said. Joking as I began, and then very much not, my throat drawing tighter with every syllable. "My beautiful Felicita. You know if anything actually happened to you I would go full-on Orpheus. I would drag you back. I would . . ." *Melt into sand without you. Disintegrate into stars.*

"Me, too," she said, and cinched an arm around me. "My one and only sister."

I think we really believed that love could work that way. That we could hold each other fast to the surface of the spinning world.

We shaved the hours away, minute by endless minute, until seven p.m. came and time started melting like a sno-cone.

It was eight and we were trying to fill our stomachs, enough so we wouldn't be trembly but not so much that we'd barf. Nine p.m. and the sun was gone. We blinked and it was 10:30 and we were waiting for the bus, so twitchy a woman waiting with us— clear vinyl backpack, green powder to her brows—offered us some pretzels. Half past eleven and we were lost in the scented shade of the occultist's house, combing the grass for four-leaf clovers.

Sharon arrived just behind us. She saw what we were doing,

dropped onto the grass, and joined the hunt. None of us found any luck before Marion showed.

Her bruises had faded to ugly smudges of yellow and green. She looked brittle as a candy stick, with a raw vitality to her that made me think of a frayed and sparking wire. I stared at her until I understood: it was Astrid's gift. While Fee and I were making ourselves sick trying to suppress it, Marion must've been tending her portion of power like a strangler vine. My stomach gnawed on itself. It would be hard for her to give that up.

"Let's get this over with," she said.

We retraced our steps, trooping through the dust and the dark. The library's antique air made me feel like I was breathing through rough cotton. Astrid was with us, a presence at our backs, ahead of us, pressing in from the sides. We scaled the attic ladder.

The moon was just right for our purposes, leaner now but satiating in a way I could feel to the bottom of my witch's soul. Now that the moment had come, now that we were here, I felt curiously calm. As if everything that was about to happen already had.

The hour turned. Marion kneeled. The working began.

The spell unfolded with the gripless texture of reenactment. Blue flame, gray mirror, white wax. Until Marion snapped her knife open and lifted the rabbit.

It was wild this time, and skinny despite the season, sides heaving beneath its mottled coat. It fought and fought, twisting in Marion's grip, finally jerking its head into a broken angle to bite her. Even through the pain of its yellow teeth she was silent. The rest of us hissed in dismay as her blood hit the wax.

With a decisive stab her knife went in. But it must've been too dull, or the creature's neck too sinewy. Dying, it twisted free; Marion wrestled it back. She held it more efficiently this time, sawing away so fiercely a spurt of arterial blood hit my knuckles. I dropped my needle and had to scrabble in the dust to find it.

The spell went on, but the chain had come off. The magic felt loose and messy, a drafty house where any kind of weather might come in. When Marion began the incantation it sounded different than it had the first time. Harsher vowels, cruder consonants. She laid the salt circle with her bleeding hand, lit the waxed mirror. The entire room wobbled with spiking heat, and that was wrong, too. There must've been an error somewhere, a gap. *It's not gonna work,* I thought. Glad and terrified at once. But no, look: there was Astrid Washington, her gold-dust eyes peering up through the glass. She smiled, lips drawing back from teeth as white and uniform as seed pearls.

I tasted acid and apple. This was where the summoning would make its hairpin turn into banishment. If Marion could pull it off.

Her eyes were vacant with effort, her shoulders slumped beneath the heat. She signaled to us and we sliced our palms, dropping to our knees to press them to the floor. I felt compacted grit loosening beneath my blood.

Marion laughed. A sound so high and wild I felt it shuddering through all three of us, connected by an invisible net of blood magic. And we *knew.* Right then we knew Marion was going to betray us.

She spoke Astrid's full name, her voice filling like a wineglass with rich red satisfaction. She took a deep breath.

And she made a terrible mistake.

Dipping her hand into a hidden pocket, Marion pulled out

something that pooled brightly over her fingers, glinting in the moonlight like one of the devil's golden hairs. Below the glass, Astrid stopped smiling.

I craned to make out what Marion held, pinching my needle tight. She worked her fingers like a cat's cradle, the thing unfolding between them into a veil fine as fog.

Sharon charged the circle, but this time its borders held.

"Don't do it," she cried desperately. "Marion, *no!*"

Marion paid her no mind. Holding the drifting veil above the manhole of mirror, she began to speak.

"I charge you, Astrid Washington, to do my bidding. To serve me. I charge you to bind yourself to me. To be my helpmeet and my—my familiar."

Fee gasped. Sharon cursed with such ferocity she was making a spell of it, the words spilling out in a cool blue mist. Even Marion stumbled over what she'd asked for. A mediocre witch standing in a table salt circle, her hopeless plan revealed: not a banishment, but a *binding*.

Marion dropped the veil. I blinked and saw how she meant it to go. This delicate piece of fey magic, god knew where she'd gotten it and what currency she'd paid, would fall over the silver-blonde crown of Astrid's head. It would fix itself to her, sticky as cobwebs, and bind her.

That wasn't how it went.

Almost before the veil left Marion's fingers, Astrid was raising her own to meet it. Its translucent weave clung to her skin, glowing as it made contact. And if *I* were Astrid, I would've done exactly what she did next. Which was this:

You summon me to do your bidding?

We couldn't hear her, but her lips moved so crisply there was no question what was being said.

You summon me *to serve* you? *To bind myself to your worthlessness and be your helpmeet? Would a lion put her head down to be bound by a mouse? Would the lightning bow to the lightning bug?*

The whole time she spoke, she was smiling. It was worse that way.

You would have me be, she said, "your familiar?"

The last two words we heard. We heard them because in one smooth motion Astrid hefted herself through the glass, crouching on its edge with her toes still dipped into mirror world. The room became so *small* with her inside it, so vivid with the scent of witching.

"Stupid girl." Her voice was a crow-feather scratch, hoarse and glimmering. "I and my book have been your only teachers. You have no magic you didn't take from me."

Marion was shaking. "I—I charge you—" she began, and with a languid hand Astrid flung the binding veil.

It stuck to Marion like cling wrap, visible for an instant then drawn into her skin. She pulsed the color of yellow gold before it was absorbed completely. The room's odor of blood and sweat bent beneath the stench of big magic, well water and bitters and clove. Marion reeled against the circle's edge but couldn't cross it. It was a prison that held them both.

Fee was at my shoulder reciting her Hail Marys in three languages. Sharon paced the edges of the salt, looking for a weakness. Seeing them *trying* shocked me into motion, into remembering something I'd nearly forgotten: we weren't entirely helpless.

I grabbed Fee, pressed my mouth right up to her ear. "We still have a piece of her power," I said frantically. "If we can just get Marion out of the circle . . ."

Fee's eyes widened. Some idea had struck her. "Broken," she said. She turned to face me, putting a hand to my heart—to the place just over my heart, where my necklace charm hung. "All broken things wish to be whole again."

She began to chant.

Draw tight the power of three
Add blood to a loving cup
And if ever the trio should part
Let the river swallow them up.

It wasn't a spell. Not a real one. It was a rhyme Marion made up on a day we harvested water from the river at sundown, the brawny silver city stretching over our heads. We'd been happy and hopeful and a hundred years younger, our silly broken-heart necklaces clasped freshly around our throats.

I was still wearing mine. Despite everything, we all were. Fee chanted the rhyme again, and this time I joined her.

All of this—Astrid's escape from the mirror, Marion's binding, the chant—seemed to happen at once, boiling into one burning-metal minute. Fee and I were screaming now, repeating the rhyme.

Marion's eyes met mine across the salt line. Then her lips were moving with ours.

That was when it began to work. The chant, multiplied by

three, fizzing with the unwieldy charge of Astrid's borrowed magic. My broken piece of charm grew hotter, every cut edge simmering against my skin. Fee's and Marion's were glowing like the center of a flame. The heart's divided pieces drew toward each other, chains straining around our throats as they tugged us right up against the circle's edge. Like calling to like, something broken longing to be whole.

Together we spoke the final piece of the rhyme. A fractional breath and then an explosion, submerged and soundless, as the three of us fell together in a tangle.

Everything was heat and hair and a neon confusion, my vision scribbled over with streaks. Marion's skin was sour against my lips and I laughed with relief, because we'd done it, we'd pulled her out.

Then I blinked the light away and realized she hadn't left the circle. We'd been dragged in.

Fee, Marion, and I lay together, bound by the healed heart, and Astrid stood above us. Her yellow irises had eaten the whites of her eyes away. She had the two-toned glare of a bird of prey.

Being looked at by Astrid Washington felt like being studied by two entities. One was a woman, an occultist, a human being who had walked and breathed and lived. The other was a thing of steel or living stone, hammered by time and magic into a terrifying flatness. A cynical, efficient being that wouldn't think twice about breaking us down for parts.

Astrid took the knife from where it lay on the floor. She looked into each of our faces—one, two, three—then bent, knife in hand, over Fee.

"*No!*" I writhed in an attempt to protect her, cover her. Astrid laughed, flipping the knife so its blade was in her hand.

"You've got a traitor in your coven," she said, giving it to Fee hilt first. "Needs must."

Fee took the knife, not limply but with slow focus. Marion's face was a void, her eyes blank as eggs. If Fee had gone for her then, I think she would have turned her neck willingly to the blade. I was babbling terrified lies—*Fee, Fee, you don't have to*—my own voice an irritant I couldn't make stop. But Fee was quiet.

She looked at Astrid Washington and spoke almost steadily. "You and Marion are bound now. You bound her, with that net. Which means if I kill her, you'll die, too. Right?"

For two raggedy heartbeats Astrid's face was perfectly composed, and I thought Fee had overplayed her hand. Then the occultist's eyes widened and she screamed, a sound too wretched and raking to have come from a human throat.

She grabbed her head in both arms and folded in half at the waist, so her hair dragged over the floor. As soon as her eyes were off us I ripped myself free of the bonded necklace, its broken links dragging bloody beads across my neck.

Marion's mouth was loose, her eyes unfocused.

"Break the circle," I told her in a savage whisper. "You laid it, you can break it."

She didn't speak or move. I wasn't sure she heard me.

"Marion, you idiot." Fee shook her by the shoulders. "Wake *up*! Break the circle and we'll figure out the rest. We can still fix this. We can still end this."

Marion jerked to life, her hollow eyes burning. She spoke through clenched teeth. "You think I want this to *end*?"

The occultist straightened. In a sinuous dart she snatched the knife from Fee's hand and stood above us, her hawk's eyes shining like reverse moons.

"What to do, what to do," she whispered, eyes switching between Fee and me. She tapped her temple with the tip of the blade.

My head roared and rattled. She was looking at us like a cook considering her kitchen. We were nothing but the ingredients she had at hand: one witch she couldn't touch, two that she could. And a knife. She would pulp us if that was what it took to devise an escape hatch. My thoughts raged, all my joints went putty-soft with terror. Then a thought cut through the clamor, cool as river water.

I could kill her.

Not Astrid. She would fillet me faster than I could lift my hand. But Marion. Maybe I could steal just enough time to kill Marion. If she died, Astrid died, too. The circle broke. We were free.

In a freight-train flash I saw my arm on her throat, pressing down; my needle remapping her arms' undersides; the heavy salt bowl coming down on her head. Celluloid squares from a horror film. And I knew I couldn't do it.

So I did the next worst thing. As quickly as the idea seized me I took Marion by the shoulders and waist and heaved her body through the mirror.

In my memory it happened in silence. No sounds of effort or surprise. Marion's eyes and mouth stretched wide, her throat trailed our broken necklace chains. Her body shrank as she dropped into the mirror's greenish depths and was gone.

Astrid had time only to take a step toward me, both hands grasping, then the strength of the binding pulled her in after. I felt the locomotive huff of the circle breaking, then the empty-socket shock of Astrid's magic being ripped out of us by the roots. Fee gasped, Sharon swore, and I screamed with relief and terror. My scream set the mirror's surface to shivering. Not entirely glass, not entirely a door.

I slammed my fist into its center.

It gave against me. My heart sank with my hand, plunging into its dreadful jellied coolness. Then it rebounded and broke. My hand sang with pain and the cracks shuddered outward until the whole mirror was a glittering spider's web.

I cradled my hand, all gloved in red, and looked at my brave Felicita.

She was staring at me with open horror. She would've *died* before doing what I'd just done. But that was the thing: I wouldn't let her.

CHAPTER TWENTY-EIGHT

❯

The suburbs
Right now

Three girls done up in witch baby drag, their faces challenging or sly. My mother, my aunt, and a girl who'd smashed flat a quarter century of time like it was a pop can, stepping across it untouched.

She'd been here, inside my house. Biting my cookies, creeping through the dark, stealing my parents' befuddling golden box. Maybe she'd stood right here, looking at the place where her image bent back.

Who *was* this girl to my mother that she'd held on to her photo this way? There but not there, kept in a place where she would see it every day and remember what was hidden.

My dad turned in his sleep, spoke a muffled word against his pillow, and was still. I slipped from the room.

My panic was cooling, that first jolt of fear drifting away. I could still observe the shock of it, the impossibility, but I'd run out of the energy to *feel* them. Caught in this state of unnatural calm, I stepped into the bathroom and flicked the wall switch.

I stood off-center in the mirror, sickly beneath the white

light. It was scalding, surreal, it flooded every silent corner. The photo was a little crumpled now, but I held it up. In case Sharon was right, and mirrors were dangerous; in case they were a conduit through which I could reach this girl. Maybe yesterday I'd have been self-conscious doing it, but now I looked straight at my reflection and spoke.

"I need to talk to you."

There was no ripple, no mist, just an exhausted bleach blonde holding a creased photograph.

"I'm coming to find you."

I took my dad's keys from his bedside table and pulled on a T-shirt dress and didn't realize I'd forgotten shoes until my bare foot was bending around the brake pedal.

The girl could be anywhere. Just the knowledge of her transformed the night, fermenting its air like drifting bacteria. All the cars on the road seemed to be following me, all the shadows clotted like black cream. Lifeguard stands became alien monoliths, looming over the sinister mirror of the public pool. I passed the tinny lights of the Denny's, the white bubble of the Amoco, the dying mall lording over its empty lots. Slow through downtown Woodbine, where the bars had long since closed and the quaint pools of lamplight were no match for the dark.

She could be anywhere; she could be gone. But I doubted it. The space between us yawned like an open line. I braked to a soft stop in front of the train tracks. Before I could drive on, the passenger door opened.

The girl climbed in.

She was realer than I remembered. Jawline peppered with zits, hair tangled and greasy at the scalp. She might've been plain if not for the intensity of those pale wolf's eyes. I could smell her, a layered accretion of body odor and dirty hair and the bergamot undertow of my mother's perfume.

"Drive," she said.

I thought I was too resolute to feel afraid, but my body knew better. My foot was jumpy on the pedal and my limbs quivered like plucked strings. Her presence was a constant scratch, her regard a spotlight that singed my skin. She'd known my mother once. Been young with her. And if my mother really was in trouble, I'd bet this time traveler knew something about it.

The radio was keening about a pink, pink moon. I switched it off. The girl's silence made its own kind of noise, a bass pulse of *here*ness that thudded in time with my heart. At the last stop sign before the forest preserve, she pointed left.

"That way."

When she lifted her arm I caught another breath of my mother's perfume. The image of this stranger standing at my parents' vanity, drained face smiling as she sprayed it over her pulse points, raked over my neck like a fingernail. It seemed a greater violation than her teeth in my cookies, her hands in the closet safe.

We could be on our way to my mother now. My breath quickened with anticipation, edged with bitterness. Maybe she and the stranger had been together all this time. We were driving along the suburb's unincorporated edge, a realm of sprawling houses and overgrown backyards with a reputation for lawlessness akin to that of international waters. For every kid who got arrested out here, there were five more who insisted you couldn't legally get arrested out here.

"There," she said.

There was an unlit turnoff cut between the trees. Alone, I wouldn't have seen it. I went slowly, tires chewing over gravel, until she pressed a hand to the dash.

"Stop. Turn off the car."

With the headlights out the road in front of us flattened to a gray sea. But the moon was high, the gravel pale, and its contours rebounded. I made out the place where the path veered right and out of sight.

"Where are we?"

She didn't reply. She was going through some silent deliberation, her breaths shallow as an animal's. "I don't know if you're ready," she whispered.

"Ready," I said, and bit my lip. It felt too intimate, our voices meeting in the dark. "Ready for what?"

The girl looked down. I had the sense that she was gathering herself, like the thing she needed to communicate was bigger than she could hold.

"There are fairy tales," she began, "in which girls trade pieces of themselves away for the things they want. Love, riches." She looked at me. "Information."

I pressed both hands to my jittering knees. "Just tell me what you want from me."

"You've paid enough," she said fervently. "If I had it my way, this wouldn't cost you one single thing."

A wave of self-pity washed over me, warm as bathwater. "What wouldn't?"

One of her eyes was in shadow. The other was a cup of liquid light. "Answers. To all the questions you've asked, and all the ones you never thought to."

"Who *are* you?" I said.

"I'm your friend, Ivy. Don't worry. Don't be afraid. You'll understand soon."

The way she said my name—why was that the part that scared me most? Maybe it was how she looked when she said it: like she knew me. Like we shared a whole complicated history. My brain was sodden with fear but busy, too, ticking like a game-show wheel.

"If I want this," I said. "If I want answers—what happens next?"

"We walk up the path." Her voice was on the edge of trembling. "We turn, just there. And I take you to a place where you can know everything."

The car keys were imprinting into my palm. "Why not here? Just tell me here."

"Doesn't work that way."

I looked to the place where the road bent right. It was high summer, the trees too thick to see what lay behind them. I looked back at the girl who knew my mother, and had walked an unfathomable road to sit beside me. "What's your name?"

She paused, and something shifted behind her eyes. "My name is Marion."

I had the oddest feeling the name hadn't been at her fingertips. That she'd had to dredge it up, like she was a ghost who'd already divested itself of the trappings of the living. But *I* knew that name. I could summon it in my mother's voice, and Aunt

Fee's. A taint of secrecy hung about it. They'd only ever spoken it at that register reserved for hidden things.

"Marion," I repeated, and put my hand on the door. "Let's go."

The night was still, just the faintest breeze hushing like an endless exhale. This was the way I'd first seen Marion: as a pale shape moving through a nighttime wood. She was clothed now, jeans and a blue peasant shirt that didn't fit her. I kept her in my sight and one fist tight around my dad's keys. The gravel was murder on my bare feet. The third time I sucked in a pained breath she glanced down and spoke a few careless words.

They hung in the air like a sparkler's trail. I smelled dark sugar and burnt hair and felt a silky tautening beneath my soles, as if the rocks I walked over were smoothing themselves into a hot glass road. I yelped, jumping back, before I realized it wasn't the path. It was my feet.

I lifted one, then the other. When I tapped a nail against my callused right heel I heard an audible glassy click.

"Holy . . . how did you do that? What did you do?"

Marion looked at me blankly, like I was interrogating her for breathing. "You're welcome," she said.

I high-stepped down the road, lifting and resettling my feet like a dog in snow boots. Such a small change but it made my whole body feel foreign to me. *Separate* from me, my form and my consciousness never more sharply defined. My brain rebelled from what she'd done, from being near her at all. But my skin was *awake*, attuned to her every motion, and the shimmering possibility that she might do something impossible again.

We hit the turning. The gravel broadened, giving way to clean pavement. A long driveway that ended at a house, big and white and silent. All the windows were dark, but the front door hung wide open.

CHAPTER TWENTY-NINE

)

The city
Back then

When I walked into our apartment my dad was asleep on the sofa, a whiskey tumbler balanced on his chest. There was ice in the glass and the record he'd put on was still turning. The Flamingos played eerie and sweet, tinting the stale air gold.

He lifted his head groggily. "Dana?"

"Go to sleep, Dad." My throat was raw as meat.

"Where've *you* been?" He sniffed. "Jesus, what have you been rolling in? Is that blood on your shirt?"

"I said *go to sleep!*"

Intent thickened my words into a roux. He fell back against the cushions, out cold, and stayed that way.

We'd scrubbed the round room. First on our hands and knees, because we were stump-stupid with shock. Then, when she woke up enough to do it, Sharon used a scouring spell. The occultist's book was gone, fallen through the mirror with Marion. We took everything else that had been hers and fled the library, sliding through the waning dark. By three a.m. we were gathered beneath the scratchy overhang of a parking garage.

"Not *ever*," Sharon was saying. "You got me?"

I watched her like bad TV. I could hear her, but I couldn't make her words connect into anything with meaning.

"You don't even know my last name," she went on. "Let's keep it that way. You saw nothing, you know nothing. They'll make their way to you, once her parents report it. If you send them to me I'll make sure you regret it."

Them. "Who?" I asked.

"The *police*, you doorknob."

A breeze blew over us, lake-water cool. The scent of it flushed something crucial out of the great blank in my head.

"Eighteen," I said dully. "It's Marion's birthday today. She's . . . she was . . ." I blinked my sandy eyes. "She's eighteen."

Sharon brightened right up. "Seriously? Holy shit, that's lucky. We might actually get out of this. They won't even put her down as a runaway."

"You're *horrible*," Fee said. Her arms were jacketed tightly over her ribs. "Horrible. I hope you . . . I wish you . . ." She pressed her lips together tight before anything dangerous could escape. "I do not wish you well," she finished.

"How nice to be sixteen and blameless," Sharon said. "What a luxury to think regret can wipe your slate clean. That girl built her own casket, honey. And the blood on your hands is as red as the blood on mine." She shook her head. "My hand to god, I wouldn't be sixteen again for the world."

In the days that followed, pieces of what Sharon said came back to me, like bits of tape I hadn't known I was recording. It all played out like she'd told us it would.

First came days of nothing. No supernatural visitations and no police, either. A peace so false and sinister it almost broke me.

Then, right when I thought it would never happen, a cop. A full two weeks had passed when a man with hound-dog eyes and an ill-fitting suit showed up at the fish shop to talk to Uncle Nestor. Fee was working that day and he talked to her, too.

Maybe my uncle knew more than he let on. He'd seen the maze of deep cuts on my left hand, already settling into scars, and the changes in Fee, invisible but impossible to miss. But he never asked us. He underplayed our friendship with Marion, and the man's interrogations were perfunctory at best. Sharon was right again: Marion was eighteen. It wasn't their job to care what happened to her.

We looked on from a distance as they drew a silhouette of a girl and colored it in: Delinquent. Depressed. Disappeared. A girl who left home the day she was legal to do it, and dropped out of sight.

That's how Marion vanished twice. The first time it happened because of me. The second time, it was the world that buried her.

CHAPTER THIRTY

)

The suburbs
Right now

I followed Marion over moon-drenched pavement, toward an
open front door that felt less like an invitation than a warning.
Like a house from a fairy tale, drawing you in with food and rest
before you realize you're a prisoner.

She led me past the tinted windows of an SUV, a basketball
hoop in freshly poured concrete, an Ariel doll lying facedown in
grass. Then through the front door.

The house was open-plan, with a high timbered ceiling and
great flanks of shining windows. In the daytime it must've been
a hotbox of light. From the entryway I could see a sunken living
space and a staircase curving to the upper floor, and a short hallway
that led to an unlit kitchen. The house smelled like new appliances
and floor wax and something else, a drowsy scent that nibbled at
my brain and made me catch myself on the wall, fingers fumbling
against the hook where a glittery unicorn backpack hung.

"Oh, right," Marion said, and spoke close to my ear. Three
syllables that set off a bracing burst behind my eyes and burned
my confusion away.

"What was that?" I caught her wrist. "What did you just do?"

She shook me off with a hiss, strange eyes flaring. Just as quickly they cooled. "Be careful," she said, conciliatory. "Don't surprise me. Don't just *touch* me like that."

I put my hands behind my back and followed her through the house's first floor.

The furniture was showroom plump, the painted walls had an impersonal shine. I didn't think the house had been lived in long. A mirror hung in the hall that led to the kitchen; I could see the glint of its beveled edge. But when I walked past, it didn't reflect me.

I stopped. Moved a hand in front of my face. Nothing. The hall was dark and so was the scene through the mirror, so it took some squinting to make out that they didn't match. Inside the mirror, to my left, was a half-open door, and straight ahead a familiar striped shower curtain.

I was looking at my own bathroom. The mirror was as good as a window and even though I'd already suspected Marion could see me through it I wanted to smash the glass with my fists. But she was watching from the kitchen to see what I would do. I kept walking.

Pots of limp herbs lined the window over the sink beside a cobalt finger bowl inside which jewelry glittered. I pictured the person who'd last washed dishes here stripping off their rings. On the kitchen island was an open *New Yorker* and a pottery mug with an inch of coffee in it, its surface iridescent with oil. The room stank of unrinsed takeout containers and garbage gone bad. I guessed the mess was the only thing in this house that belonged to Marion. The sliding patio door was open all the way, letting in a breath of lilac and chlorine. An icy rectangle of swimming pool glowed against the dark.

"Why'd you leave the doors open?"

"I don't like enclosed spaces." She said it dryly, like a joke, and hoisted herself up on the counter.

"Whose house is this?" When she didn't answer I picked up the *New Yorker* and read aloud the name printed on its mailing label. "Who is that?"

She eyed me steadily. "You want to meet him?"

My stomach twisted. "He's home?"

Marion nodded toward another brief hallway leading off the kitchen. I could make out a few closed doors and the latticed front of a pantry. "Go say hi."

"Is he . . ." *Okay*, I was gonna say. But what came out was, "Is he alive?"

For a protracted second, she said nothing. Then, "Yes, Ivy." Nice and easy, no sign of irritation. "He's alive."

Ashamed I'd asked it, not sure I believed her, I walked toward the hall.

"First door on the left," she said.

I turned the knob and pushed the door lightly open. There was a nightlight plugged into a socket, a tacky amber seashell that cast a glow over the man stretched across the floor in a white T-shirt and boxer shorts. He was on his back, arms gently outspread, oriented so the bottoms of his feet could be seen from the door.

I screamed. It was a half-swallowed, just-saw-a-cockroach kind of scream, because even as I opened my mouth I could see he was breathing.

"He's alive," she said again, from the kitchen.

"What did you *do* to him?" I pressed a hand to my corroded throat, remembering the feeling that hit me when I walked into the house. That knee-buckling sense of imminent blackout that Marion banished with a couple of words. Whatever the spell was, it was environmental, airborne.

Her voice floated my way, she didn't move any closer. "He's *fine*."

I found it hard to focus on the man's face. It seemed obscene, almost, to look at him when he couldn't look back. I focused on his hands instead, and the clean white front of his shirt. Had she dragged him here, or is this where he'd fallen?

"Wake him up, Marion."

"No," she said, affronted. "I need his house."

I stalked out to face her. "This is vile. How am I supposed to trust you after you show me this?"

She ran her tongue tip between her teeth. "If I didn't show you these things, you *shouldn't* trust me."

"Are there other people in the house?"

"Does it matter?"

"It matters to them!"

"I'm asking if it matters to *you*. They're not dead. While they're sleeping, they *won't* die, or age, or thirst. They're as safe as it's possible to be in this world. Their house fulfills a need, and I'll give it back when I'm through. So. Does it matter?"

"Of course it does," I said stubbornly. "They're human beings."

"And there are just so many of them."

And god, her voice was so *light*. She laughed at the look on my face and said, "Ivy, they're inside a dream. Okay? A good dream, all of them together—a mom and a dad and a kid. There's a photo in the bathroom, the three of them in one of those boats, those fancy Italian boats." She waited.

"Gondola," I said curtly.

"Gondola. Yeah. They're dreaming of the day they rode in the gondola."

I wiped a hand over my mouth. "So this is what witches do, huh? They just fuck with people's brains to get what they want?"

"I'm an occultist," she snapped, "and *nobody* can do what I can do. Well." She shifted her jaw, forward and back. "Almost nobody."

I swallowed, tasting the tease in her words. I had to help these people, and I would. But a few more minutes of sleep wouldn't kill anyone.

"Who else?" I said. "My mom?"

She made a dismissive noise.

"Who, then?"

"Now that is a really big question."

She reached behind herself. With a magician's flourish, she revealed the golden box.

The back of my tongue sparked like I'd just bitten into a lemon. Seeing it in someone else's hands made my brain hiss, *Mine.* But when I reached for it, she pulled it away.

"Not yet."

"What do you mean, not yet? What are you waiting for? Why did you take this?"

"Ask the question you're not asking. Ask me: What does it hold?"

I swallowed. "Well?"

She slid off the counter. "Come with me."

I followed her outside, across the patio, to the jeweled lip of the pool. She set the box on the concrete and unbuttoned her jeans.

"Take off your clothes," she said.

"Why?"

"The pool is half the reason I chose this house." Her shirt went over her head. "It'll make it easier."

"Make what easier?" But I was already stripping.

"Into the pool," she said when I was done.

The water was spit-warm and deeper than it looked. Wet leaves churned around my ankles as I regained my feet. Marion bobbed beside me, blue-lit and unreadable.

"I've thought about this a lot." She sounded a little breathless. "If you're in water, I think that'll help."

She put the box into my hands. Even against the lucent water it held its own light. "It's dangerous, yeah?" I asked hoarsely. "Whatever's inside this?"

She nodded.

"How do I open it?"

"Blood." Marion held something else now: a knife. She must've pulled it from the butcher block in the kitchen. Her eyes were wide, their irises flattened to nothing by the moonlight. "Want me to do it?"

"No."

I gripped the golden box and I was not the girl I'd known myself to be. Not cautious, not full of fear. I was hungry, I was burning, I was ready to dive. I took the knife, gouged its tip into the fattest part of my thumb, and pressed the bleeding place to the golden box. "Like this?"

But I already knew.

The box didn't glow or hover or hum. It just warmed to my skin, loosening like a tablet of wax. I could see the seam now, and the catch, as easy as if they'd always been there. There was another body treading water beside mine but she was far away from me now, apart. I was alone.

I slid one nail into the seam, my guesses flickering like a shuffled deck: old letters, photos, a notebook written in my mom's illegible hand. A magic button, colored rings. I didn't feel like Pandora, I didn't fully believe I was on the verge. I still thought what lay inside the box was something I could pick up and hold.

I undid the catch and lifted the lid.

And woke up.

PART II

CHAPTER THIRTY-ONE

)

Elsewhere

Dana pushed Marion and watched her fall, down and down through the wind-colored corridor of mirror world. The last thing Marion saw before closing her eyes was Dana's fist coming down on the glass.

Good, she thought.

But that was when she believed she would die.

Marion was right. Astrid Washington was an extraordinary witch. The realm she had created for herself, this catchment for her soul into which Marion fell, was the image of the house she'd died in down to its last lintel.

Its halls were lined with doors that opened onto rooms full of books and bedding, chess sets and hand mirrors, bone-china cups and sugar lumps pitted like old ivory. Its windows framed a flat plane of ominous sky: the house was forever snared on the violet edge of the late August evening when Astrid Washington had died. *Mostly* died. There was a ballroom below where a winsome tune played, a billiards room and a conservatory and a dark-wood bar, the bottles behind it intricately cut and their contents bottomless.

Marion drank from every one of those bottles eventually. Their liquors were bitter or treacly or sharp as a lightning bolt, lancing her tongue and making her remember a time when she'd *lived*, beneath a true sky, out in the teeming world.

She couldn't get drunk, but she drank anyway. She played games alone, like a child left to its own devices. This was when the worst of her grieving had passed, the first spate of desperation at her entrapment. It came in waves, the horror of what had been done to her—ejected from the world and set down in this afterlife waiting room. In between were long periods of a kind of surreal peace. She ran through dim halls and tried on clothing dug out of trunks. She lay in wait for a sleep that never came, she spun over the polished boards, dancing alone to that deathless, maddening music. Alone, alone.

You couldn't die here. When she first arrived Astrid used a particularly ruthless magic to remove the net that bound them; in another place it would've killed them, too. Some things weren't meant to be undone.

Not that it mattered much. Bound or not, they were stuck with each other.

Astrid was an inconstant captor. The madness of long confinement had stolen over her like a powdery decay. After a period of towering rages she left Marion to her own devices. Sometimes when they came upon each other in the house's halls Marion could swear the woman had forgotten who she was. She grew to despise Astrid the way you'd despise a sun that only shows itself once a week, for an hour, leaving you colder each time it goes away.

The occultist's twilit kingdom was a place that stripped from you every nonessential thing. And after all of that was gone—Marion's grip on reality, her earthly desires, all the flesh she could spare, and the last bit of color from a sun that was lost to her—what remained was this: an endless IV drip of rage. It warped her sight and made her fingertips tingle.

But rage wasn't *useful*. So Marion tended it until it grew into something that was: ambition. A furious desire to escape this place and make Dana pay for what she'd done. Marion had the will. Now she had to discover the *means*.

Often she held the cheap gold necklace in her fist, a once-broken heart united, swinging from three chains. The fine file of the heart's edges was caked with a dried rind of reddish brown where it had scraped across Dana's neck. Marion scratched the blood off with a nail, collecting the flakes in a snuffbox.

And later, when she found the spell inside one of Astrid's books, she knew why she'd held on so carefully to Dana's blood.

It was a scrying spell.

Steadily Marion poured water into a heavy silver bowl. She sprinkled its surface with Dana's blood and spoke the words and waited to see what would come. There was a haze, pearlescent, then a figure came into view: Dana's red hair. Her angry mouth.

Bent over the peephole of the scrying glass, Marion watched.

CHAPTER THIRTY-TWO

The city
Back then

The last of summer burned itself away. The leaves turned and fell in what seemed like a single weekend, trampled into sludge and then gone. Fee and I were still together all the time, but it was different, the space between us filled for the first time with things we didn't dare say out loud. Maybe if my dad hadn't been sick we would've had the fight we needed to have. Gotten it over with, figured out who and what we were on the other side. But he was, and we didn't.

We stopped doing magic cold turkey. Though our abilities were our own again, Astrid's power-up stripped away, we didn't dare use them after Marion.

The world on the other side of magic was so flat, so gray.

When we were sophomores nobody noticed us. But we went back junior year reeking of elsewhere. By then Fee topped five feet ten, with a brick shithouse build that affected the general population like a stupefying gas. Burgundy mouth, black clothes, this waving mass of hair that gave you the impression of an angel's fallen sister.

Within a week she had a secret girlfriend, a Polly Pocket–size blonde who cornered me in an empty girls' room to thank me for covering for them. It took me a second to realize she was thanking me for being Fee's *public* girlfriend, the fake one who'd take the heat.

"No problem," I muttered. All the garbage I'd thought would happen—the slurs written in lipstick, the hallway shoulder checks—never materialized. I moved through school the same as I always had, in a bubble of my own making. And nobody was about to mess with Fee.

I paid a tithe for what I'd done to Marion, of course. I paid it out in sleep. My dreams were an endless round of salt and blood and broken mirror, soundtracked by a rabbit's death cry.

But I had other things to worry about. My dad was dying. First he was functional sick, shuffling to the corner for Pringles and tallboys and Nicorette. Then he was housebound sick. Then Uncle Nestor was holding my hands, talking about a future I refused to look at straight.

My dad hung on through a miserly spring that softened grudgingly into June. I opened my eyes one pale blue Tuesday and knew, just by the plasticine quality of the quiet. I called Uncle Nestor before I'd even opened my dad's door.

My uncle held me tightly as the EMTs carried him out. My dad. My dad's body, that he'd used too hard and loved too little.

Uncle Nestor was talking to me.

"You'll always have a home with us," he said. "As long as I'm alive, you'll have a father."

I tried to focus on his face. "Thank you," I said.

I felt like a girl in a storybook, packing my bag. That's the fantasy, right? Your parents need to be eliminated for your life to change, so you can go live in a boxcar or a cottage in the woods or a magical school for the broken. When I unzipped my suitcase on Fee's bed, later, I knew by her expression I'd done it all wrong. I'd grabbed odd and senseless things and it made her worry about me.

My father died on a Tuesday and I moved in with Fee and Uncle Nestor that Thursday. I turned seventeen a few weeks later. It didn't take long for my entire childhood to feel like a dream.

The fight Fee and I were putting off happened one year after the second summoning. The day before Marion would've turned nineteen. Fee woke me when the sky was still silver, whispering into my ear. *Let's go to the lake.*

We snuck out together like we used to, like we hadn't in months, walking east through the dawn. Fee dropped to her knees and looked over the water, toward the place where the world bent out of sight. Finally she sighed, running both hands through her tangled hair.

"Tonight. We have to at least try."

"Try." My head was still toffee-sticky with sleep. "Try what?"

Fee looked at me with a face so naked in its grief I finally saw how much she'd been hiding from me. "To find Marion."

My heart started to pound. "What are you talking about?"

"I think about her all the time. When I look in a mirror. When I can't sleep. When I, I don't know, when I feel *good* for one minute, I think about how she doesn't." Her eyes were pleading. "I don't think I can live with myself if we don't try."

"She's dead," I said shrilly. "My god, Fee—all this time you've been thinking she's *alive?*"

"She can't be dead. If she were dead, that would mean that you ... that you ..."

"That I what? Say it."

She looked back at the water.

"Do you need me to be the bad guy?" I asked her. "I'll do it. I'll be that for you, if that's what you need. But first you have to accept this: Marion's gone. *Dead.* And it was either her, or all of us."

She moved her head restlessly. "We don't know that. We don't *know* what Astrid would've done. We didn't *see* Marion die."

"We didn't have to."

"I replay it in my head, all the time, and I ..."

"*Stop.*" I dropped my head onto my knees. "I replay it all the time, too. The only way out of that circle was to kill her. It was the only way out of the mess *she* made, that she refused to even try to clean up. Sometimes I think a knife would've been kinder. The way I did it ..." I twisted my head to look into my best friend's sorrowful eyes. "It probably wasn't quick."

I pictured it sometimes. If the fall didn't kill her, Astrid would've kept her alive until she found a way to unbind them. Maybe she tortured Marion first. Maybe she left her to wander whatever half-world I'd banished her to until she suffered and faded and perished, like a girl in an old ballad.

But there was no death I could imagine for her that was worse than the alternative: that she'd actually *survived.*

"Honestly, Fee." Suddenly I couldn't speak above a whisper. "I couldn't bear it if she were alive. It would be unbearable. To think of her alive, and trapped, and, and, *kept*, by Astrid. Alone. I *can't*. She's flesh and blood, Fee. She *can't* have survived it."

I looked at her for confirmation of what I knew to be true, needed to be true. For absolution. She took a shaky breath.

"Marion is dead," she said. Gazing across the water proud as a figurehead, her voice so stern you would've thought she was the one convincing me.

I breathed in, the succubus weight of guilt finally easing. "She's dead."

We watched the gulls rise and fall, cartwheeling through the air and nipping at the waves. Fee whispered a prayer for Marion, and neither of us speculated aloud on whether she'd died in a place that prayer could reach.

CHAPTER THIRTY-THREE

)

The city
Back then

High school ended and Fee and I moved into a studio apartment on a grim block of Broadway, across from a century-old jazz club whose sign filled our apartment with green light.

She dove headfirst into real life. An apprenticeship with the yerbera in Pilsen, a job with the parks department, a series of relationships with girls who weren't sure whether to try to win me over or keep an eye on me.

It seemed so easy for her to keep her eyes set on the future. But I could barely see to the end of the day. I worked six shifts a week at the Golden Nugget, gone by six and back by four, then I had the whole evening to fill. Half the time I was alone—our place was too small to bring anyone home to, and Fee was never single for long. On the nights she was out I'd make coffee and play records from my dad's collection and feel a treacherous relief when the sun went down. I liked to sit in the dark and watch the jazz club's sequined sign glitter and blink, like a hard-luck woman in a balding green dress.

I got fired from the diner on a Sunday, ten months after graduation, for knocking a full cup of coffee into an alderman's lap.

The guy was a regular, a showy tipper with a carnival barker's voice and cheeks like red taffy. He wasn't seated in my section, but he'd touched my waist when I walked by, given it a hard pinch. "Filler upper?"

His fingers burned through my polyester work shirt. I was riding on a few hours' sleep, my head still swimming with slow, rose-colored dreams. I got the pot, filled his cup, and knocked it smartly over with the spout. It wasn't until he shouted, stumbling out of the booth, that I realized what I'd done.

"You did that on purpose." He sounded stunned. "She did that on purpose!"

My boss, Sergio, rushed over with a wad of napkins. One of the waitresses trailed behind, carrying a little dish of pink ice cream.

"Get outta here," Sergio muttered. I was already untying my apron.

I grabbed my stuff and was hustling toward the door when someone stopped me—physically, she sprang from her booth and got in my way.

"Hey. Nowak."

I blinked at her: a face from another life. "Linh."

Linh who worked at the Metro; Linh who could talk to the

dead. I hadn't seen her since I'd gone begging for help with Astrid a few years ago.

"That was awesome," she said. "You could not have chosen a better asshole to pour hot coffee on."

Linh was in her mid-twenties, bangs grazing her brows and eyeliner so hard-edged it could've been sprayed through a stencil. She wore a scissored-off sweatshirt that read GO TO HELL KITTY and her hair was black to the tops of her ears, fading at its ends to watered apricot.

I looked over my shoulder to see if Sergio was coming. "Thanks. I just got fired, though. I think I'm supposed to leave."

"You should get promoted. That guy's the neighborhood scumbag. He tried me at a bar once, asked if I dated white guys. I said sure, maybe, but I don't date *bright red* guys."

"Hah." I was still bracing for Sergio's meaty hand on my shoulder. "So I'm gonna go."

"Wait." She bit her lip, almost wistful. "Can I buy you breakfast? Not at this shithole, obviously. Boycott. I haven't ordered yet, we could walk somewhere."

I wondered what Linh was doing in this deeply uncool family restaurant, alone, instead of at some hip dirty-spoon diner with her actual friends. I let myself consider the possibility that she was lonely, too.

We walked to a Swedish pancake place a few blocks away. Linh put so much sugar in her coffee it seemed like a joke, then sipped and gave a nod of satisfaction.

"Coffee's good here."

"You can still taste coffee?"

She gave me a lofty look. "The dead love sugar. They're more likely to talk to me when I've got it on my breath."

"Really? That's cool." For the first time in ages, the thought of something supernatural *didn't* wring my heart. "So, do ghosts—do they just come up and start talking to you? Or, how does it work?"

Linh put down her cup. "It's never a good thing when a spirit comes looking for me. It's way, way better when I'm the one doing the courting. And when one does find me, I'm never the point, you know? It's always somebody else's haunting. Most of the time the dead are doing their own thing, and it's the living who are desperate to reach them." She smiled at me faintly. "Here's the part where you ask about your dead. If any ghosts are still hanging around you."

An image hit me with the force of a sucker punch: Marion at my shoulder, running phantom fingers through my hair. I gripped the table so hard I rattled the dishes.

"Hey. No." Linh put her elbow in a coffee spill, reaching across to grab my hand. "I didn't mean to freak you out, that's just the question everyone asks. Like people wanting free rash advice from a doctor. You're clean, I promise you. No ghosts."

I looked down, focused on dragging a triangle of crepe through a puddle of lingonberry without letting my fork shake. My mother and father joined Marion in my mind's eye, gathering behind me like a bouquet of fog roses. It was almost soothing to imagine Marion in the dust tones of the dead. Too often she appeared to me in shades of mirror-world green, or—far worse—in the colors of a living lost girl.

Don't don't don't, I told myself, the closest I ever got to prayer.

Linh kept her eyes pointed politely toward her plate. "It's a funny thing," she said, as if I weren't unraveling. "No matter how much sugar I eat, my own ghosts won't come near me. I can dig through three generations of someone else's dead to find a long-lost recipe for jollof rice, but I can't even ask my own—"

She cut herself off. Stared at her plate while drawing her nails through her bleach-and-apricot ends. Then she looked squarely at me. "Your problem with that spirit. It got worked out?"

I laughed unhappily. "I wouldn't say that."

"I felt bad about what I did. Sending you away. I should've at least listened."

"I'm glad you didn't. Nobody came out of that situation okay."

"You're not okay?"

The way she asked it, I think she actually wanted to know. So I told her.

"I have no job as of today, and even when I did I could barely afford my half of a studio. My parents are gone. I have *one* friend, and she'd never ever say it but I know I'm deadweight. And every morning when I open my eyes, I think, 'Man, I can't wait to go to bed tonight!'"

I laughed. Linh didn't. She raised her cup of wet sugar to her mouth, and I could see her working out what she wanted to say.

"Do you need a job?" she asked.

"Really?" I leaned forward. "*Hell* yeah. Is the Metro hiring? I'll be nineteen soon. Is that old enough?"

"Not the Metro. This would be more of a . . . freelance thing."

It took a second to click. "Oh. Sorry, no. I don't do magic anymore."

That stopped her, fork halfway to her mouth with a hunk of smoked salmon. "Don't, or can't?"

"Don't. Won't."

"You want to talk about why?"

I shook my head.

"Fair. *But.*" She held up a hand, violet nails cut to the quick and rings studded with chunks of blue kyanite. "Before you say no, listen to my pitch."

"You've got a pitch?"

"*And* I'm buying you breakfast. Have more coffee, the refills are free. So. Magic." She cupped her chin in her hand. "It is the loneliest thing in the world."

A dozen different memories hit my head at once, an overlapping movie montage of the way it was when I was in a coven of three. *No,* I thought. *It's not.*

Or was Linh right? Even when we started together and ended in the same place, there was a point in each spell in which you had only yourself and the magic. *It's like giving birth,* a practitioner had told Fee once. *If you're lucky, you go in with a partner and come out with a child. But in the middle, you're alone.*

"Almost no one in this city can do what I can do," Linh went on. Not bragging but getting it out of the way. "So I don't have a circle, you know? Not a power circle, at least. What I have instead is a business."

"A business for practitioners." I crossed my arms over my chest, leaning back on the wooden bench. "But I don't do that. You need a secretary?"

She looked me up and down, like she was fitting me for something in her head. "Some of the stuff we peddle is real, but some is just theater. I need someone who knows what it looks like when it works, how it feels. Someone who can make people believe they're seeing the real deal."

"You need a faker."

She crinkled her nose. "I need someone who can appreciate the theatrical side of magic, you know? Make people *want* to believe."

"*Oh*. You need a bullshitter."

She grinned at me.

Briefly I turned my eyes to the pressed-tin ceiling. "I'm not wearing any pointy hats, Linh. Also I'm allergic to cats. I don't own a single cape. You sure you want me?"

She laughed. "You've got that red hair, man. It's, like, *red*. My grandmother would've chased you down the street to take your picture. Hundred bucks a gig, and you're never there more than two and a half hours. Sometimes less than two."

I unfolded my arms. "Hundred bucks?"

"That's after my cut."

"What's a *gig*? How many in a week?"

She only answered the second question. "Realistically, two. Sometimes three, though. Our busy time's about to start—May through September. I've got one tonight, you can come with me. Decide after you've seen how it works."

I'd already decided. I didn't even ask what I'd be doing. I'd learn soon enough.

CHAPTER THIRTY-FOUR

)

Elsewhere

Marion spied on Dana without pity. She glutted herself on Dana's life, the way she drank tea and scuffed her boots through fallen leaves and let her temple rest against the scratched windows of the train. Real tea, real windows. Dana slept and ate and pissed and bumped up against other people, and even when it looked miserable it also looked *real*. It stropped Marion's anger to a diamond point.

Seeing everything she'd lost almost broke her. It *did* break her, and when she pulled herself back together she understood everything with an aftermath clarity.

Dana had the whole world. A city full of strangers and colored lights and her hand on a pit bull's satiny skull, kneeling on the sidewalk to pat it with its owner standing impatiently by. The rattle of the elevated train shaking rain into her hair. Hash browns eaten hot with ketchup dregs, *showers*.

She had every single thing but this: the foresight to be ready. The ability to see Marion coming, before it was too late.

CHAPTER THIRTY-FIVE

)

The city
Back then

Bachelorette parties. That was my new gig. Linh farmed me out to tell fortunes, to read auras and palms, to do spooky little party tricks for drunk girls sipping cosmos through scrotum straws, crowned in glitter dicks.

I thrifted a long white dress someone had probably died in, and before each gig painted on two sinister circles of blush and combed my hair down my back like a Waterhouse print.

"Very Victorian plague child," Fee said when she saw me. She didn't fully approve of my crab walk back into magic—or its shady cousin—but she stopped with the eye rolling pretty quickly.

Because the weird thing was, I almost liked the work. I wasn't bad at it, either. The magic I pretended to wield was so *campy*, everything I did was with a wink. Sometimes I caught hold of some true insight—the beaming bride with the frigid feet, the maid of honor with poison in her heart—and leaned into the feeling like an ex-smoker coasting off secondhand fumes. But nothing I touched in those days bore more than a passing re-semblance to the scorching white searchlight of true magic.

Working parties turned my nocturnal tendencies into a full-on lifestyle. I ate dinner in the middle of the night and slept the day away with a T-shirt over my eyes. It was good in summer, waking up to the golden hour, but once October hit I never saw the sun. When Linh reminded me the work would be slow for a while, I knew I had to figure out something to get me through until spring. I started filling out applications at places around my neighborhood, the bracing void of the future pressing in.

My last job fell on a strangely warm Friday in November, just after our Halloween mini-rush. Another bachelorette, I was told, but when I got there it just looked like a house party, bottled beers and hummus tubs and people smoking out the windows. Spoon was playing when the bride opened the door. She was a Black woman in her mid-twenties, tank top and over-alls and big sexy glasses.

"You're the reader, right? I love the look."

She led me through her apartment to a bedroom at the back. The windows were open to the unseasonably warm night, naked ash trees pressing their hands against the screens.

"Okay, so." The bride lifted a shoulder. "Set yourself up. I'll bring you some food. Beer or wine?"

"Water. Please."

When she was gone I looked around the room. Fistfuls of beaded and copper jewelry spilled out of the etched Ti-betan singing bowls that lined the dresser top. A jewel-toned abstract hung above a platform bed, indifferently made with

Mediterranean-blue sheets. I scanned the slanted bookshelves. Ah: academics.

The bride returned with a paper plate wilting beneath smears of dun-colored dips, grain salad, an oily pool of pesto, then left me alone. I sat on the windowsill watching the trees. An hour went by and the music cycled from R&B to new wave to soul to a cheesy radio song that made all the unseen guests go *Whoo*. I wondered if the bride had remembered to tell her friends I was here. Finally I crossed to the bookshelf and chose something, settling back on the windowsill to read.

> *Come into the garden, Maud,*
> >   *For the black bat, night, has flown,*
> *Come into the garden, Maud,*
> >   *I am here at the gate alone.*

The door opened. An inch, apologetically, then all the way.

For the first time in ages, I had a rare flash of sight: I saw his aura before I saw him. Blue, blue, blue. Fee's words ghosted by me, from the day we did that very first spell. *You look like you're gift-wrapped in sky.* I know I stared at him too long. Until he laughed, and came into focus.

A white guy in his early twenties, probably, lean with a deep farmer's tan. White T-shirt, Elvis Costello glasses, a dark wedge of rockabilly hair.

"Your aura," I said without thinking. "It's the prettiest color I've ever seen."

He laughed again, a little startled. "Is that . . . a pickup line?"

"No," I told him. Clipped, gathering myself. You didn't flirt at these things. For all I knew he was the groom.

He saw the book I was holding and brightened. "I love that poem."

Through the door a new song came on, bubblegum pop, and a swell of voices sang along. He tipped his chin toward them and began to recite. "'And the soul of the rose went into my blood, as the music clash'd in the hall.'"

My shoulders went up. "Oh. You don't have to—please don't do that."

"*Don't* be the asshole quoting Tennyson to girls at the party?" Hanson kept singing, distantly. "Has it ever worked?"

"Like, *ever*? I bet it worked for Tennyson. No one else, though."

Without meaning to, I smiled. "Did you want a reading or what?"

"Prettiest aura you've ever seen. Where do I go from there?"

"Well," I said, remembering with a warm rush that I'd already been paid. "That depends how much of a taste for bullshit you've got. I could tell you all about your aura and what it means. I could read your palm as a chaser."

"But it's all bullshit, huh." He sat on the bed, knees pointed toward mine. "Aren't you not supposed to tell me that?"

His eyes were brown and his hands were big around the neck of a bottle of Rolling Rock. He had excellent hair. "Here's what I'm not supposed to tell you," I said. "It's real. Magic is completely real. The bullshit part is believing anyone would ever want to hear their *actual* fortune."

He grinned, not believing a word. "What's your name?"

He was cute, I decided. He was tall. I didn't really think he was the groom. I could already see the way he'd look at me just before unlocking his apartment door, the shy, conspiratorial smile. I foresaw the shaggy contours of his place. Its clutter of books and papers, its messy single-guy scent of deodorant and takeout if I was lucky, cat piss and black mold if I wasn't. I didn't care so much, I just wanted to spend a bright stripe of hours inside that sky-colored aura.

"I'm Dana," I told him.

I knew by the way his body shifted, eager and pleased, that he could see the decision in my face. "It's nice to meet you, Dana," he said. "I'm Rob."

Some of the things Rob said to me. In November and December and in the new year.

"God, it's so *red*. It's like a crayon." We were lying in the freeze-dried grass of Winnemac Park, Rob hanging over me so I didn't have to squint against the winter sun. "That's the first thing I wanted to do when I saw you. Get my hands in this hair."

At the Peking duck place down the block from my apartment, his glasses fogging over with steam. "You're my girlfriend, right? I thought you were, but then I woke up worried in the middle of the night."

Standing in the Powell's on Lincoln Avenue, whispering in my ear as I browsed the overstock table. "I used to work at the shop on Fifty-Seventh. I still have a key."

Lying on his futon by the window, street light coming in. Early February, each of us pretending we didn't remember it was three months exactly since we'd met. "I know you don't want me to say it." His breath warm in my hair. "I know you're not ready to hear it. But, Dana . . ."

I sat up, into the light. I'd gotten lucky, his place smelled like books and coffee and the must of wet laundry. And like *him*, a scent that had crept up on me, that made me equal parts restless and inflamed, oppressed and *heady*. Sometimes when Rob was sleeping and held on to me too tight, my brain said, *Run run run*. When he was awake he kept hold of me so lightly. Like I was a sparrow on a palm, a wild thing that might take off at the first sign of curling fingers.

Now I stepped swiftly from his bed. "You don't know me that well."

He sat up to look at me. At the blurred planes of me, he didn't reach for his glasses. His face was in shadow, his torso lit pale as a piece of statuary. "I know you as well as you'll let me. I want to know everything."

"That's a childish thing to say. Also, a lie. Nobody wants to know everything."

His hair stood up like a wave in a surf video. "Fair. But I want to know *more*. I love—I love all the things that I know. Can I say that much?"

My body was hot and cold, stay and go, stalled in place by opposing pressures. "You know all the good stuff and almost none of the bad. I love things about you, too. Okay? I love enough things that I feel sick thinking what it'll be like. When you know the bad things about me."

When I said *love* his face sweetened. When I said it again, I knew I wasn't going anywhere. At least not tonight.

"What could be so bad?" he said softly. Twenty-three years old but somehow younger than I was at nineteen. "Are you married? In the mob? Do you stand on the wrong side of the escalator? Did you kill someone?"

I laced my hands behind my neck, hoping he couldn't hear the tremor in my throat. "I'm not doing this on purpose. It's not an act, I'm not *trying* to be mysterious."

He put his glasses on then and really looked at me. "I would never think that of you. I'm just asking you to trust me a little. To let me know you better."

My grad student. My earnest man. He still liked to smooth my hair over the pillow when I was falling asleep.

"Okay," I told him, and climbed back into bed.

"Okay?" he said, into my neck.

I breathed. "Yes."

I brought Rob to meet Uncle Nestor. He showed up with a bottle of wine that was five bucks better than what we usually drank and taught everyone how to play cribbage. Fee had already met him a few times, and by the end of the night my uncle loved him, too.

In May I felt off, perforated, the world coming at me in incorrect ways. Food smelled oddly *sweet*, like a bad banana. I was waiting tables at a Greek restaurant in Lincoln Square, walking distance from Rob's place. On a Thursday night in June, too hot, the gamey fug of saganaki sent me flying into the bathroom to vomit.

When I came out my least favorite waitress was waiting for

me. Phoebe of the rat-black eyes, the coke-carved frame, the only girl on staff who spoke Greek so the owner let her get away with red murder.

"It's Gabriel's, isn't it?" she said. Gabriel was a fifty-something line cook who liked to follow girls into the walk-in cooler. "If you're nice I'll give you a ride to Planned Parenthood."

"Don't fucking talk to me," I said, shouldering past her.

"Ex*cuse* me?" Her lip went up. "Hey. *Bitch*."

There was a ringing in my head, icy-thin and high as planets. It was star song. A memory from the night I first opened my hands to magic.

A book of matches was tucked into the pocket of my apron. I pinched one free, snapped it, spoke two star-bright syllables. Phoebe screamed as the sconce beside her head burst, raining glass pieces over her hair.

I ran the block to Walgreens, and peed on the stick in a bar bathroom. The light was so murky I had to turn and turn it before I could see the results. Then I wrapped the stick in toilet paper and shoved it deep into the trash.

Leaning my forehead against the damp wood of the door-frame, I listened to the jukebox whirring on the other side of the wall. *Give me something*, I thought, *some clue*. Through the door came the opening strains of "Stratford-on-Guy."

I took a cab I couldn't afford so I could get home quicker. From the street I saw Fee moving in the window. I took the stairs at a run and slipped halfway up the second flight, coming down hard on one knee. The jolt made me clutch at my stomach, thinking for the first time of what I carried. Not the idea of it, but the actual fiddlehead curl.

Fee was already crossing to the door when I opened it. She'd heard me fall.

"What happened?"

I held on to her like a failing swimmer. "Remember when we were kids and we knew one of us would die young? Like your mom did, when you were born, and she left my mom all alone?"

Her eyes were already wet. "I remember."

"I'm pregnant."

My best friend breathed in, not quite a gasp. She wrapped her arms around me tightly and held me in the green light.

CHAPTER THIRTY-SIX

)

Elsewhere

The occultist's house was a realm between life and death, made rotten by its own changelessness. Marion was on the eve of eighteen and Astrid was thirty and the hour struck 8:46 and the eggplant light of a long-ago night still fastened itself to every window. There was no center to anything here, no *heart*. The liquor didn't make you drunk, the music didn't move your soul, the food evaporated on your tongue. Even the flavorless fruits of the conservatory had no pits in their middles, just black cavities.

The exception was the library. Whether Astrid dreamed them into being with a staggering grasp of their contents, or whether they possessed their own enchantment, her books were complete. Tangible, legible, brimful of the only sustenance Marion still longed for: information.

Among the flaking grimoires were histories, spell books, myths and legends. A witch's garden of poisonous blooms. It didn't matter in the dreamhouse whether Marion was a natural, whether she had meet intentions or the strength to bear the costs or a coven to back her up. This place *was* magic. She absorbed its dreadful atmosphere. It thinned and hardened her, it turned her over time into something as juiceless and hollow as the conservatory's damson plums.

Into the hollow place she tucked charms and curses and cantrips, incantations and celestial bylaws. She used to welcome any chance to prove herself worthy of magic, ready to suffer or die or kill for it. Now she was simply practical. Knowledge and faith are all you need, plus will tempered by time into steel.

And when she wasn't working, Marion kept her jealous eyes on Dana's expanding world. She honed her fury, kept its light alive. Rage and time were the only currencies left to her, and she used them. Knowing that when the moment came, she would be ready.

Time in the scrying glass moved triple-quick. Dana got pregnant, she got married, she gave birth to a boy who slipped out quick as a fish, with a thick mist of hair and eyes that stayed blue. Her belly was just starting to swell again when she left the city for a dustless house in a suburb with a witchy name. *Woodbine*, whispered Marion's nimble brain. *Honeysuckle, false grape, Virginia creeper.*

Her second pregnancy was harder than the first. She was big in the middle but spindly everywhere else. Nothing she ate stayed down. Marion felt no pity, not ever. But as Dana's time drew nearer she did feel *some*thing. An electric anticipation, a pleasurable dread. Marion knew something Dana did not: this one would be a girl.

The pain began in the night's raw center, plucking Dana

from sleep and reducing her to a keening animal. The mile between house and hospital was a beaded string of red lights. They rushed her through the halls in a wheelchair, a shrieking tick with chopstick limbs, then laid her flat in a green-walled room.

Astrid scorned Marion and her spyglass. But here she was at Marion's shoulder, watching alongside her. All that interested the occultist anymore were the bitter rules of life and death. Marion knew she was lingering to witness Dana dying.

When Death walked in, Astrid hissed through her teeth. It took the form of a smoky, dark-furred dog, purling in the room's sterile corners, one sly eye on the woman on the bed.

Yes, thought Marion, and *No*. Her breath caught, her heart knocked against its cage. She felt—*human*. Almost, again. Her eyes ached and Astrid hovered at her shoulder and they watched the skin of the water to see who would win.

Dana looked boldly back at Death's hound. She seemed to recognize it. Her mouth was moving but you couldn't hear her over the machines, and the blunt, frightened efforts of the people working to keep her spirit inside her skin. None of them understanding that all that really mattered was her mutinous staring contest with Death's dog.

Dana's skin was porridge-colored against her garish hair. She took great hanks of it in her hands and pulled, pulled.

She *pushed*.

CHAPTER THIRTY-SEVEN

›

The suburbs
Back then

There was a moment just before Ivy came when the whole world went porous. When the weave of it stretched and I could see the great yawp of nothing behind and I stopped being afraid because I could *feel* her. She needed me to be brave.

There's object magic, sympathetic magic, spells you cook or coax or speak into being. Luminous magic and magic so cruel that to wield it is to wrap your fist around a blade with no hilt. And there's magic born out of pure will, voiceless. No, not *pure*: will muddied and thickened with grief and terror, and love in all its forms.

With all my compromised will, and all my callused heart, I reached for the creature swimming, struggling at the center of me.

Come, I said to it. *Little one, come.*

The thing—baby—twitched in its casing. It was afraid. I knew what it was afraid of and I glared again at that panting black-eyed dog. *Not yet*, I told it. The force of the thought made it cower in its corner. *Someday, someday. But not yet.*

The creature turned once on the floor. Then it slipped, smoke-like, through the world's loosened weave. When it was gone I spoke again to my child. *Come. I'll keep you safe. If you'll come.*

Ivy came. With a rooster-red comb-over and the scathing eyes of someone looking to lodge a complaint about all *this*, everything, the big and the bright and the cold. She couldn't cry right away, the cord looped around her throat like a two-strand necklace, but I knew we would live.

When they finally put her in my arms I thought of wishbone halves and walnut shells. *Loosen your grip,* I told myself, on reflex—never wanting Hank to feel smothered, never wanting Rob to worry I'd die of it if he got fed up and left me—but she was so new she couldn't even see me. I held on as tightly as I wished.

It came to me at night. In those endless early days, in those fragile starlit hours. When I nursed before dawn, the only person awake in the world, the fear of what I might have done rolled over me. That I could have *altered* Ivy somehow, her nature or chemistry. That, in reaching out to her with love and will and magic, I'd woken in her something that should have stayed asleep.

I considered it with terror, I imagined it with pride. Across the years the anxiety dimmed but it never blinked out. And when she was six, Ivy proved my suspicions correct.

CHAPTER THIRTY-EIGHT

)

The suburbs
Back then

Ivy Chase was six years old. She loved ducks and drawing and butterscotch pie and, lately, the purple bounce house she'd jumped in at her friend Shawna's birthday party.

Every night since then she'd fallen asleep fast, so she could spend more time in the bounce house dream. She'd been perfecting it for a week and tonight it was glorious. The house was as sheer and daunting as a ship. The air smelled like funnel cake. The grass was so plush she bent to run her palms over the rubbery-soft blades. If her mom could just *see* how awesome this was, she would understand Ivy's birthday party needed a bounce house, too.

Still inside the dream, Ivy's body pulsed with a thrilling realization. There was no reason Mom *couldn't* see this. She was right across the hall.

Ivy had begun to suspect that her dreamlife—vast, lucid, entirely moldable, though she wouldn't have used any of those words—was unusual. It was Aunt Fee who tipped her off. Ivy was going on and on about a dream she'd made, and auntie's face was going stiller and stiller. When Ivy broke off, uneasy, her aunt smiled.

"That's awesome," she'd said. "Tell me about another one." But Ivy said she couldn't remember any more.

She wasn't thinking about that right now. Within her dream-world she was queen. She could, if she wished to, turn the grass blue or make the cloudless sky rain Dippin' Dots, or have a puppy run right out of the bounce house and into her arms. There was no reason she shouldn't be able to reach her mother, too.

She could, when she concentrated, feel her mom across the hall. That was one of the nicest things about dreaming: even though they weren't with her, Ivy could feel Mom, Dad, and Hank asleep. They were three different kinds of warmth.

Standing in the velvet shadow of the bounce house, she closed her eyes and felt for the blue, bottom-of-the-fire heat that was her sleeping mother.

There. Ivy got hold of her. She tugged, and she didn't even have to tug that hard. Her mother stepped into the dream.

Her face was vacant. She stood on the grass, eyes clicking emptily from one thing to the next, squinting away from the sun. Then they clicked onto Ivy.

"Hi, Mom."

Her mother's pupils spread like ink spots. She opened her mouth and Ivy heard two sutured screams: one in the dream and one out of it, across the hall.

The shock woke her up. Also the *noise*. A breath, two, then her mom flew in wearing a tank top and underpants, her hair streaming like a Valkyrie's. Ivy's eyes were open but Mom still put a hand to her heart, like she wouldn't believe her daughter was okay until she felt it beating. Then she scooped Ivy into her arms.

"How did you do that?" she asked in a fierce whisper.

"I don't know," Ivy whispered back. Then, defensively, "Do what?"

Mom pulled away, sliding the backs of her fingers over her wet cheeks. Ivy could see her thinking.

Then, slowly, Mom's eyelids shut. Her mouth was loose and her head drifted on her neck like seaweed. Ivy watched her, heart running like a rabbit. At least a full minute passed, then Mom opened her eyes.

"Did you lose that watch Dad gave you?"

Ivy felt confused, then annoyed. Her dad had let her borrow his diving watch for a game, and yes, she'd lost it, but that had nothing to do with anything.

"Hey." Mom tapped her knee. "You're not in trouble, Ivy-girl. I'm just . . . here, I'll show you."

She moved like a wading bird through the low sea of golden nightlight, then crouched in front of the bookshelf. On the bottom row, lying horizontally across the tops of the other books, was a copy of *The Westing Game*. Mom picked it up and pulled the watch from its pages.

Ivy looked between her and the watch, trying to find the trick. "How'd you know it was there?"

"How'd you pull me into your dream?"

Ivy set her jaw. "You first."

Mom smiled. Really smiled, the with-teeth kind that made

your belly feel warm as a dragon's. Until right then Ivy still thought she was in trouble.

"Tomorrow morning," Mom said, "we'll both tell each other how we did it. Deal?"

They shook on it. The next day, Ivy's second life began.

CHAPTER THIRTY-NINE

)

The suburbs
Back then

"Some kinds of magic are for everyone. Growing things, the weather. The moon belongs to all of us. Fingernails, spit. You can keep yourself like a garden."

I wouldn't tell Ivy yet about the weeding you had to do. There was enough of me in her that she'd find out for herself soon enough.

"Some kinds of magic are just for you—the magic that grows in your blood. Everyone is a well fed by different springs, different traditions. Folk magic, myth magic, we've got lots of that in our tree. You have to be careful, you've gotta keep your eyes off other people's paper. Your aunt and I . . ." Here I tiptoed around the great ravine at the center of everything I ever told my daughter. "We learned when we were young not to siphon off springs that don't belong to us."

"Siphon?" Ivy's smooth little forehead furrowed.

"Steal. Borrow, if you're trying to make excuses for it. But you're not. When you're older we can dig more into what's ours. For now let's stick with the stuff that's universal."

I'd thought the well I drew my magic from had been permanently tainted by Astrid's gift. That if you X-rayed me you'd still see her shadow cast over my bones. But the magic that came back when I worked with Ivy felt so *pure*. It ran through and out of me like clean sweat.

Magic was friendly to Ivy from the start. Fee and I started with softballs: healing tinctures, cleansing rituals, the guideposts of the tarot. Luck tokens, memory charms, energy manipulations that had her screeching with delight, making fingersnaps of firelight hop from candle to candle.

Ivy was a good pupil. She didn't approach working with Fee's warmth or Marion's skinlessness or my bubbling sense of agenda. Magic to her was a living book, full of stories and secrets and maddening contradictions. She liked the grind of it, the physical preparation that came before the bang.

The hard part was convincing her to hide it from Hank. She longed to bring him into our secret but Rob put his foot down hard. Rob, who only knew this much of my history: that I had a youthful fling with the supernatural, and a girl I knew had died because of it. That sometimes after a nightmare I went away from him, deep within my skin, until the poison was diluted enough for me to resurface.

Hank made hiding it easy on Ivy. He was a sunny kid who preferred to see the world in black and white; gray shades simply didn't register. They were my fairy tale, my Day Boy and Night Girl, one sweet and thoughtless, the other curious and tart. As they grew up, one with magic and one without but both so good, I felt lucky. I was so *lucky*.

What if I was allowed to be lucky?

Following the night of the bounce house, Ivy promised never to pull me into her dreams without my permission. After that she didn't really talk about her dreaming, and I figured it was something she'd outgrown. Until the midwinter morning she woke me, frantic, having dreamed of a strangled tree.

I remember the white smoke of our breath, the tamp of our boots over snow. Her small shape in Hank's hand-me-down coat with the corduroy collar, leading me through the forest preserve. Our search ended at a leafless hazel tree wound around with a mass of sticky, spiky vines, the only green thing we could see. There was a circle of empty ground around the tree, not quite a clearing. Within that circle was a feeling of wrongness so thick and physical you could almost scratch your nails across it.

We cleared the vines, yanked and salted the roots, and burned everything we could carry. It didn't cross my mind until we were done that interfering with the tree could've been dangerous. In the pale blue snow light, working beside my determined daughter, I'd been unafraid.

"What exactly did you dream?" I asked her later.

She shrugged. "I told you. I saw the tree, and I knew where to find it."

"Have you had dreams like that before?"

Another shrug, and a nonanswer. "I don't remember all my dreams."

There was something so solemn, almost druidical, in Ivy's hearing the call of a suffering tree. Thinking about her accessing magic that ancient gave me the feeling of a swimmer drifting past the place where the seafloor gives way to the deep.

That night I couldn't sleep. Ivy wasn't even ten and I could no longer fathom the contours of her abilities. Nor did I trust her to tell me the whole truth if asked. Where did the borders of her lucid dreaming lie? Could she spy on other people's dreams? Walk through them? Shape them the way she did her own?

She wouldn't, of course. I knew she wouldn't. So did it really matter if she *could*?

The question kept me up until morning.

"I could just do it."

Ivy at ten, fists balled in frustration because I'd told her she would not, under any circumstances, hex a classmate.

"But you won't."

"How do you know?"

"Because," I said, willing my words to be a protective net, an ordinary kind of mother's magic. "I trust you, and you trust me. And I'm telling you what you already know: hexes are dark magic. They don't come free."

"Of *course* she wants to curse her enemies," Fee told me later. "What ten-year-old wouldn't?"

"And she wants to scry," I said sourly. "Or as she puts it, 'spy on people to see what they really think of me.'"

I knew what Fee was gonna say before she said it. "You have to tell her about Marion. Give her a chance to understand *why*. Right now she thinks you're holding her back for the hell of it. Don't let her set you up as an adversary, not with this."

She'd said it a dozen times before. And I replied like I always did.

"Of course I'll tell her. When she's a little older, we'll tell her everything."

It was my shame that was really stopping me. Fee and I both knew it.

She's a good kid.

I repeated it to myself like it was gospel. And it was true, but that didn't alter the fact that Ivy was drawn to morally questionable magic like a bee to the lip of a Coke can. She was curious, heedless, troublingly fearless. And she was stronger than me. Corralling her abilities into small workings felt increasingly like trying to direct divine fire through the claustrophobic tunnels of an ant farm.

Working magic had set her apart from other kids her age. She was too self-possessed, too immune to other people's influence. She had soccer friends, camp friends, school friends, but she didn't really have *friend* friends.

Until a family moved in across the street the year she turned eight. A single dad, a toddler, and a freckle-faced seven-year-old cannonball named Billy.

I hadn't actually realized Ivy was lonesome until he showed up, and they merged like two raindrops meeting on a window. She nodded with great seriousness when I reminded her that magic was a secret even Billy couldn't know. Months became years and there were no explosions but I wasn't an idiot: the little boy from across the street knew something.

I looked out the window once and saw them in the grass at the end of the yard. Both were keeping an eye on the ground between them, with an absorbed stillness few grade schoolers possessed. I couldn't see what they were looking at.

Then Billy's face opened up into startled delight. Ivy grinned at him and he grinned back. I knew how pride looked on her and I *knew* she wasn't showing him something ordinary.

I upgraded my assumptions. The boy from across the street knew everything.

My appendix burst at the worst possible time. Rob was on a work trip, Fee and Uncle Nestor were visiting family in San Antonio. Hank was going through some kind of emotional upheaval he refused to talk about, and Ivy was being an adolescent nightmare. I didn't have loads of mom friends, so I turned to Google. *Twelve-year-old daughter incredibly defiant normal?*

The next day Ivy came into the kitchen, brandishing my laptop. The search was pulled up. "First of all," she said, "learn how to erase your search history. Second, I'm not defiant, I'm *assertive.*"

I stood too fast, lunging to yank the laptop from her hands. Just as quickly, I was bent over my knees, gut neon with pain.

Ivy crouched beside me, grabbing my hand. "What is it? What hurts?"

I showed her with my fingers, gasping.

"Uh-oh." She looked scared and a little thrilled. "I bet it's your appendix."

She wanted to try a healing charm and I said absolutely not and she was still sulking when a neighbor showed up to drive us to the hospital. Ivy stayed until late showing me videos on her phone, then got a ride home from another neighbor. I had to stay overnight, my appendix so thoroughly ruptured my whole gut was shot through with poison.

"People die from this," a nurse told me, with too much relish. She was pissed because I fought everything they wanted to do. I needed Fee here, running interference. I needed Rob to come take me home. I was furious at them for being so far away.

Rob couldn't get a flight home until the next morning, but the kids were old enough to keep each other alive for a night. It was fine. It should've been *fine*.

When I got home, I knew right away that it wasn't.

CHAPTER FORTY

>

The suburbs
Back then

Ivy's mom was a total freaking hypocrite.

She talked all the time about balance and responsibility and being careful what you put into the world and blah blah blah, when all along you just *knew* she'd done some bad, bad things.

You could see it in her refusal to talk about the web of scars on her hand. The abrupt silence that fell when Ivy walked into a room where Mom and Aunt Fee were talking. The stormy weather that blew through the house at random, and made Dad say, *Guys, give your mom some space.*

Most of all it was in the look on her face when Ivy pulled something off. Ivy was so good now, so *strong,* her mother's pride should've grown accordingly. Instead she seemed to shrink as Ivy expanded, becoming more watchful, more controlling and afraid. If she could've lassoed Ivy's ability and broken it like a colt, she probably would have.

Ivy was certain it had to do with the thing she wouldn't talk about—the thing she'd done. She waited for Mom to let something slip, or Aunt Fee to spill the secret. And when neither happened, she made other plans.

She was waiting for a night when both her parents were out. If it made her feel a little guilty that it finally happened because her mom was in the hospital, well, guilt was rarely a useful emotion.

It was just past eight. Hank was on the other side of the wall watching *Battlestar Galactica* and her room was soft in the gloaming.

Ivy propped a mirror against her footboard. She pressed a blend of clarity oils into seven crucial places. She looped a thread of dark hair around her right ring finger—spirited off of her best friend Billy's shoulder—and incanted as she used that fingertip to trace a sigil over the mirror. Mist spilled into the glass, displacing her reflection. She made her voice cool and commanding.

"Show me what Billy's doing right now."

Out of the mist, like a photo dipped in developer, a boy with freckles and wet dark hair appeared. When she made out what he was doing—pulling a shirt over his head, damp from the shower—Ivy squeaked and yanked the strand off her finger.

The boy in the glass gave way to a many-toned nothing, a galactic vista that tinted the room with gauzy light.

Ivy counted breaths, waiting for them to slow. She could smell her own sweat beneath the bright spice of frankincense.

It had *worked*.

But that was just a test, to see if she could. Now it was time to do it for real. It might not work the second time, she reminded herself. The question she wanted to ask was fuzzy. But she didn't know enough to ask a better one.

Ivy took another strand of hair and twined it around her finger. This one was the same color as her own. She'd pulled it from her mother's hairbrush.

She retraced the sigil. Her door was locked, Hank had headphones on, and still the words came in a heavy whisper.

"Show me Mom's secret."

This time the mist caught the question like a pond catching a rock, an impact then a widening ripple. When it smoothed out what Ivy saw in the mirror was a girl.

She darted back, bare legs catching on the humid wooden floor. She just barely kept herself from ripping the red strand free. Through her panic the girl hung motionless in the mirror, odd and definite, framed like a portrait somebody dug up from a thrift store. Fish-belly skin and blonde hair and a look of forbearance. It almost seemed like she was looking back, but that wasn't how scrying worked. Ivy gathered her nerve and moved closer. When she did the girl followed the motion with her unsettling eyes.

Ivy gasped. "Can you . . ." She coughed the nervous scuzz away. "Can you *see* me?"

Of course she couldn't, scrying was a one-way mirror. But the girl said, "Yes."

Just one word, in a voice that sounded like something dug up from the back of a basement.

They watched each other a while, the patient apparition and the child with the butterfly bandage stuck to one knee.

"Who are you?" Ivy asked. She tried, but the command she had summoned was gone.

"I'm an occultist."

Ivy drew back, impressed. *Occultist*. Definitely a cooler term than her mom's bland, beloved *worker*.

"What's your name?"

The girl's dusty voice was gaining strength. "What's yours? Name for a name."

Ivy narrowed her eyes. "I bet you already know it."

"Clever Ivy," said the figure in the mirror. "I'm Marion."

The compliment gave Ivy a shot of blunt courage. She squared up. "What do you have to do with my mom's secret?"

Now the girl—woman? Ivy couldn't decide—smiled for the first time, dry lips stretched around even white teeth.

"I am your mother's secret."

CHAPTER FORTY-ONE

)

The suburbs
Back then

Something was up with Ivy. She hadn't been easy for a while but at least she'd always talk to me. But after I got home from having my appendix out she wouldn't even *look* at me. It was late summer and she should've been running around with Billy, frantic to drink up the last drops of the season. Instead she was holed up in her room.

On the third day of this I marched in and closed the door behind me.

Right away she was furious. "Get out of my room," she hissed, slapping shut the notebook she'd been writing in and clutching it to her chest. I'd come in ready to be patient, but her tone rocked me back on my heels.

"*Your* room," I snapped, my own father's words clawing out of me, back from the dead. "When did you start paying rent?"

Her face reddened and she sprang to her feet.

"I said get *out* of here! You . . . you . . . *monster!*"

The world spun. One dizzy turn, and on the other side of it my life had changed.

"Why did you call me that?" I said, when I could speak again.

"You know why."

Of course I did. The real question was how she'd learned what I had done. I gamed it out and saw a dozen ways to make things worse. The only trick I had left was the truth.

I showed her my hands. Gently I pressed one to my belly, above my stitches, and layered the other on top. Then I backed up until I was pressed against the wall. "Talk to me, Ivy-girl. What happened when I was away?"

"*Nothing,*" she said, her voice full of adolescent rage. "Something happened twenty years ago."

"Who told you that? *Who?*"

Something in my voice must have cut through, because her expression flickered with an emotion other than fury. "I got a letter. There was no name on it. I burned it, you can't see it."

Goddamned Sharon. I closed my eyes, relief and terror running through me like spiked lemonade. "Tell me what you think you know, and I'll tell you the truth."

"Yeah, *right.*" Savagely she bit a piece of skin off her lip. "I don't want to hear anything from you. Except . . ." Her eyes flared with hope. "Tell me it's not true. Tell me you didn't *push* your friend into Hell."

I used to be so good at lying. When it was a mechanism of survival, growing up with my dad, it came to me like breathing. All it took was absolute commitment and the kind of steel-cut nerve nobody expects to see on a girl. But I was rusty these days.

"I did what I did for a reason," I began, and Ivy's eyes widened.

"Oh, my god," she said. She'd wanted me to deny it.

"Baby, let me *finish*—"

"No!" she said, so loud it surprised both of us. Then, "Get *out!*" she screamed, and flung up a hand. I staggered back, into the hallway, the door clipping me hard on the bridge of the nose as it slammed.

She wouldn't let anyone in. She turned her music up if we tried to talk to her through the door.

Fifteen years into our marriage, I finally told Rob what happened with Marion. I gave him the shape of it, the worst details scrubbed away. His response wasn't what I expected.

"This is what you were referring to, wasn't it?" He had his glasses on but his eyes looked unfocused, grave. "All those years ago, before Hank, even. That night I wanted to tell you I loved you."

I didn't pretend to have to think about it. "Yes."

"You should have told me then," he said, and left the room.

That night I woke from a dream I couldn't remember, my body ringing with panic. I needed my daughter. I needed to hold her, see her face. When I stepped out of our room I saw a strange light coming from under her door. It was the chill shade of a scrying glass.

I crossed the hall in three bounds, unlocking the door with a panicked charm that made the index fingers on both my hands stiffen and curl.

Ivy sat cross-legged on the floor, a mirror propped in front of her. The slow gauze of scrying still lay over her irises, and she didn't react to my presence right away. In the mirror's dim pool hung a face, a neck, shoulders, glimpsed from the side so they were indistinct.

My scarred hand rang with remembered pain. This time I grabbed something on my way to the mirror.

It was a boot. Ridiculous. I stuck my hand in it like a big gothic hoof, shoved Ivy out of the way, and swung the boot into the mirror. The figure was gone but the glass still held a light-shot mist. It was the room's only source of illumination. When the mirror broke we were left in the dark.

CHAPTER FORTY-TWO

)

The suburbs
Back then

For the fairy-tale span of three nights, Ivy talked to Marion. Every night she learned new things. What her mother did, who she really was. The hell Marion had lived in, all these crawling years.

I've watched you from the start, she told Ivy. *I burned with pride to see your gifts grow. I know you're the one who will save me.*

Ivy was smart and brave and powerful enough to find the girl her mother had tried to kill. Now she and Marion would figure out a way for Ivy to bring her home.

All day Ivy was reading, searching, looking for anything that might help them. When her parents were asleep she returned to her mirror and to Marion.

When you're scrying, the surface you use becomes your singular point of focus. The rest of the world simmers to gray scale. Ivy only registered a glimmer of motion to her right before something pushed her to the ground. A swinging object, a hideous *crack,* and she was crouching in darkness.

It's a shock to come out of magic that way. Everything felt

as chopped up and perilous as the mirror. Then the world came back into focus.

Her mother stood over her. On one hand she wore a big black boot.

Ivy was furious. Then she was *glad*. Her mother was just the person she wanted to scream at. "What are you doing in here? I told you to leave me alone!"

Mom flicked on the bedside lamp. By its light her face looked shiny, puffy with crying. "Save it. You need to eat something."

"*Eat* something? That's all you have to say?"

"You lied to me about getting a letter." Mom sat on the edge of the bed. "We're going to talk about what's really going on. But first, yes, you need food or you'll feel like absolute garbage."

Ivy goggled at her, talking about food like the world hadn't just blown to pieces. "You think I don't already feel like garbage?"

"Yell at me later. Right now I'm gonna get you some crackers. And water."

"Fuck water," Ivy said. It was maybe the first time she'd ever said that word in front of her mother. "I don't need water, I need to fix what you did. *That's* what matters."

Mom moved a hand over her forehead, restlessly. Her voice had nothing in it. "There is no fixing what I did."

"I'm not gonna stop till I've done it," Ivy said fervently. "You can't stop me."

Her mother didn't reply right away. She wasn't moving but you got a jittery feeling looking at her, the sense of detonations going off inside her head.

"*Mom*. You've got nothing to say to me?"

"I never should've taught you any of this." Mom's voice was low and certain. "I shouldn't have even used the word *magic*."

Ivy's stomach burned. "I didn't need you to help me find magic."

"I gave you words for it. Spells and intentions and . . ." She looked at Ivy pleadingly. "I helped you grow strong."

"I was always gonna be strong."

Mom shook her head. "It didn't have to happen this way. Just by working with you, I . . . *corrupted* you. My magic—it's not clean."

Her mom had never talked like this. She'd never looked like this, stripped-down and sorrowful. It was horrible and it made Ivy feel as if she were falling but it also gave her a flash of how it might've been all along, if her mother had been willing to show herself unarmored.

"Mom." Ivy could hear in her own voice an appeasing note. She hardened her tone, hardened her heart. "I can fix it."

"How *exactly* are you planning to do that? Eye for an eye? Are you gonna kill me?"

Her self-pity brought all of Ivy's fury roaring back. "I'm gonna do what you should've done twenty years ago," she said. "I'm bringing Marion home."

The name hit Mom like a hand grenade. "Ivy," she said wretchedly. "There is no bringing back the dead."

"The dead?" Ivy frowned. "Marion's not dead."

CHAPTER FORTY-THREE

)

The suburbs
Back then

I felt a great unraveling.

The truth tore through me and it ripped every stitch I'd made from that day to this: from the minute I'd pushed Marion through the mirror and given her up gratefully for dead, to right now, watching my child confirm what I'd refused to believe.

I felt myself reaching for magic. Words to calm my racing heart, to make every breakable thing in this room burst. But magic was what had opened the doors in the first place, and let the wolves come in.

Ivy didn't see that I'd been shattered. She saw me the way I'd taught her to: as a stoic, as a foe, someone to love and rage against, to trade half-truths with.

"The thing is, Mom, you can't stop me," she was saying. Not taunting but coldly certain, her voice pulling me back to the here and now. "I'm bringing her back. All I need is a mirror. You think you can hide every mirror from me every day for the rest of my life?" Now she let a smirk in. She was too young, too strong, she couldn't help herself. "You can't do shit."

My vision went bright with anger and very very clear, like I was looking at the world through red Saran Wrap. She was twelve years old. Sheltered, self-righteous, threatening *me* with a living nightmare.

What Ivy brought back wouldn't be Marion. It might be *shaped* like her, but all the parts you couldn't see would be twisted, broken, sucked dry across the unfathomable years. She would be a *monster*.

But—to know she was out there, and do nothing. That would make me the monstrous one.

"Magic that big would break you," I said in a voice I barely recognized. "It would grind your bones for its bread."

She blinked. Good. She *should* be scared. She should be terrified.

"You can't—" she began, a little wobbly, and I cut her off.

"Can't stop you. I heard you the first time."

Because Ivy was right, I'd have a hell of a time stopping her. I'd have to lock her up to keep her from tearing her mind and body to pieces trying to wield whatever terrible spell Marion had whispered through the mirror. She was so much stronger than me.

But there was one thing in this house that was stronger than her.

I could feel now that it had been waiting for me since I was sixteen. The golden box, a creature that slumbered with half-open eyes. I'd been told long ago I would need it one day. Now that day had come and my whole body felt heavy with sorrow.

It was wrapped in a torn Sleater-Kinney T-shirt, tucked

into a shoe box on the top shelf of my closet. When I returned to Ivy's room her posture was unchanged: shoulders up, fists balled, head down. Her eyes hooked onto the box.

"What's that?"

I held it out, setting in motion a story that had already been told. "Take it."

She yanked it from my hands like it was hers to begin with. She looked *so much* like me. Suspicious and hungry, heart humming so hard you could see it through cotton, skin, bone. She turned the box over, looking for the catch. "What's inside?"

I was breathing hard. I was the witch with the apple. "Open it. Just needs a drop of blood."

With her teeth she ripped a cuticle away, leaving a thin white furrow that filled with red.

"Touch it," I said. "To the box."

It wasn't dramatic. The box was solid, then seamed, the lid lifting on a hinge. I thought it would be gold inside, too, but it was lined with a gleaming, rosy-colored wood. The longer I looked the more the color seemed anatomical, its iridescence the queasy sheen you find on deli roast beef.

"I love you," I said. "And I cannot let you destroy yourself over this."

My voice was indistinct, my words anodyne. She didn't seem to hear me.

"I love you," I repeated.

Then I spoke the incantation.

It had been recited to me once, on Maxwell Street when I was sixteen. I'd written it down, but a couple months later I burned it. It was fossilized in my head alongside Fee's childhood phone number, the Empire Carpet theme song, the expression on Rob's face when I told him I was pregnant the first time.

Fury propelled me through the first half. Then it was the sheer terror of using magic to mess with my kid's brain, and wondering if I could cause literal *brain damage* if I tried to stop.

I don't want to take too much away, I told the box. *All I want you to hold is her memory of this. All the awful, dangerous things, all these tainted memories of magic.*

But everything that matters is a little dangerous. All magic is tainted—tinted, shaped—by *something*. And the box was a fairy enchantment. I should've remembered fairy bargains are poison to the root.

Ivy was still staring into the box when I spoke the incantation's last thorn-tipped syllable. "What is—" she began, then stopped, eyes flicking to mine, welling with fear.

"Mom?" she whispered.

"It's okay." I was trembling. "I'm here."

There was a moment, I was sure of it, when she understood what I'd done and seared me with a look I'd remember until consciousness stopped. Then she went still, the box cradled to her chest like an open mouth. Her body twitched and kept *twitching*, as if every memory had to be yanked like a weed.

It was horrible. So horrible I moved her onto the bed and covered her body with my own. She writhed beneath me and made no sound.

I looked at her rigid face and remembered drawing pictures with our fingertips in sheets of falling rain. I heard her screaming at the stench of the blemish charm Fee taught her to make when she was eleven, and crying when she managed to turn her hair bright orange instead of pink before the first day of sixth grade. I felt her quiet beside me in the soccer fields at midsummer gathering the flowers only we knew about, that opened in the rift between the sky's lightening and the sun showing its face. The memories blossomed and withered, and now they belonged only to me.

I heard the clap of the awful box. When I looked it was closed and seamless and Ivy was asleep. Her chest moving slow and even, her eyelids smooth as suede. A damp whip of red hair wrapped around her neck like an umbilical cord. I started to nestle against her, then stiffened and drew back. Gently I lifted her hair, sweeping it over the pillow and pulling the sheets to her shoulders.

Rob was sitting blearily at the top of the stairs outside her room. I could tell by his face he hadn't been there long. "Hey," he whispered, reaching up to touch my hip. "Did the hostage negotiate?"

Shame pooled in my stomach. It nested between my teeth like a capsule of cyanide.

"It's done," I said, and slid past him down the stairs, to lie sleepless on the couch until morning.

When Fee saw me on her doorstep at six a.m. she cursed softly and beckoned me in.

She'd always been my mirror, always let me know when I'd gone too far, been too impatient or too unkind. When I was done talking her face was slack as a dead woman's, both palms pressed flat to the table. "What did Rob say?"

I shook my head.

Fee closed her eyes. "Go home to your husband. Go home to the child you've . . ." Her face spasmed. "Go home, Dana."

I could hear Rob making coffee when I walked in. I'd looked at Ivy before leaving the house and she was lying as I'd left her, color good and heart rate steady. Still I lingered a while at the foot of the stairs, watching her bedroom door.

I found Rob in the kitchen. "Hey." His tone was cool. "What's going on?" He looked irritated and weary but still like he *knew* me, and I tried to hold it around me like a coat. The last time he'd ever look at me that way.

I started talking. The whole time I kept my eyes on the window, and the clumsy fly that bumped around its upper corner. Then my story was through and I was refocusing on his face.

He'd looked at me with confusion before, with exhaustion, even disgust. But never with all three boiled together, into something that might have been hate.

"Are you gonna divorce me?" I whispered.

He twitched back like I was dirty. Like he was looking down on me from a long long way. And later he'd apologize for it, and months after deny he'd even said it, but he did. He did say this: "Of course not. If I left, *you'd* get the kids."

So: open the box, right? Restore everything you've stolen.

"Do not touch that box." Fee's voice, sizzling across a bad connection. "I know you're tempted, but you can't just erase this."

"Why? What did you learn?"

"Common sense," she snapped. "She's too young, her brain is too flexible. If we're *lucky* she'll be fine, just . . . minus some memories. But we can't flood her system with god knows how much information."

"Till when? How long do we wait?"

"There's not a manual, Dana. What did Rob say?"

"He hates me."

She sighed. "I'm almost at the shop. Stay home today, try to map the fallout. I'll come by tonight."

We waited in blistering silence for our daughter to wake. Finally we heard the creak of the upper hall, the toilet's flush. Then she was walking down the stairs humming something. She walked in, saw us sitting there like mannequins, and did a double take.

"Whoa. What's up?"

Rob got up and folded her into a hug. "Everything's fine," he said unconvincingly.

"Dad," she said after the hug had gone on too long. "*Dad.*" Then, craftily, sensing she held some mysterious advantage, "Can we go to Walker Bros.? I want a Dutch pancake."

She could've asked for the moon.

We were only alone for a minute that morning, washing our hands in the women's room. All morning I'd been searching for changes in her face. When our eyes met in the mirror, she squirmed and rolled her eyes.

"*Mom.* Stop *staring* at me."

My heart seized. "Ivy."

Her brows drew down at the panic in my voice.

"Rooibos, lavender, bay," I recited. "Lead dark hearts astray."

Her mouth squished into an embarrassed line. "You're being weird," she whispered.

The bathroom door swung shut behind her.

Ivy's friend Billy came by to see her an hour after we returned from breakfast. For days she'd been too busy locked inside her room to spend time with him, and I'd felt sorry for the kid. Now the sight of him filled me with terror. He was the only person besides me, Rob, and Fee who *knew*. What would happen when he tried to talk to Ivy about stuff she couldn't remember?

I turned him away. He came back the next morning. It was early and I told him Ivy was asleep, but when I turned she stood behind me on the stairs.

"Who was that?"

"Billy," I said without thinking. She had a clear line on the door and would've seen his face.

"Who's Billy?"

My body processed a single moment of compressed white shock. Then horror seeped in.

I'd wondered what Billy knew, and for how long, and I guessed I had my answer now. Magic must've been a part of their friendship from the start. It must've been at the very root of them. Her best friend and everything he was to her, fed to the golden box like another ripped-up weed.

"He's nobody," I said. "Just a boy on the block."

CHAPTER FORTY-FOUR

)

Elsewhere

Escape had passed Marion by, so swift and close the heat of it kissed her skin. She could have raged at the loss, but what truly grieved her was what Dana had done to Ivy.

That surprised her; she wasn't built for sentiment. But Marion had watched Ivy all her life. From the day she was born.

Marion curled into herself like a boxer protecting her head. She drifted a while, disarmed by sorrow. She dreamed the deep-sea dreams of a thing that doesn't truly sleep.

It took her a long time to look again into the scrying glass. When she did the girl was older.

Who *was* this remade Ivy? Her lips pinked with drugstore gloss, her features gawky. Without magic to shape it, her restlessness had curdled. She was fretful, armorless, wandering.

Marion watched Ivy stumble, unprotected, through the worst years to be a girl. She watched scar tissue form over the broken places in her head. Still clever but robbed of her confidence, still curious but deprived of her faith in the world's ability to truly surprise.

Ivy was fourteen, fifteen, sixteen. Then, in a blink, seventeen. The age Marion was when she met her disastrous coven.

Time could pace and blow outside the walls of Astrid's house and never find a crack. The place was Tupperware-tight. But when Ivy turned seventeen, Marion's mind leapt the walls and sang like an arrow through the future.

Dana would die. Ivy would die. If Ivy had daughters they, too, would die. Would Marion hang over her glass like a spider through it all, glutting herself on their shadows? Would she remain deathless, forever almost-eighteen, sealed in a dream-house that smelled eternally of rose dust?

No.

Marion found the occultist lying on a fainting couch the color of blood on ice, hair puddled over its velvet like a saint's penumbra. Her eyes were open but a great distance away.

Marion jabbed a foot into the deadish woman's side. "Wake up."

Astrid's eyes focused with a reptilian snap.

Marion held out the spell book. The occultist's book she stole from a dead scholar's handbag, long ago. She dropped it with a thump on Astrid's chest.

"It's time."

Astrid blinked slow, contemptuous blinks. "Time," she said dismissively.

Marion curled her lip at her jailer, her fellow prisoner—she never could decide which—and dragged her onto the carpet by her saintly hair.

"It's time," she repeated.

"Flea-shit speck," the occultist spat. The air around her was heating with a summery wobble but nothing had happened yet. She was slower than she used to be.

Marion kneeled to pick up the book from where it had slid. She was in reach now and the occultist slapped her hard, twice. Marion absorbed it, pressing the book into the hand that had struck her. "Open it."

The book had a sick sense of humor, just like the woman who'd bound it in the skin of a charlatan clairvoyant. Marion used to believe it showed you the spells you needed to see, but of course it was only ever showing what Astrid wanted to give you.

She remembered clutching it in trembling hands right after she'd arrived here. Her last source of hope, and she'd felt so brilliant to have held on to it through her tumble. Fireworks popped in her temples as she opened it, seeking some cure for her imprisonment. Smearing fingers over her swollen eyes, she'd leaned close to the page.

To purify lanced boils, it said.

When Marion looked up the occultist had been watching her with the merry feline hatred of the meanest girl at school. She'd opened the book a dozen times since then, and found one mocking spell after another.

But *Astrid* hadn't opened it. And Marion would bet her unnatural life she knew what kind of spell Astrid most wanted to see.

"You come to me with orders and with talk of time," said the occultist, as sneering and sure as the queen of a fallen country. "Remember that I rule this place, and you are bound to *me*."

Alone among her attributes, the occultist's thrilling, razor-backed voice still held the power to magnetize Marion's spine, to make her draw in small and tight and afraid.

She shook it off. "You rule nothing and nowhere. You're a queen of smoke. Everyone who knew your name is dead, and no one else will ever learn it. *No one* is coming to release you. It's over. Open the goddamned book."

"Sheep scat. Eavesdropper. Rank slut!"

"Yeah, yeah," Marion said, no stranger to Astrid's rants. "But I'm right, too."

"You are *nothing*."

"I am what you made me."

"No," Astrid replied, decisive. "Here is the last thing I will tell you, the very last. You were always an apple without a core. Why else would you have stolen another worker's book?"

"There's nothing you can tell me about myself that I don't know. After all this time. I know a few things about you, too." Marion looked into the occultist's faded eyes. "You're tired, Astrid. We're *tired*. Let's make an end of this."

The two weary witches considered each other. Astrid breathed in but didn't speak. She sighed instead, her cruel and beautiful face settling into new furrows, as if passing time had finally found a gap in their eggshell world.

She took her book from Marion's hands. Slowly she traced a sharpened fingernail over the book's fearful binding, then inserted its point delicately among the pages. She opened it.

Their pale heads pressed close as they read the name of the spell.

To unravel your cage.

The occultist had nerve. No one could say she didn't. After a pause just long enough to skim the spell, taking in its dimensions, Astrid began the incantation that would unwind their world.

As she incanted Marion closed her eyes against a vast melancholy. Inside the tender dark of her head she watched the walls come down and time drift in like salt, which gnaws you to nothing then eats the bones. She saw all the dimly, deeply recalled treasures of the occultist's brief life fur over whitely, then shudder to dust.

Maybe Marion would unwind with them. Maybe she'd bob like a bottle, shoot like a star, evaporate or explode or hold on tight, too used to consciousness to give it up so easily. She didn't open her eyes, even when Astrid clawed at her—with terror, in the end? With gratitude?—and when the clawing stopped she still would not open them.

Ivy, she said. *Ivy.* And a third time, *Ivy.*

Marion thought she'd seen too much to ever be scared again, but there was no terror so pure as what seized her when the grip of Astrid's fingers broke apart with a sensation of pattering sand.

She held on to herself amid a whipping storm that wished to reduce her, too, to stardust. Its fingers plucked her clothes to tatters, then molecules. It didn't matter, there was so little she'd ever been allowed to keep. Only the righteous burning sword at her center, because Astrid was wrong. She *did* have a core. It was intent on a single end.

Ivy.

Knowledge and faith are all you need, plus will tempered by time into steel. All of you yearning toward what you seek. Marion felt whipping wind, gritty with the remains of the released occultist. For a bright empty instant she felt nothing.

And then.

Vastness. A world without walls.

She opened her eyes onto stars. True ones. Stars in a real sky and a tepid breeze that ran over her like . . . like a goddamned *breeze*, it was itself and there was nothing like it, not anywhere. All around her was the massive breath of night and inside it she felt drunk and sick and wild.

She was *out*. Astrid's world was dead, and she hadn't died with it.

Marion's feet were bare. Beneath them was the wet black grain of that shining-dark *stuff* machines poured out to make roads in summer. *Asphalt*, she thought, and laughed. She looked up into a bell jar of endless sky, up and up, to the place where three stars gathered in a row.

That meant something. It was called something. She was reaching for the words when the sound she'd registered only in her spine, as a tingling rising anxiety, became a white-eyed monster bearing down on her.

Fixed halogen gaze and clunky bullet of a body, tearing the air. Marion froze in a fog of toxin and terror before the monster changed course, screaming away from her, and only when it was still did she think, *Car. I almost got hit by a car.*

Instinct sent her toward the trees. The lash of branches and everything that tore at her was a gift, she was laughing at the *wealth* of it, the pain of opened skin and the itch of sweat and the sheer spiraling pleasure of the wind on her naked skin.

She smelled water—or heard it, maybe, all her senses were shaken up like a cocktail—and it washed her clean of anything but the desire to submerge herself. Out of the trees and over an abbreviated bank, then she stumbled face-first into a sluggish creek, sinking ankle-deep into its bed. The rest of her floated with the current. It gentled her, seduced her. She was laughing and delirious, slapping at her body just to feel that she had one.

Then: a pen-sharp point of light, cast on her from the trees. Two shapes lingered there, watching her.

People! Marion hadn't had to be human in so long, but she welcomed it. Every new thing. She shouted at them, something goading, something crude, wanting them to come closer. When they didn't answer she felt, not fear, but the first inkling of a grander awareness: she was just one animal again, in a world full of them.

She reached for magic first, but it didn't come. That wasn't too surprising, she was out of practice in this place. Next she reached for a big stick.

Then the light went off and she could see the people looking down at her and one of them was Ivy.

Marion would've needed a different kind of heart to feel it swell, to feel it break. But it did ache to see the girl so close, so real. She had Dana's hair, a gentler riff on Dana's ruthless face. All the certainty of her younger self had bled out with her magic. Marion was flush with triumph, drunk with thrill, but laying eyes on this tipped-out version of Ivy sobered her up.

You don't remember me, she wanted to say, *but you will when I'm through.*

Not yet. They had world enough, and time.

Marion had forgotten she was naked until Ivy took off her own shirt and threw it to her. She snatched it up, her brain already unraveling its scents.

She let the girl leave, for now. "Thank you, Ivy," she called, and was gratified to see her startle, looking back over her shoulder in the moonlight.

Good. This was the start. Marion had to get her bearings, had to move at proper speed. She'd been watching when Fee warned Dana against simply reopening the golden box. It could break Ivy again, and worse. She had to be lured back into the thickets. Magic had to glitter a while at the edges of her sight. The seeds must be planted and coaxed from the soil before she was ready to receive everything.

With one hand she would give Ivy back her magic. With the other she would pick Dana to pieces. She would plant a bomb in the middle of her lovely life and make damned sure she heard it ticking.

PART III

CHAPTER FORTY-FIVE

)

You bob in the blue embrace of a suburban swimming pool. Bleeding, stripped to your skin, holding tight to a box made of gold. You lift the box's lid and come

undone.

Tell the tale of the Golden Box.

Once upon a time there was a prince and the girl who loved him. But a wicked fairy stole his memories away and locked them inside a golden box.

Try again. Tell it crooked.

Once upon a time there was a mother and the daughter who loved her. But the truth swept the scales from the girl's eyes. The mother could not bear to see the truth of herself in her daughter's face, so she stole it away. And locked it inside a golden box.

What comes back first? Scent. Juniper and bay leaves toasting in a skillet. Your mother's hands, one mapped with scars, crushing the herbs in a mortar.

Stars, bigger than the ones you know. Magnified until you swear you can see silver star-children coasting down molten rivers, chased by the rippling flags of their celestial hair.

There's true, your mother says, *and there's story. Both have their uses.*

Was her voice ever so patient, her focus so squarely on you? Is this a wish or a memory?

Memory. More are coming now.

Some kinds of magic are for everyone. Her eyes blue agates but warmer. *Growing things, the weather. The moon belongs to all of us. Fingernails, spit. You can keep yourself like a garden.*

Schoolroom. Hot dust and body spray and uncapped marker. Your teacher stands over you looking at the green mess of your planting. Each child has a box of soil into which they've pushed seeds. Impatient, you helped your seeds along. Now your box is jungly with sprouts, days too early. Your teacher—who has a feeling about you, who doesn't like you and can't say why—drops your box into the trash.

Your brother, whipping your bare legs with a kitchen towel. *Shut up, I barely touched you!* Later your mother catches you harvesting hair from his brush and slaps your face, the first time she's ever hit you. *It's not a weapon,* she says as you weep gustily. *If you work against your brother, against anyone, it stops.*

How could it stop? Bees and clouds and dirt don't stop. Your pulse goes, your hair grows, your hands and head and heart sizzle with a sweet green static that lives in and around you, that your mother and your aunt call *working.* You can shape it, direct it, but you can't say no to it.

You pull out of the memories just enough to feel your fragile body, red meat and star stuff, floating in the hyaline eye of the pool. Someone floats there with you. Someone is holding you tight. Then you're off again.

Walking through a field at night. Your mother is beside you and the grass is hip-high, parting around you in itching curtains. Again, same field, but you're taller now, the grass no longer an enchantment but an annoyance around your knees. Your aunt's just ahead, Carhartts and pruning shears. The moon is a scanted scoop, a day or two from full. Your nose pricks, anticipating the work of separating herbs from grasses in the pale dark.

Come on, auntie. Not even a flashlight?

Not even a candle, modern girl.

The memories come faster now.

Here's one, a memory from before you could make them, your mother's voice imprinted onto your infant mind like pine needles on wax. *Swim, little one, into the deep, Mama is tired and wanting her sleep.*

Stalking through the woods in a sundress, looking for fairy houses. Knock twice on ashwood to wake it, thrice on larch. Leave an offering.

Nightmares after a slumber party. Stripping the bed, laying down fresh sheets sprinkled with lavender water to keep bad dreams away.

Blue flowers shaped like tongues. Something brackish on the burner. Blood beading on your knees. The memories make a flood and the flood makes a river and you're rising on it, spinning like a leaf, threatening to waterlog and go under.

Someone speaks in your ear. *Ivy. Strong girl, clever girl. Make yourself into a fortress. Make yourself into an ark. You're a safe, you're a sailboat, you're a hot-air balloon. Hold tight to your edges. You're a raincoat.*

You don't know how you do it, but you do: you tuck your mind away. You make it weathertight. You tread the flood and like Prospero you find on it an isle: a memory so clear and crystal-cut you can beach yourself on its shores, and rest.

Freckles. That's what comes.

You're little enough that your hair hangs down your back, uncut. You forgot how heavy it was. You're wearing overalls that belonged to your brother and a T-shirt with a hole at the neck and you're crouched in the spring dirt. There's a sticky patch at the corner of your lip that you touch your tongue to absently. Maple syrup.

A boy is watching you. Yesterday there was a moving truck parked across the street and today a boy with curly brown hair and freckles and a Peter Pan smile. He's spying from the gap in the fence line.

You're young, but old enough to know the capital R *Rule*: Don't let anyone see the things you can do. They belong to a world that belongs to *you* (and your mother, and your aunt) and you don't show anyone, not ever. Not your soccer friends or your recess friends or your nature camp friends, and if Hank asks any questions you send him straight to me.

But it's spring now, this very day. You could feel the change when you woke up. That limbering of the world's bones, every branch and bud humming with promise. The season has an impatience to it that makes the working easy. The sun isn't fully up and the rest of the block shouldn't be either, but here's this grinning stranger, just your size and lit up with curiosity like a Christmas bulb.

He kneels beside you. You should try to hide what you were doing, to deny it, but you're too proud, too hungry to share this secret: that you can do things other people can't.

Laid out in front of you is a patch of clover. With touch and will you're giving each clover new ambitions, coaxing them into unfurling a lucky fourth leaf. The luckiest among them have five. You comb your fingers through and find one, give it to him.

Holy moly, he says, in his scratchy voice like Peppermint Patty's. *Show me again.*

From the start, you and Billy were magic.

It's always summer with him. Flashlights and frogs and the burn in your legs as you chase the ice-cream truck. Even your winter memories have the molten texture of June. It starts with magic—with yours, showing off at last; he has no aptitude—but after a while magic isn't the point anymore. Not the *doing* of it, just the secret. It binds you together more tightly than a spit pact, it gives your expanding play world shadows and deep ravines.

Most days you're just silly. Most days you ride bikes and build forts and buy massive bags of Jelly Bellies at the mall and eat them at the movies. But some days you show him the things you can do and he watches with awe and no jealousy, the two of you glowing with your gift.

And wound through all of it, a rising awareness that plays in you like a song. A shimmer that grows into a feeling no word can hold.

And then, at last, a kiss. In the creek, in the violet hour. Wet lashes and freckles and Popsicle mouths.

You want to balance here, inside this pretty summer dream, but the flood takes you away. Now the way grows rockier, and you remember things it wasn't so bad to forget.

Hanging over a mirror, tracing its surface with a fingertip, your heart beating delicate dread. Because you love your mother. She's your *mother*, impatient and wry. The green tree you shelter beneath; a tough nut to crack. But she's a liar, too. She has secrets, gaps in her history she thinks she's so good at hiding. She wants you to turn down the dial on your magic, to dole it out in teaspoons. If you could just confront her, dig up proof she wasn't always the good witch she pretends to be, maybe she'd finally tell you all the things you're dying to know. Maybe she'd stop clipping your wings.

On a late summer night you pluck a big piece of magic off your mother's *don't even think about it* shelf and you make yourself a scrying glass. From its depths rises a phantom rendered in shades of butter and ice, whispering to you. *I am your mother's secret.*

Your mother's secret will be bigger than you thought it would be. It will be more than you wanted to know. But your curiosity is just a little bit louder than the warning bells ringing in your head.

I knew your mother, says the pale-lipped ghost. *I was young with her. All the years since then I've been pacing the halls of Hell. Would you like to know how I got here?*

You love your mother. You're old enough to know she's imperfect and smart enough to name some of her flaws and sure you see her as clearly as anyone could.

Until you learn what she did, and it alters you like a chemical reaction.

You're close to the end now. The flood of memories is ebbing, it's only knee-high.

That last fight with your mother, words popping between you like firecrackers. Her arms folded, her face closed and weary, then flaring with horror and revelation.

She puts the golden box into your hands. Its cool metal turns to something living when it meets your blood, a wicked mouth that wicks you up. Your mother's eyes are wet and full of remorse, like the killer who cries as their dagger goes in.

The box strips away the best and strangest pieces of you. It shaves you down into a different girl. Your mother makes you into someone who is *easy*, and then finds herself incapable of loving what she's made.

It's done. You know every last secret.

Now. Open your eyes.

CHAPTER FORTY-SIX

)

The suburbs
Right now

I woke up screaming.

Someone was touching me. Their lips were close to my ear. "Ivy. Ivy, are you—"

I screamed again. Words this time, charged with terror and the need to *not be touched*. The speaker's words cut to a shout and I heard the awful thud of a body meeting an obstacle.

I tried to turn toward the sound but there was no ground beneath me. I thrashed until I realized I was in a pool, floating bodiless in water like blue light. I made the mistake of looking up and the stars were so *god-awful close*. I knew they were looking at me, a thousand thousand silver eyes I couldn't hide from. I sucked in a breath to scream them away and took in a mouthful of bright water.

It tasted like death. I tried to cough it out, to breathe, but my neck didn't work right, no part of me did, and I swallowed more water. I was under it now and kicked for the surface, but I went down instead of up, my cooked brain turning tile into sky. I beat my palms against the bottom of the pool like it might give way.

I was drowning. Too airless to float, too weak to swim. My body turned and I gazed through the chlorinated blue dome that would kill me. The golden box had closed again, fallen to rest on the tile. I wrapped one boneless hand around it. The other drifted above me. My fingers moved, my mouth formed a word I didn't know, and I shot to the surface with such force I was out to my ribs before I splashed down again.

This time I kept my eyes on those horrid, orienting stars, breathing to cleanse myself of the taste of drowning. The water that would've killed me now held me like a flower in a cup, but I'd never forget what it tried to do.

The blue was veined delicately with red. The red drifted and became pink clouds and it was so pretty I didn't understand why my whole body had gone electric with warning.

Then I saw the girl floating in the pool. All the pretty sunset clouds were coming from her head. I remembered the terrible thud and knew I'd done this somehow, that the words I used to force her away from me had thrown her straight into the wall.

The realization worked on my brain like an adrenaline shot, making room for my name, and hers, and that of the boy I'd loved when I was twelve years old and of my mother, who had taken from me more than I even knew I had.

My throat was too ravaged to scream again, so I paddled to the side and dragged Marion's body out.

The instant I was clear of the pool, I understood *why* she'd had me open the golden box inside it. When I could feel my body again—the sodden weight of it, the exhaustion, the old bug bites and new abrasions—everything in the world turned up to eleven.

The sky spun like a disco ball, the pool glittered like diamond dust. I smelled grass, chlorine, rain. But I also smelled the gasoline in my dad's car on the other side of the property and the plastic torso of that far-off Ariel doll and the shallow breath of the three sleepers in that big, silent house. There was confetti under my skin, my blood was seltzer water. I wanted to unzip myself and float away.

I could jump back into the pool or I could do something else, something faster, that would purge the effervescence from this oversized night.

I could cast.

I didn't think, I *reached,* and what reached back was the cottony border of the sleeping spell Marion had laid on the house. Now that I could really feel it, it no longer seemed drowsy and sweet. It was a stale blanket, heavy as stone, laid over people's brains. All because they were unlucky enough to have a house in the woods with a swimming pool.

I caught hold of that gnarly blanket between fingers and teeth, and I ripped that fucker in half.

Now. Marion. I turned her over, naked back to gritty concrete, feeling carefully along the dark gash at the back of her head. My CPR was rusty, like, *only seen it in the movies* rusty, but I figured if I pushed hard enough, the water would come out.

I pictured the liquid caught in her chest like a tributary map. As I pressed the heels of my hands into the gaunt V below her breastbone, that map glowed in my sight. *Out*, I thought, placing a palm lightly over her ribs.

The water bubbled from her mouth in a gummy stream. Marion coughed, explosive, and rocked onto her side. For a minute she lay there, gasping, as I tried to get my head around what I'd done. Then she swiped a hand over her mouth and raised it to the back of her head.

"Stitch, stitch," she said.

I couldn't see the wound closing but I could sense the disturbance around her skull. There was a *busyness* to her magic. It skittered like a rat king, a thing of too many limbs and unnatural motion. My mouth dried.

As her magic worked she watched me, fingers probing her healing scalp. When it was done she sat all the way up, a naked witch with a crown of blood.

"I'm sorry," I said breathlessly. "I didn't mean to hurt you."

Her face was keen as an unsheathed blade. "Do you remember now?"

There was so much to remember. But I knew she was asking if I remembered *her*. The scrying glass and the dark room and the tales she told. "I remember."

"And you understand how strong you are."

I nodded, but I didn't. Not really. I couldn't take in everything I now knew about myself. All the fragile restored pieces of knowledge and thought and experience moved in and out of focus. I had the sense my head would be blooming with things lost and recalled for a very long time. Maybe the rest of my life.

Marion misread my silence as awe. "You can do anything," she said softly. "It's okay that you can't control it yet. I can help you. We can . . . Oh, Ivy." Her eyes shone. "Just think. Think of what we could do."

"We," I repeated.

"If you want." Her chin came up. "If you want, you could come with me."

"Where?"

She looked, I thought, uncertain. "Where do you want to go?"

"I—I don't . . . I need . . ." I stammered, shook my head.

I needed time alone. To let the sharp edges soften, the new information settle. She wanted me to think about what came next, but all I could see was my mother's face sizzling above me, underlit by the glow of the box. And what about everything that came before that night? All the tenderness, everything we were to each other before she took it all away. Those memories were still too radiant to look at, too hot to touch.

And Billy. All those years with him, all those wasted years without. I was twelve when I forgot him. Can you really fall in love when you're twelve years old? Even thinking the word turned my stomach to melted ice cream.

And magic. Magic? Fucking *magic*!

The bitter, the sweet, the shining. I tried to breathe but the newness hammered at my head and suddenly I was gasping.

"Shit." Marion moved closer, but didn't try to touch me again. "Get back in the pool. Or, wait. Cast something."

"Like what?" I rubbed frantically at my head. It spun like a carousel, I couldn't focus on any one spell.

"Just, anything." She looked around, spied her clothes on the ground. "Here, I've got matches. We'll do an energy spell."

She grabbed her jeans and when she did a phone dropped from their pocket with a smack. It fell glass-down, so I saw its case. Klimt's *Judith*, wear-faded to white across her belly, so familiar to me my eyes were tearing before I recognized what it meant. It was my Aunt Fee's phone.

I looked at the case, then at a suddenly silent Marion. She was waiting to see what I would figure out, and what I'd do.

Again I recalled standing in front of my aunt's house after visiting the shop, that sense of eyes crawling over my skin. Now I knew it was Marion who'd been watching me. Clear as a movie playing out I saw her standing in an upper window, blunt fingers tapping out a reply on my aunt's phone. A text that made me believe—made me want to believe, *allow* myself to believe—that my mother and aunt were together and fine and just being selfish.

"Where are they?" I said. "Where's my mother?"

"Do you care?" She said it so swiftly. "Now that you know what you know, do you honestly care where she is?"

My voice was shaking. "Did you hurt them?"

"They're not dead." Her mouth showed a slip of humorless smile. "I'm not that merciful."

"My god, Marion, what did you do to them?"

"Your mother crushed you," Marion hissed. "Forget what she did to *me*. Since you were a child she's been trying to kill the witch in you—the powerful fucking witch in you, whose abilities make her look like a birthday magician. But I was watching you, too. And *I* was proud. And *I* dug my way out of Hell to return what she stole, to turn you back into *that* Ivy, a witch who was questing and hungry and true. And here you are, wasting your breath on the woman who gutted your magic like it was a *mackerel*."

My hands went up like I could keep the words from reaching me. But I must've thrown something at her, too: the pain in my head, the resentment of knowing what she said was at least halfway true. She rocked back, a queasy expression rolling over her face.

"Okay," she said tightly. "You get *one* for free."

But maybe she saw something in my face that told her more was coming. Her fingers pinched the air, I could feel the approach of her magic on little rat feet. I was too new at this, my current and former selves still crashing into each other like ball lightning. I wasn't gonna be fast enough even to duck.

Then a hard square of yellow light fell over her, leaving me in the dark. In the second-floor windows, one of the sleepers I'd roused had turned on a lamp. Marion looked toward it, blinking.

I ran.

Straight down the sloping lawn, into the trees. I broke through them and remembered I was still naked, plunging through a civilized suburban wood transformed into a brambly hell. The only thing I'd grabbed in my panic was the golden box. It was sickly warm in my hand. By some miracle my feet didn't hurt, then I remembered: Marion had charmed them.

Don't see me, I thought as I ran. *I'm Nobody. See me not.*

I used to read so much poetry, old and new. A fluency with language and metaphor and outdated forms of speech was good for magic. A memory rose like an apparition: my mom reading a hypnotic bit of Tennyson aloud and then laughing, telling me a story about how she and my dad met.

I physically shook the memory away. Sorrow wasn't speed. Pain wasn't invisibility. I sensed Marion could follow the drift of grief, the perfume of anger.

I heard her, not far behind. Then closer, so close the edges of the leaves I raced through were whitened by the light she carried. Some kind of glowing wizard orb, probably. Or maybe just a flashlight.

I'm Nobody. See me not.

I wasn't just running away. I was running *toward* something. I felt an unnamed destination pulsing ahead, with a sense of nightlight safety and reaching arms, and when I got there it was a hazel tree.

Beneath the tree's summer crown I pressed my hands to its bark, breathing its good green breath and feeling the rootless pieces inside of me settle. All the Ivys I was or used to be. Marion was so close I saw the hard arc of the light she carried, but it didn't penetrate the circle of the tree. *My* tree, that had called out to me in dreams when I was ten. Seven years ago my mother and I untangled it from a piece of bad work some other witch had woven; now it would protect me. I palmed its trunk and closed my eyes and heard Marion run right past us.

When she was gone, I said my thanks and set off again.

I'm Nobody. See me not.

I fell into a rhythm of words and the tattoo of my toughened feet. I felt my path corrected by an awareness of the moon, and tasted like sugar in my molars the places where human things cut through the trees. I followed that ache back to the road.

Don't see me, I thought, as I dashed onto black asphalt.

And screamed.

CHAPTER FORTY-SEVEN

>

The suburbs

Right now

The car that almost hit me swerved madly but stayed off the grass, coming to a halt about thirty yards away. Somebody kicked open the driver's door and stepped out.

"Ivy, *what the fuck!*"

Nate's eyes were moon-size, one of them circled by a yellowing patch of bruise. I could hear Haim spilling out of his car radio.

"Nate." I thanked, kind of, whatever forces had sent him my way. "I need a ride."

He stalked over and gripped my arm, fingers digging in above the elbow.

"Are you insane? Is there a cult of *naked effing forest women* in this town? And you're all trying to get me locked up for *vehicular manslaughter?*"

Then he yanked his hand away with a yelp. I wasn't sure what I'd done, but my temples throbbed and I knew it was something. I stepped forward. He took half a step back.

"Don't grab me again. Ever."

"Okay," he said dazedly, looking between me and his fingers. "Sure."

I darted a glance back at the woods. "Look, I really need a ride. I wouldn't ask if it wasn't important."

He gave a short nod and I followed him up the road. There was a girl in his car, gaping at me. A sophomore, I was pretty sure, with a dark red bob and this spare Charlotte Gainsbourg kind of beauty.

"Hi," I said, climbing in, then turned to scan the woods. As Nate took the car out of park, Marion broke through. Low to the ground, like she'd been creeping.

"Hey," the sophomore said thinly. "Do you see that?"

"Drive," I said. "*Drive.*"

Marion was up now, watching from the shoulder. It was awful to see her and worse when she was out of sight.

I perched between their two seats, watching the road. The thin spits of white line soothed me, issuing at intervals like pages from a printer.

"Um." The girl shifted, not quite looking at me. "I've got workout clothes in my bag. They're not clean, but . . ."

"Thank you," I said. "I don't care if they're clean."

She passed back a wad of black activewear and I wriggled in. Just being clothed helped. Not with my modesty, which I seemed to have left in my life before the golden box, but with that skinned, raggedy feeling of *muchness*.

"Was that the same girl from the other night?" Nate's voice was tight, abrupt.

"Yeah," I said. "That was her."

A long pause. "So she did know you."

"Yes."

"I don't understand it," he said quietly, to himself. Then, "Are you gonna be okay?"

He asked it in the way people do when they want you to say, *Yeah, of course*, so I met his eyes in the rearview mirror and said, "Yeah. Of course."

He was driving toward my house, but I couldn't go there. Marion would be right behind me. I didn't want to imagine what she'd do to my dad if she had to go through him to get to me. Nowhere seemed safe enough, but I knew where I *wanted* to go, so I told Nate, "Drop me up there."

He stopped beside a grassy, moon-gray hill that unrolled to meet a row of fenced backyards. "I can go another couple blocks. You don't want me to drop you off at your house?"

I pointed at the back of Billy's place. Big yard with a rambling vegetable plot, and a badass tree house he helped his dad build the year after they moved in. I'd spent hours in that tree house. "I'm going there."

"Billy Paxton's house." He almost managed to say it neutrally.

"Thanks for the ride," I said as I climbed out, and meant it.

"No problem. But hey, Ivy."

I looked back at him, his solemn fringed eyes and the blood-bruise stipple over his pretty mouth.

"I won't tell anyone about this. I promise."

"You probably will, but that's okay." I smiled at the sophomore. "Thanks for the clothes. I'll get them back to you."

"They're yours," she said, in a tone that reminded me I was

striped with welling scratches and rank with sweat and chlorine.

I could hear Nate's music switch back on as I walked away. The mystery of me, all my naked panic and the slithering girl who'd followed me from the trees, was already fading from their sight. Soon I'd just be a startling shared interval in their predictable suburban night. I smiled to myself and ran toward Billy.

One of his bedroom windows overlooked the left side of the house. I searched for convenient pebbles to toss and found massive decorative boulders. Then I remembered who I was dealing with and sprinted to the front.

He was sitting on the porch with his head tilted back, white T-shirt and pajama pants and an empty matchbook in one restless hand. I could smell burnt-out matches but no cigarette. When he saw me, he moved to his feet so fast I knew he'd been waiting.

Our bodies collided at the bottom of his steps, my nose in clean cotton tinged with sulfur dioxide, his buried in my chemical hair. Our breathing rose in sync and I clung to him, pressing the golden box into his back.

"What happened?" he murmured. "Something happened."

I rose on my toes to reach his ear.

"Can we go to the tree house?"

Billy stiffened and pulled away to look at me. "The tree house." His eyes so wide, so full of hope, it could break your heart. "Ivy. Do you . . . do you . . ."

"I remember."

He collapsed a little. "I thought you did. When I saw you

running up the lawn. You look—you look like yourself. Not that you didn't before, I just—"

"It's okay. I know."

He gathered me up, pressed his nose to my neck. "You even smell the way you used to."

"Like what?"

His voice was muffled by my skin. "Like wild things."

My eyes burned. His hair was so soft on my cheek.

"What made you remember?"

"Let's talk in the tree house."

He nodded, but he didn't let go. "What happens if you forget again?"

"I won't."

"How can you know that?"

"Tree house," I repeated.

"Okay," he said softly, then sighed. "It's been a long time. Let's get something to cover the cobwebs."

We walked into the house still half-entwined. Everywhere he touched me was electric, everywhere he didn't was waiting to be touched. Gremlin tap-danced our way, then froze, darting a sniff at my feet before racing off into the darkened den.

"You don't smell *that* weird," Billy whispered, looking after him.

I laughed a little, very quietly. "It's not . . . it's spellwork, on my feet. I'll explain."

His brows went up and his hand tightened around mine. We moved like a two-headed animal up the stairs, to a linen closet with a squeaky door. I should've been down where his dad wouldn't see me but neither of us wanted to let go. On the way out I took a windbreaker from a hook, something with a pocket to tuck the golden box inside.

There was no ladder to the tree house, you had to climb the tree itself. I went first and Billy threw the bedding up piece by piece. It was damp inside and strewn with dead leaves but it smelled the way I remembered. A little like my old cigar box, plus rain and must and that dense green scent at the base of a leaf stem. I layered two comforters over the old boards, arranged the uncased pillows, and waited for him.

I was right, this was the best place we could be. It was built with skill and love and it was even weatherproofed, one shed-size room with a peaked roof and three windows and a doorway you had to kinda swing yourself through. Better than that, it was nestled in the branches of an old oak that had held me so many times as I grew. We would be safe here.

Billy pulled himself inside. He looked at me, then around the little house. "This was a good idea."

"I know."

Of course I used to pretend this was our *actual* house, his and mine, and around the time I hit ten I dreamed it as a wedding house, the place we'd live in when we were married. Not that I ever told him that. The air shimmered with the ghosts of our younger selves, our secrets, our heads side by side on the wooden floor. All the times I wanted to kiss him or hoped he'd kiss me. The walls and our faces were patterned with leaves turning under moonlight.

"Come here." I reached a hand out and tugged him down, the last of my energy tipping out like spilled salt as we went horizontal.

"You asked me what happened," I said. "All the things I couldn't remember—everything about you, about magic—my mother stole them from me. And she locked it all inside a golden box."

I could feel the whole warm line of his body beside mine. "That's not a metaphor, is it?"

I shook my head, slipping the box briefly from my borrowed jacket pocket to show him. It felt like a loaded gun. "I do believe she thought she was protecting me. I just don't know if that's good enough."

"I'm so sorry," he whispered. "That's . . . I'm so sorry."

"I can't sleep yet," I murmured. "The person I thought was in my house the other day, she's someone my mother knew. Another witch. My mom and aunt have been gone for days and I'm sure she has them, or hurt them, I don't know. We're safe while we're here, but I have to find them." I pressed my fingers to my eyes. "I can't even keep track of what I know, what I could use to find them. I could scry, I could sleep . . ."

He nodded. "You should sleep, you need it. I'll stay awake, I'll watch over you."

"No, I mean, I could sleep to dream." An ache filled my rib cage as I made another connection. "I've spent years believing I didn't even have dreams. But that was one more thing the box took. When I was a kid, I could do *anything* when I dreamed. Even pull people in with me."

"Ivy." His eyes were so soft. "I know."

He did know. I remembered now. When Billy was a kid, he had nightmares. They tended to start up after his mother called the house, erratic bursts of maternal interest that never lasted long. When the nightmares got bad, I'd pull him into my dreams.

We smiled at each other, and when he kissed me we were still smiling.

Until we weren't. He was beside me, then above me, propped on one arm. He ran a hand firmly down my body, rib cage to thigh, then held me there and pulled me up, closer. We kissed and kissed and it wove the air to silver and the silver touched every part of our skin, until he sighed against my mouth and said, "Oh, my god. *Finally*."

"Second kiss," I said.

"It was better. It was even better."

We laughed together in the dark. Everything outside was a barbed-wire knot, but we were in here. I didn't know joy and sorrow could lodge together so tightly. I didn't know how to accept all my mother had taken from me, how to think about everything I'd gotten back.

He was running a hand over the sleek flank of my borrowed activewear. "*Shit*. I'm gonna have an exercise video fetish now. Tell me to do a push-up, okay?"

I laughed and kissed him again. I felt like a kid who'd come into sudden possession of an ice-cream truck: *all mine*. Then I rolled away, because I needed my brain right now and otherwise I'd never stop. Billy nestled in behind me, his arm across my chest. "Sweetheart," he murmured into my dirty hair.

The endearment filled my chest like honey, the kind of drowning sweet you could lose yourself in. I tried to think cold-water thoughts, *any* thoughts. I heard Marion again, when I asked if she'd hurt my mom and aunt.

They're not dead. I'm not that merciful.

Not dead, but not here. So, contained. Somewhere. I sat up. "What is it?"

"I have an idea. A place we can check." I looked at him. "Can we take your car?"

CHAPTER FORTY-EIGHT

>

The suburbs
Right now

Billy's car had a busted AC. All the windows were down and the wind came roaring off the highway, pummeling my head and making it easier to hold my thoughts away from me, where they wouldn't hurt. My sense of time was pulpy. The car clock said 3:07 but that had to be a lie. The night had already stretched so long.

Maybe Marion was packing extra minutes into every hour to make room for me to come find her. To find *them*. She and my mother and Aunt Fee had lived through a nightmare. Now I was going to look for them at its source.

We'd climbed down from the tree house and Marion wasn't waiting for me. Billy grabbed keys and shoes and a bag of pretzels just in case and still she didn't come. But that didn't mean her eyes weren't on me.

We hit our exit and a few minutes later we were driving through a college town. Campus was a warren of lawns and pedestrian walkways and parking garages. We got as close as we could and I still couldn't see what I was looking for.

"I'm gonna find a place to park," Billy said, turning his blinker on even though it was the middle of the night and there were no other cars in sight.

"Wait," I said. "Pull over here quick."

When he had I turned to him and took his hands and said, "You know you're not coming with me."

"Ivy," he began, and I shook my head.

"If I'm right, and they're there, I can't be focused on protecting you."

"You wouldn't—" He cut himself off, thought about it. "But if she . . . what if she comes at you with a candlestick or something? You need someone watching your back."

"It's not gonna be a candlestick. And if she knows . . . I mean, look at us." I waved at the space between our bodies, a zinging arena of heart arrows, basically. "She knows who you are, to me. She could use it."

He dropped his head. "I hate this."

"This is what it is to be with a witch," I told him. "You have to let me be stronger than you."

His eyes went wide and he kissed my knuckles. "With you," he said, grinning. "With a *witch*. I've known you were stronger than me since I was seven. It's awesome. I just hate that I'm a liability. I wish I could help you."

"You *are* helping me. You're my getaway vehicle, right? Also my getting-there vehicle. Also my—"

He kissed me. "I'm your ride. So I wait here. Watching my phone in case you need me."

"Wish me luck," I told him, and stepped out of the car.

When I was alone I could let myself feel afraid without worrying he'd try to stop or follow me. I slipped around the side of a concrete building. I was starting to mistrust Google Maps when I saw the narrow sidewalk.

It ran beneath old lamps, their bulbs the safety-orange of construction lights. At the path's end was a house built to such sinister specifications I didn't need to see its sign to know I was there. I'd read about it on the drive and learned it had been closed for a long time, for renovations. But there was no scaffolding, no sign of work in progress. Just an unlit house on a lawn of clover in the center of a dark campus. I reached the end of the path and stopped.

The library's front door was open. Just like the house in the woods.

I walked on.

Everything I'd cast so far had been by instinct. I'd reacted, I'd panicked, I'd reached for what was right there. I had this idea that I would use an unlocking charm to get into the library that had once been the occultist's house. Now that I didn't need it the magic gummed up in my head like gauze on a nosebleed. I spent it on a charm for clarity of sight.

It made the moonlight brighter, turned the volume up on all the edges of things that wanted to lie flat in the dark. I stepped into a foyer scented with old books. As I stood there getting my bearings a headache began to form, so dispersed and metallic it felt like I'd breathed in silver dust.

Another old/new memory shouldered its way to the front of my brain: I knew this feeling. I was bobbing in the wake of someone else's bad magic.

I followed it. My mother had made this walk, or something

close to it, the night she'd pushed Marion through the mirror. A dreamer's version of this place had been Marion's cell for more than twenty years. I felt their footsteps alongside my own as I walked over dusty inlaid floors, past bookshelves, beneath stained-glass windows casting eerie shapes on my skin.

I ascended two flights of stairs on the trail of the awful feeling, my headache blooming into a full-body tremble. At the bottom of the third flight, I looked up. I saw nothing but drifting dust motes and moonlight but the thought of climbing filled me with a deep-space terror. I took three breaths and began, shoulder set against the raw edge of recently worked magic.

All was silent, all was still, but my heart beat in quick hard pulses, like the steady squeezing of a fist. I came to a halt below a trapdoor cut into the ceiling. Up there was the source of everything, and still I couldn't hear a sound.

The trapdoor popped free with a shotgun bang and a ladder rattled to the floor inches from my head. When my heart had descended back into my chest I looked up.

More dust. More moonlight. I set a foot on the ladder and climbed. It was quiet. My head broke even with the ceiling and I saw their bodies lying on the floor.

I hauled myself up and staggered to them. My mother and my aunt lay on their backs. Aunt Fee's right eye was bruised and my mother's face was covered with what looked like rug burn along one side. Their hands reached toward each other but didn't quite meet. Their eyelids jittered with dreams.

It wasn't a natural sleep. Even before I touched them, shook them, pleaded with them, I knew they wouldn't just wake. The whole room was filled like a cup with enchantment. When I tried to get an arm under my mother her body was stone-heavy, sodden.

I touched their faces and thought of the sleepers in the house in the woods. This spell wasn't so breakable: I reached for its edges and it had none. I plumbed for its bottom and felt deeper water than I could dive through.

But if they were sleeping, there was a chance I could reach them. I could fall asleep right here and pull them out of Marion's nightmare, and into a dream of my own. One they could wake from. I had no time for it—Marion couldn't be far—but no better ideas, either.

I lay between them on the attic floor. Eyes closed, I reached for the lucid dreaming that had waited for me across five long years, locked with all the rest of my magic inside a golden box.

CHAPTER FORTY-NINE

)

The suburbs
Right now

Three sleeping witches, lined up in a row. Two twitch in the grip of an uncanny slumber. The third—slotted between them, her head lying below the almost-grasp of their outstretched hands—is just now drifting away.

Below them, but not too far, a fourth witch is on the move. She runs over clover, she sprints beneath rows of stately trees, setting their branches to rattling. She was young in this place, long ago, a little girl with a lonesome, devouring heart. If she has a heart now it's impenetrable. A black-lacquered curio that bends the light away.

As she runs she passes a car at the curb with a boy inside it. His heart is the kind you can almost touch, lit up with fear and love and a dozen kinds of anticipation. He doesn't see the fourth witch passing. She chooses not to be seen, and he only has eyes for the girl with bleached hair.

The fourth witch is coming. She's almost there.

+   +   +

Here's how it was, falling asleep on the attic floor.

I closed my eyes and dwelled a while in the dark, coaxing it closer, asking it to steal over and displace the sour fog of Marion's magic. The dark softened to my will. It sifted, it stirred, it turned lightly over into sleep.

I knew how it should go next, how it had always gone, when I was young and dreaming was my kingdom. The dark would unpack itself like a trunk of costume clothes, spreading out into colors as soft as watercolor on an eggshell, drifting like curtains in a breeze. I could walk forward and touch them, all these sea and sky colors you couldn't name, that shifted in your mouth when you tried. An infinite number to walk through, into a dream.

But this time when I fell asleep there was only one curtain waiting for me. It wasn't misty or stormy or sunrise-tinted, it was pure oxidized red, not drifting but *boiling*. It looked like the entrance to Hell.

I could feel them behind it, two kinds of heat. My mother's self-contained layer of cobalt fire and Aunt Fee's mellow autumn sun. So I walked through the bloody curtain and into the dream Marion had put them inside.

In the dream she'd made we were in the attic still. But it was transformed by spellwork into a nightmare.

It was, I understood, a memory.

In the center of the room a dream version of Marion incanted over a mirror. A slaughtered rabbit lay beside her, bleeding over the boards. My mother and Aunt Fee, teenaged and terrified, had their backs pressed to the walls. A fourth, black-haired woman stood between them, with a face like a flint.

I'd hoped to make a dream of my own, to catch them in. But this dream was so *insistent*, so desperate with the odor of blood. There was no room in my head for anything else.

I'd heard the story of the summoning once, from Marion in the scrying glass. It was different when I saw it play through.

I witnessed Marion's attempt to bind the occultist, and its fallout. I saw Astrid Washington, solid malevolence crowned with fairy hair. Mom and Aunt Fee's battle to save Marion, which ended with all three in the circle. Fee's courage, Marion's catatonia. And my mother's decision, so fast you couldn't see it coming, to push Marion over the lip of the mirror.

I saw at last how she got the scars that covered her hand. And I measured the gap between the portrait of her that Marion had painted—monstrous, deliberate—and the furious, agonized girl I watched banish her friend from this world.

By the end I was frozen. Transfixed by horror and the wicked math of it: four witches then three, without even a body to show. I put my hands to my mouth as I comprehended the cruelty of what Marion had done: she was making Mom and Aunt Fee relive the very worst night of their lives.

I had barely caught my breath when the dream reset and began again. Blood, wax, smoke, and misery vacuumed away, four witches reset to the start like gameboard pieces.

As with any horror movie, it was less awful the second time through. I could think now, I could move through the room like a spectator in a haunted house. The longer I was inside this dream the more I could make out its contours and its rules. Marion had built it edgeless as an egg. My mother and aunt were living it, inside their younger forms, but I couldn't make them see me.

I tried to extinguish the flame of Dream Marion's lighter, smudge the salt circle, pinch my mother's arm. Marion's incanting took on a locust drone, and everything I touched was smoke or porcelain. I looked frantically for a weakness and what I settled on was the rabbit. Before the poor thing could be sacrificed again, I scooped it up.

It was solid, it was soft, it was kicking wildly in my grasp. I pushed the creature into my dream mother's arms.

It bit her. That beautiful piece of dream magic, feral even in its re-creation, sank its teeth right into her forearm. She was sixteen when the animal lunged but *herself*, Mom-aged and familiar, as the bite came down.

The pain had shocked her real self out of the shell Marion put her in. She dropped the rabbit, which zipped into a corner. Before she could recede, transform, I grabbed hold of my mother like she was Tam Lin, like only my grip could keep her from disappearing. I held her, feeling her body trembling, saying, "Mom, Mom, it's me." The dream melted to smoke until only we remained, and my aunt wrapping her arms around herself, sitting on the misty ground.

My mom backed away from me, talking to herself. "It's not her," she was saying. "It's another dream."

"It's me, Mom. It is."

"You're a phantom. Or maybe it's *you* under there." Her voice went venomous. "Marion."

"You need to see me," I said shrilly. All the times she

looked right through me clawing at my skin. "You need to believe me."

"Ivy-girl." Aunt Fee's voice was a balm over my heart. "How are you *here*? Dana, it's her. Can't you feel it's her?"

My mom's face stained with a complicated hope. "Ivy," she whispered.

We didn't have time for anything but getting ourselves out, but I was too angry to stop myself. "I know everything," I told her. "The golden box and Billy and—everything."

"Everything." Her face was a study in contrasts. Twisted mouth and glistening eyes and cheeks red as a slap. "Everything?"

"Yes."

"*Oh.*" The word was a cry, pressed into her palm. Eyes squeezed shut for a beat, then she looked at me. "Do you remember . . . that day in the forest preserve, with the deer and her fawn?"

I gritted my teeth. "Yes."

The dream shifted, shaping itself into something new. We stood together on gray grass beneath a nothing-colored sky. Aunt Fee pulled up a few blades and held them to her nose, watching us like an edgy referee.

"The bounce house," my mom said. "Remember that?"

"Don't try to manipulate me."

"That rash you got brewing a luck charm. And, oh, my god, Ivy. Do you remember the hazel tree?"

Lips mashed together, I nodded.

She looked like a political prisoner. Radiant with purpose, circles around her exhausted eyes. "Writing your first—your first cantrip. Staying up all night at midsummer, drinking coffee milk." She laughed, wet and brief. "Finding your fairy stone."

"Forgetting Billy," I said. "Lying to Hank. Losing half my mind."

Her radiance dimmed. "Yes."

"Why?"

"If you know everything, you know why." Her voice not challenging but hopeless. Then her eyes widened. "Oh, god. She put you here. Marion."

"I put my*self* here. I found her, and I found you, too. For god's sake." I stamped my foot before I could stop myself. "When will you ever stop underestimating me?"

The sky broke open over our heads. The raindrops that pelted us felt like cottony hail, and dried on our skin like rubbing alcohol.

"Protecting you," she said, eyes huge. "Badly, foolishly. Getting it all wrong. But never . . . never without love."

"Does love count if you can't feel it?"

"I messed up. But I always loved you. Always."

"*Loved* me," I said harshly. "You took half of me away from myself and stuffed it in a *shoe box*, then you didn't even like what was left."

Her chin trembled. "That can't be what you think."

"Five years, Mom. Five years of trying to get you to look at me."

"I was ashamed, Ivy! I am *ashamed*. I—maimed you. But I was gonna fix it. Eighteen, your dad and I agreed. When you turned eighteen, we were gonna tell you everything, open the box—"

"Marion fixed it. And everything's still broken."

"I'm so sorry. For all of it."

She was crying. My mom, who never cried, not even when Hank accidentally slammed the car door on her fingers. And it was what I needed to hear. It was what she owed me. But it was so *little*, so late, I couldn't bear it.

"Just stop," I said angrily. "We don't have time for this."

Her face was so tentative, so un-Mom-like. "It might be all we have time for."

"What's that supposed to mean?"

The cottony rain was thickening, hardening. It pelted our skin like bits of sea glass.

Aunt Fee put a palm out to catch some, brow furrowing. "Ivy, is this *your* dream?"

"Still mine," said Marion. She was standing a little ways away, holding an open umbrella.

My mother moved so her body was between mine and Marion's. Her breathing was audible, terrified. I winced as the raindrops started to *hurt*, not sea glass anymore but slivers of freshly broken bottle.

Then I breathed in sharply because I realized *I* was making it rain. It was my hurt and anger doing it. And once I knew that, it wasn't so hard to turn Marion's umbrella into a massive black bird that clawed at her, making her shriek. She changed it into a cloud of black smoke that drifted away.

Now all four of us were cowering beneath the vicious rain. I knew it was mine but it was harder to change than the umbrella, because it came out of a fury I was stuck with. I couldn't disappear it, so instead I *stopped* it in midair, all the cruel little drops shining and still. Then I drew them together. I think I wanted a piece of offensive magic, some big glass dagger to cut our way out of this piece of shit dreamspace. But the dream was still of Marion's making, I was only working within it, and what the drops formed instead was drawn from *her* head: the great circular mirror from the summoning, the one my mother had pushed her through.

It was already the size of a manhole, and the air still teemed with glass rain. The drops kept adding themselves to the mirror, its surface making a crystalline gnashing as it grew.

"Oh, hell, no," Marion said as it crawled closer to our feet.

She broke the dream.

As soon as I felt its borders give, tipping my consciousness back into my body, I was rolling to my feet. Staggering, dizzy, but up. I'd not been in it for even an hour, while Mom and Aunt Fee had been lying flat for god knows how long. It took them time just to open their eyes.

Marion could've killed them then. My body was primed for her to try, my head pulsing with the risk. But she could've killed them all along, and hadn't. I watched her watching them with utter disdain as they moved weakly on the floor.

"Are you okay?" I said.

My mom coughed. Dusty air in a dry throat. "Marion," she said. "Please."

"Don't you dare," Marion snarled. Her face looked more human with anger in it, but it flared fast and was gone.

My mom said her name again, so quietly. "Do what you want to do, but do it to *me*. Not Ivy. Not Fee. You've got nothing to punish them for."

Marion's smile was audible, lips pulling wetly back from white teeth. "My god, Dana, when did you become so *fucking* mediocre? You can't even tell a solid lie. I watched you. I never stopped watching you. A year after you pushed me I watched you and Felicita sit on the sand and agree between you that I was dead. You both knew that wasn't true. You *both* decided not to save me. What was it you were doing instead? Oh, right. Giving fake palm readings to drunk girls."

"Just us, then," my aunt said. "Let Ivy go. However you want to finish this, let's finish it."

I stepped forward but Marion spoke before I could, her words an eerie echo of what I was about to say.

"Listen to yourselves. Ivy is a better witch than both of you put together. *She's* here to save *you*. Stop pretending she's the one who needs your protection."

"Yeah, Mom," I said. "Just stop."

My mom flinched at my tone, but I ignored her. I had eyes only for Marion.

"What is it you want?" I asked her. "What did you come back for? What are you here to do—kill us?"

I got the strangest feeling, when she looked at me, of being looked at by something I couldn't entirely see, that was using her eyes as peepholes. Something cold and slow and utterly lacking in some crucial human thing.

"Death is too easy," she said. "Death is a *milk bath*. I thought the worst thing I could do to her would be to take you. Make you mine. Help you become so *bright* she could see from any-where what she'd tried to kill in you. What she'd lost forever. But now." Those otherwhere eyes ran over my face. "Now I think the worst thing for her would be to lose you. I mean really lose you."

I willed the women in this room who loved me to stay out of this, to be still. "Are you gonna kill me, Marion?"

"I could."

"Maybe." I took a step closer, then another, close enough that she could reach me. We could reach each other. "If you didn't, though. If I . . . if I went with you, where would we go?"

Her jaw shifted. She didn't speak and didn't speak, then the words all came abruptly. "There are legends about matriarchal societies that still exist. In lost places. On islands or deserts or deep in the trees. Little worlds with ancient roots. Places where women work and magic is revered and you can live your whole life without going farther than a mile from home."

"Is that what you want?"

The slow cold thing that wore her face peered at me. "I don't know. I don't think so."

"What do you want?"

"I don't want anything anymore," Marion replied almost before I'd finished talking. She pushed a fist to her sternum. "But I can still *feel* the place where I wanted."

"I think," I said softly, "that what you wanted was to save me. And you did. You did it *right*. You put me inside water, you held me in your arms. You talked to me when my mind was going to pieces. You didn't let the magic blow up my brain." I held out a hand to her. "You saved me."

"Don't patronize me," she said.

I didn't move. An endless second passed, then she reached out and took my hand.

I dug my nails into her skin with all my strength, until I was sure I'd broken it. Before she could twist free of me, or cast, or wrap us back up in some terrible dream, I stuck my other hand into the pocket of Billy's jacket, pulled out the golden box, and pressed it to the place I'd drawn blood.

Marion *laughed*. Eyebrows up, a laugh of true surprise. She looked like a teenage girl then, a real one, flawed and gifted and magical and incomplete, just like me.

"I didn't think—" she began, but the box opened its hungry mouth and she stopped and I never would know what she'd meant to say.

As she gazed into its empty heart I spoke over her the incantation my mother once spoke over me. Then I told the box, "Let her forget us. Take from her Dana Nowak and Felicita Guzman and Ivy Chase. Let her forget . . ."

And I stopped, because I didn't know what else to give to it. What would be a mercy, what would be a punishment. What Marion might be longing to lose.

So I handed her the box. She couldn't take anything back now, my words couldn't be unspoken. She looked like she wanted to slap it to the floor but she took it instead, bringing her mouth in close and whispering something I couldn't hear.

The box began its work. It was horrible to see, but sometimes the only way to show your reverence is to witness. By the end of it I was holding my mother's hand, and my aunt's, all of us watching together as the golden box snapped shut and Marion lay down to sleep.

We took the box and left her there on the moonlit floor. Stripped of her vengeance and who knew what else. It didn't feel good to do it. We didn't know whether we were abandoning an amnesiac or a round of live ammunition. Maybe both.

And maybe I was finally old enough for magic, because I was starting to reckon the costs of it. That I'd carry around this guilt, and a piece of the witch who'd forgotten me, until I was dead.

CHAPTER FIFTY

〉

The suburbs

Right now

Billy and I lay on our backs in the creek, watching the stars. The water was just this side of too cold, glowing Pop-Ice blue.

That was Billy's idea. He showed me pictures online of a bio-luminescent bay, so I could put one into the dream.

"Are you ready to wake up?" I asked.

"One more minute," he said, squeezing my hand. "Hey. Look."

He pointed to a place where the stars were bending closer, too close, as if they wanted to watch us, too. My shoulders tensed and gently I pushed them back into their places.

Sometimes my dreams did things I didn't ask for. I figured it was my subconscious at play. But I knew it hadn't happened that way before the golden box.

Outside the dream our bodies were asleep in Billy's tree house. None of our parents had caught on yet that it was back in use, the one place that was just ours. My dad had been overprotective of everyone since the morning I returned home with Mom and Aunt Fee, all of us shell-shocked, smeared with scrapes, sweat, bruises, blood. And Billy's dad still hadn't forgiven me for ditching his son five years ago. Since we couldn't tell him what really happened, I was trying to win him back over slowly.

For now, we had the tree house. Billy's car. And my dreams.

I held his hand in the luminous water, closing my eyes as it eddied around us, lifting me up.

"Ivy." His voice was level, but sharp enough that I dropped my feet to the creek bed—disgusting in life, paved with green river stones in the dream—and looked to where he was pointing.

The stars were watching us again. Really *watching* us, their alien gazes prickly sharp. It was a sky identical to the one I'd almost drowned beneath, panicking in the swimming pool after I opened the golden box.

Billy planted his feet beside mine and put his arms around my waist. "Let's wake up now, okay?"

I nodded, focusing on my breaths. Then I looked down at the water and cried out. The vivid blue creek was gone. We were submerged waist deep in pliant mirror glass.

"Look at me." Billy's voice was soothing, firm. He was the solid point around which the dream pulsed. I clung to him.

"Let's wake up," he said.

And we did.

Outside the tree house the mourning doves were calling their peaceful calls and the sky looked like silver paper. I rolled over and buried my face in his chest. "I'm sorry," I said, muffled.

He kissed my temple. "Nothing to be sorry for."

We held on until the last possible second. Then we climbed

down from the tree house and parted ways at the gate, to sneak back into our beds.

Three weeks had passed since the longest night of my life. I kept an eye on the news, but so far nothing had come up that fit any description of Marion: no unexplained mysteries, no wandering amnesiacs found, no prodigal, supernaturally ageless daughters returned.

For my family it was three weeks of a new kind of honesty, which—in the interest of total honesty—wasn't entirely a good thing. My dad thrived in the new normal, all of us alive and together and the worst of our secrets flushed out of hiding. For Hank, though, looking reality in the face was an adjustment. He walked around all dazzled and skittish, like he'd accidentally stared straight at the sun.

And then there was my mom and me. I guessed things would be weird between us for a while. Too much had been revealed at once. But she tried. She was trying.

The thing that worked best was for us to not speak. To work together, side by side. Little spells, mainly, magic for children. Things she'd taken from me, that Marion helped me get back. Sometimes Aunt Fee was with us and sometimes we were alone.

On the other side of everything, we were not okay. But maybe someday we would be.

I had this superstitious idea that by the time my bleached hair grew out, I'd have forgiven her. In my vision of this future, we matched again. Mother and daughter, two red-haired witches side by side. I could look at her and see the mother who did love me, forgive the complicated woman who'd messed it up. She could reach for me without shame, and I could take her hand without compromise. In this dream I had.

So I waited, and let my hair grow.

I climbed into bed exhausted. My mouth was so flushed, so obviously crushed with kissing, I'd have to hide out a while.

In a few hours I'd see Billy again. We were meeting Amina and Emily at Denny's for breakfast, then he was dropping me and my bike downtown to go job hunting. He'd offered to put a word in at Pepino's, but I didn't think it was the right move to work with my boyfriend. I rolled over, smiling, then stopped.

The room was gray and mild and there was something in it that didn't belong there.

Delicately I rolled from bed, crouched in front of my bookshelf, and pulled the something out from where it was wedged between *Lunch Poems* and *The Dark Is Rising*. It was smaller than the other books, its spine blank. On the shelf it had looked like a lean black gap.

I wondered when Marion had left it for me. A little over three weeks ago, I guessed, when she broke in and took the golden box. It must have been sitting here all the days since, waiting for me to see it.

It was new, the kind of unlined book you'd find at a fancy stationary shop, bound in black leather. I didn't open it right away. There might be things inside it that were dangerous just to look at, to read in your head. But in the end, of course, I flipped back its cover.

The Book of Marion Peretz, it read on the first page. Just seeing her last name, that sliver of new information, sent a charge through me.

It was an occultist's book, half full, its pages scrawled thickly with inked notes, rhymes, rough-sketched sigils. She must've spent hours pouring her knowledge into this book, for me.

I should burn it. My mom still believed magic could be poisonous, tainted like blood after a snakebite. While I didn't fully believe that, I knew far too well there were spells you didn't cast, forces you didn't mess with.

I should burn it. I should run across the hall right now and give it to my mother. I wondered again when Marion had snuck it onto my shelf, and how I could've overlooked it for weeks.

In the end I tucked it at the very back of my bottom dresser drawer, among all my hibernating autumn sweaters.

When I lay back down I thought about Marion, who'd watched me through a scrying glass all my life. Whose memories of me were locked inside a golden box, which was itself now stashed in a safety deposit box at the bank, until my mom and I could brush up on better ways to secure it.

Marion was gone now, and wouldn't know me even if I stood right in front of her. But before I hid her book away something made me hold a hand up to the air. In recognition, in farewell, in some kind of messed-up gratitude.

Just in case.

ACKNOWLEDGMENTS

Thank you to my agent, Faye Bender, for your warm heart, cool head, and general brilliance. Thank you to my editor, Sarah Barley, for walking through this new world with me, and for your rock-steady faith in your authors' voices, ideas, and ability to tell the sometimes very strange stories we want to tell.

Thanks to Bob Miller, Megan Lynch, Malati Chavali, Sydney Jeon, Nancy Trypuc, Marlena Bittner, Cat Kenney, Erin Kibby, Erin Gordon, Kelly Gatesman, Louis Grilli, Jennifer Gonzalez, Jennifer Edwards, Holly Ruck, Sofrina Hinton, Melanie Sanders, Kim Lewis, Katy Robitzski, Robert Allen, the Macmillan Audio crew, and the entire team at Flatiron for everything you do for me and my books. And this cover! Thank you to creative director and designer Keith Hayes and illustrator Jim Tierney for turning this book into a sinister door, a concept so perfect it still takes my breath away.

Much gratitude goes to Mary Pender, and to all the agents helping this book reach readers around the world: Lora Fountain,

Ia Atterholm, Annelie Geissler, Milena Kaplarevic, Gray Tan, Clare Chi, and Eunsoo Joo.

To the generous readers of early drafts, thank you! Emma Chastain, for your wisdom and cheerleading, and for helping me to love the messy version more through your eyes. Tara Sonin, for real talk and for absorbing so much kvetching. Alexa Wejko, for genius insights that made my brain light up. Krystal Sutherland, for being the dream reader of my earliest pages and giving me fortification for the long haul. Kamilla Benko, you had better, cuter things (much better, way cuter) to worry about than reading early this time, but talking and texting with you always gives me joy and clarity.

Thank you to the caregivers at my child's former daycare. Knowing he was happy and safe even when he wasn't with me was crucial to the completion of this book.

Thanks to Natalie Hail for the perfect fake-ID shopping list. Thanks to Mike Schiele for the Polaroid wall. Thanks to Eileen Korte for the middle-of-the-night trip through a suburban Super K. Thanks to Amy Abboreno for so many things, including that radiant day when the fields flooded and filled up with teeny frogs. Magic is real, and I've always found it with you.

Love always and so much gratitude to Michael for everything, particularly for allowing me to talk at you vaguely for months on end about books you aren't yet allowed to read or know too much about. Thank you to Miles for making the world infinitely funnier, better, and brighter, and for making me excited every morning to wake up and see your face. Thank you always to my parents, Steve and Diane Albert, for everything, all of it.

ABOUT THE AUTHOR

MELISSA ALBERT is the *New York Times* and indie bestselling author of the Hazel Wood series (*The Hazel Wood, The Night Country, Tales from the Hinterland*) and a former bookseller and YA lit blogger. Her work has been translated into more than twenty languages and included in the *New York Times* list of Notable Children's Books. She lives in Brooklyn with her family.

Twitter: @mimi_albert
Instagram: melissaalbertauthor

ENTER THE WORLD OF
THE HAZEL WOOD . . .

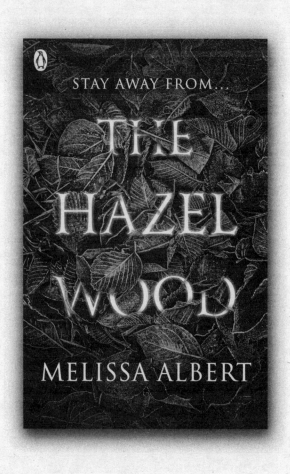

FOLLOW THE
TRAIL . . .

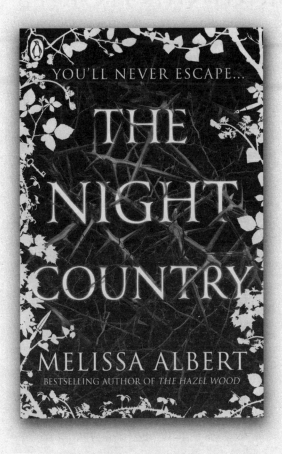

DISCOVER ALTHEA
PROSERPINE'S
ORIGINAL STORIES . . .